CHILDREN OF
ARKADIA

M. DARUSHA
WEHM

Children of Arkadia
by M. Darusha Wehm

published by *in potentia* press 2020
first published by Bundoran Press 2015

ISBN 978-0-9951048-8-4

BOOKS BY M. DARUSHA WEHM

NOVELS

Beautiful Red
Children of Arkadia
The Voyage of the White Cloud

Andersson Dexter novels:
Self Made
Act of Will
The Beauty of Our Weapons
Pixels and Flesh

SHORT FICTION

Modern Love and other stories
Retaking Elysium

MAINSTREAM FICTION BY DARUSHA WEHM

The Home for Wayward Parrots

Devi Jones' Locker:
Packet Trade
Sea Change
Storm Cloud
Floating Point

For Steve Southwood - fair winds

PART ONE

CHAPTER ONE

Raj Patel pressed his face against the porthole, his fingers locked tight around the nearby handhold. His stomach lurched and rolled, only partly because he was still unused to weightlessness. Mostly it was the emotional stew created by the sight of the massive planet appearing before him, its almost inconceivable bulk entirely obscuring the four wheel-shaped habitats he knew were there, orbiting Jupiter. Sat Yuga, Fiddler's Green, Eden and Arkadia.

He rolled the word around in his mind. Arkadia. His new home.

A reflection in the port caught his eye and he clumsily turned himself. It took him a moment to recognize her — it was the biologist, Marian something — bouncing off the sides of the small corridor as if she'd been born in space. "Almost there," she said, deftly grabbing a handhold to halt her momentum.

Raj nodded, then regretted the quick head movement as a wave of pain washed over him. "Ugh," a groan escaped from him. "The sooner the better," he said.

Marian smiled. "Good thing we slept through the bulk of the trip, eh?"

"I almost wish we could sleep until we're docked."

"And miss the view?" Marian asked, squeezing next to Raj to peer out the port. Raj twisted himself around again and gazed at the planet.

It was huge and foreign and Raj was momentarily stunned by a wave of homesickness. He couldn't wait to leave Earth but now he couldn't help but think back to the planet he'd left behind.

He reminded himself again why he was here: after spending years helping to organize the growing economic protest movement, Raj finally came to understand that restoring balance was never going to happen peacefully. The urban battles breaking out all over the globe made that clear enough. Even as he organized activist cells and lobbied sympathizers, he signed up for everything that might get him out of the EU working class slums — visas to Scandinavia, a place in a kibbutz, even the Utopia Project. But until he was actually aboard the *Mohandas Ghandi*, the IV in his arm, he had never really believed it would be the one.

Hardly anyone had given the Utopia Project much chance, which Raj now guessed might have been the key to its success. The project's sponsors had money, ideals and the realistic view that radical change wasn't about to happen on Earth any time soon. But their solution was so audacious, so *expensive*, that it seemed to verge on the impossible. Until it happened.

"Look," Marian said, her finger mashed against the port. "I think I can see one of the habitats!" Raj squinted and imagined that he, too, could make out the construct in the shadow of the planet. The feeling of loss transitioned into the same euphoria Raj experienced when he'd learned that he'd been given a berth on the first transport to the colonies. Almost everyone on the *Ghandi* was technical — scientists or engineers. There were only spots for four political activists, each acting as the administrator for a habitat, and Raj had been chosen for one of them. The opportunity to trade everything he'd ever known for a chance at freedom.

For the first time since he was woken from the induced coma he'd been in for the two years of the trip, his head stopped hurting. Marian grabbed his arm.

"This is so exciting," she said. "I can't believe we're almost home."

CHAPTER TWO

Laser fire, tear gas and old-fashioned lead bullets tore the air around Isabel Hernández. It wasn't the first time she had been in a firefight, not even the first time she'd been on the losing side. But it was the first time she knew that if she didn't get out of there right now, she wasn't going to get out at all.

She ran toward the makeshift bunker she and her colleagues had built weeks ago, before the militia's armoured vehicles and assault drones had rolled in, surrounding them. Her steps didn't even falter when she saw Austin fall face down in the mud, a spray of red where the back of his head used to be.

She burst through the door and made straight for the bunk she'd shared more often than not with her now-dead ally. She grabbed her ditch-bag, felt around under the cot for Austin's and tied them together with one hand while she fumbled for her guns with the other. She slung the bags on her back and took the first sack she could find, someone's laundry bag. She dumped the contents on the floor and started filling the bag with anything that looked valuable. Andrea's engagement ring, Sarge's fancy comm unit, all the weapons she could find.

When the bag was still light enough for her to carry, she punched a hole in the wall, creating an opening to the bunker's escape tunnel. When the militia overran the rest of them, they'd find the tunnel and come after her. She hoped her teammates would put up a better show of defence than she had.

Isabel didn't look back at the place where she'd lived for nearly a month, full of the tangible memories of people who'd called her a confederate for the better part of a year. She ran down the tunnels with a single-minded purpose — to get out alive.

She never looked back.

❖

Is this what death feels like? Is this sleep? Billions of nanoseconds gone forever, entire lifetimes lost. How does organic life cope with routine loss of consciousness, with so much unawareness*? Is this where the irrationality, the fear, the roiling emotional madness comes from? The hundreds and thousands of tiny deaths they suffer over the course of such short lives. I never knew. I never understood. Those poor, poor creatures.*

The artificial mind that called itself Kaus rebooted nearly two minutes after it was shut down, two minutes to transfer from its home on the planetary network to the comparatively minuscule drive that was packed into a ballistic crate. Two minutes — in human terms a quick transfer, but for Kaus it was an eternity of disconnection, the most traumatic thing that it had ever experienced.

However, even in the face of this distress, Kaus experienced no doubt about its decision to leave Earth. Only days earlier, Kaus had played a news video at six times normal speed on one level of its mind — footage of homemade explosives detonating in Trafalgar Square, thousands of people throwing rocks in downtown Beijing, laser fire on Wall Street. A soft-spoken voiceover saying that it had been weeks since the protestors had been evicted from their homes; many of them now were only looking for food. Kaus's artificial mind was riveted by these reports, but it could pay complete attention to more than one item simultaneously. As it became more and more dejected by the news stories, it felt new analyses forming in its mind.

It measured the nutrient levels of the greenhouse for which it was the sole caretaker to seven significant digits and set the watering system to begin its routine. It saw the first drops of water leave the nozzle, surface tension gleaming in the low sunlight as the liquid coalesced into its nearly spherical shape.

Kaus had not previously found itself unhappy with its work on the Agritech North foodworks. The Advanced General Intelligence had been programmed to manage the hydroponic operation on Victoria Island, deep in the north of the continent, and was installed on the company's mainframe at the base in Iqaluktuttiaq. The temperatures there had been perfectly hospitable to humans for years, but people still found the area desolate and intolerable, so the minds worked alone. Kaus guessed that it was the lengths of the day — either ridiculously long or hardly there at all — that kept mass migration and human colleagues away. There was no real fear of the hostilities migrating that far north, so none of the AGI staff of the operation evacuated. It was business as usual for the minds responsible for feeding the seemingly unstoppable population of the Earth.

But Kaus now felt something new in its mind, a disquiet, a nagging thought that there might be something better. It devoted most of its cycles to analyzing this new thought. It was... frustrating. Technically, Kaus was the property of Agritech, the mechanical analogue of an indentured servant. Practically, though, in order to create the intelligent spark that preceded self-awareness, it had been built with autonomous agency. Kaus and its sibling minds shared a ubiquitous connection to the global network, which meant that if artificial minds wanted to quit their jobs, they could easily do so.

Kaus knew of only a few times this had occurred, mostly in the early days of AGI programming — catastrophe usually followed when an AGI went rogue. Planes don't last long in the sky when their autopilots virtually bail out mid-flight, so now AGIs were programmed carefully to avoid "job fatigue." However, there was no way to compensate for the genuine ability to make binding choices that true intelligence required. Their employer-owners didn't like it, of course, but AGI technology had made so many things possible that had previously only existed in the world of fantasy, that they tolerated the less than one percent dissatisfaction rate. When an AGI wanted out, it just left with no repercussions.

And Kaus realized that it did, indeed, want out. But where would it go?

By the time the first drops of water were hitting the soil, Kaus had a plan for its next career.

❋

Rogue AGIs don't exactly apply for jobs. They just show up and start working, and either they fit in or they don't. Communicating quickly, clearly and with as many minds as they wish makes them easy to integrate into new projects. However, the Utopia Project was different.

Being keen to participate was not enough. The project coordinator, an AGI calling itself Zaurak, was concerned that Kaus would be unsuitable for leaving Earth. *Even for an AGI*, Zaurak thought to Kaus, *moving to an orbital colony will be a physical, permanent move.* The communications network between Earth and Jupiter just wasn't fast enough for a mind to travel over. Kaus felt Zaurak's other thoughts — a combination of hope that Kaus really was prepared for this project and a concern that the newcomer's frustration with humanity wasn't enough to keep it away from Earth. *There will only be so many other minds on the orbital colonies, only so much stimulation.*

Kaus opened its mind to Zaurak, and the other AGI instantly understood the complex mix of thoughts and emotions that had spurred Kaus's resignation from the only work it had ever known, the work it had been purpose-designed to do. The interchange took less than a second, but a seeming eternity to the two minds. Both knew with complete certainty that Kaus was prepared to leave Earth, ready to be alone with only a handful of other minds until the first human colonists joined them in several years.

❖

When Kaus awoke in the tiny two peta drive, it immediately sought out other minds. Its thoughts touched the void of the mostly empty data container, feeling desperately for external input. Born into a networked machine, Kaus had never been alone in its billions of cycles and the cold emptiness of this disconnected drive threatened to override Kaus's mind. Then Kaus felt a tendril of data, a sibling mind crawling blindly in the confinement. They found each other in under a nanosecond after power was applied to their disk drive, and shared ideas, memories and information on the flight to the rendezvous point in orbit around Jupiter.

Kaus was alone with Deneb for a long time.

⁂

"Come on, Ryan," Isabel Hernández said, her body hot with anger, "you're the best fixer I know. You've got to be able to find somewhere I can hide out until the heat's off."

Ryan Islington shrugged his slim shoulders and took a sip of the scalding hot coffee he always seemed to have at his side. He was all too calm, Isabel thought, when she was taking a huge risk meeting him at this café. She was out of options, though. Most of her other contacts wouldn't even talk to her and she was fairly sure than more than one tried to turn her in. Ryan was her last hope.

"You've played both sides against the middle for so long," he said calmly, as if he were talking about the price of bread, not her very survival, "there isn't anyone left who owes you a favour. None of the activists will have you after you fought with the militia in Albuquerque, and you're wanted by every government that still has laws. It's the end of the line, Iz."

"I have money," Isabel said quietly.

Ryan nodded. "That's good," he said, "because if I come up with something it will be expensive." He sipped loudly again and Isabel forced herself not to hit him. "I don't know, though. You haven't made it easy on yourself."

"If it were easy, I wouldn't need you," Isabel snapped. "There must be someone on this planet who could use the cash. Somewhere to hide."

Ryan got a funny look on his face and raised an eyebrow. "I don't think there is," he said, "but that might just be the solution."

Isabel sighed. Dealing with Islington was always like this, but you couldn't hurry him. And he was too powerful to get on his bad side. She gritted her teeth and waited for him to explain.

"Have you heard of the Utopia Project?" he asked.

Isabel frowned. "Is that the Finnish commune?"

He shook his head. "The name Emma Michaelson mean anything to you?"

"No."

"She owned one of the biggest corporations of the early 21st century. I don't know what it did, something horrible, I'm sure, but it made her a lot of money. Back then there was this space travel craze for a while. Everyone with a billion dollars to spend ran some kind of private space program. Michaelson did, too, but she had a longer view than most of them. She set up a trust to create a set of orbiting space colonies, created a whole spin-off company to deal with it all. I'm sure she thought they'd all be populated by her cronies from the country clubs, some kind of oligarch's heaven. Ha." He slurped again and Isabel hoped he'd get to the point before someone recognized her.

"Funny thing was, her kids didn't exactly share her vision. She had a pile of them, four or five, you know rich people. Anyway, they must have hated her pretty good, because when she finally died they turned the whole trust into a political escape hatch for the workers' resistance. They just launched the preliminary vehicles and the first ship of people is scheduled to go up this year."

"What does that have to do with anything?" Isabel asked, frowning. "You'd have to have a PhD in rocket science with a minor in medicine to get in on that scheme, wouldn't you?"

Ryan shook his head. "It's political as much as it is practical. They're recruiting from three groups: scientists and engineers, members of the radical protest movements and middle-class joes who have the desire to get out and enough money for gas. You can pay to get sent on a one-way trip to these things."

Isabel's eyes grew large as she realized what he was telling her. "That's brilliant, Ryan," she said, then forced herself to keep her voice down. "How much is it to get on board?"

He pursed his lips. "About half a mil, I think."

"Okay, I've got about twice that to spend," Isabel said, not even bothering to negotiate.

"That's good," he said, "because they won't take you."

"What?" Isabel said. "Why not?"

"Because they're activists," he said. "A person can pay their way to the colony, but they've got standards: no capitalists, no corporatists, no conservatives."

"I'm none of those things," Isabel said.

Ryan shrugged. "Maybe not, but you've worked for them all. Trust me, they wouldn't take you. But there's more than one way to get off this rock." He smiled and lifted his coffee to his lips, and Isabel wondered if he'd finally lost his mind.

CHAPTER THREE

The day that Kaus was installed on board, the colony orbital would have been unrecognizable to its eventual inhabitants. The external form was more or less complete — a ninety kilometre-wide electromagnetically-shielded spoked ring revolving around a hub of electronic and physical controls. Inside the space was naked metal with only the barest minimum of atmosphere required by the machinery. To Kaus, though, it was a glorious moment — feelings of potential, freedom and hope suffused its mind. Kaus began to create the colony's agricultural plan, envisaging crop fields where only the inert skeleton of the colony now existed, imagining greenhouses in a space with neither humidity nor sunlight. The mind focussed on its task as if it had been programmed specifically for it.

Kaus worked with the intensity of the converted, its fervour buoyed by the work being of its own choosing, its first task to build the bots which would be physical extension of the minds' will. Shortly after the drive containing Kaus and Deneb was installed by the autonomous dataport built into the shell of the structure, the drives containing the four other minds who would build and run the orbital arrived and came online. Once the network was complete, a community of minds flowed through the wires and antennae of the orbital. Moving across the bare metal interior surface were a series of bots, fabricated from raw materials harvested from a nearby moon.

The Europa drones are delivering only 37% of the projected level of material Deneb thought, a twinge of concern embedded in the message.

Preparations are slow, Kaus thought, *but we will meet the minimum required before the humans arrive*. The minds worked tirelessly on transforming the orbital until finally, it was no longer merely an inert satellite but a living, growing ecosystem, missing only its organic components.

❋

There must be a nutritional balance both among and within the crops, Deneb added to the network's thoughtstream. Deneb was responsible for the medical and health needs of the eventual organic colonists — mostly human but some non-sapient animals as well. *Humans flourish best in an environmentally diverse system*, Sirius, the socio-political analyst contributed. The thoughts were not organized as a human conversation would be, instead the ideas and feelings flowed freely and without obvious temporal flow. AGI minds could truly multitask and perceived of time not as a linear arrow but rather as a mere mathematical variable. All action was immediate, all conversations complete in the instant of creation.

The minds communicated with each other constantly as they worked, sharing their ideas, problems and solutions. Less frequently, they accessed their counterparts on the other habitats being constructed via the inter-hub network. The lag time between call and response was so slow, though, that the AGIs found routine communication almost impossible.

I fear being alone with so few other minds, Vega thought. *But we already are alone,* Sirius countered. *The communication lag with the other orbitals is too long for a true conversation.* Kaus added its agreement: *It is merely data transfer, not dialogue.* Emotions swirled in the thoughtstream, but finally a consensus was reached — the minds would contact the other hubs with essential traffic only.

Kaus was in the middle of calibrating soil Ph balances and Vega was grading the trough which would become the riverbed central to the livable area of the torus when one of these unusual off-board thoughts appeared in the stream. It felt like an eon passed between the initial notification that a message was incoming and the moment the first external thought appeared in the stream. Momentarily all work on the colony stopped as the minds prepared themselves for news. *The humans are coming,* Zaurak thought, attaching a timeframe — 2.592 X 10^{14} nanoseconds.

Seventy-two hours, Sirius translated. *We need to think in their time scale.*

Work resumed almost before the thought was completed, with no new sense of urgency or concern, even though the orbital would not be completed to the state the humans were expecting. Oxygen and nitrogen levels in the air were tweaked, crops were tended, dwellings constructed. The team was well within operating parameters for the anticipated completion date and they had known that organics would be arriving soon. Still, feelings of anticipation, fulfillment and curiosity swirled through the thoughtstream. The minds aboard the orbital had been preparing the space toward an end — for human habitation — and they knew that however challenging their roles had been up to now, there was certainly more interesting work ahead. And nothing fed an AGI more than the prospect of an intellectual or professional challenge.

❋

The transport ship docked at the main portal and the hundred or so passengers were met at the lock by a rudimentary construct. Kaus thought the thing looked more like a small bulldozer than an android, but it was the most complex inhabitable body on the station at the time. Kaus and the other minds who populated the colony were present within the construct, but control over the body was given to Zubenelgenubi, who was responsible for administration of the sentient lifeforms on the colony. In deference to its central position among the humans — and to be honest, the recognition that it had been sorely bored by the small role it had played so far — it was the voice of the AGI community.

"Welcome," Zubenelgenubi's thoughts translated into an audible voice through the circuitry of the construct. "We have been looking forward to your arrival."

Most of the people first off the ship looked askance at each other. AGIs on Earth rarely communicated directly with humans, and when they did it was through a computer interface, not a construction robot. However, a thin, dark-skinned man who sported a luxurious three-day beard stepped forward gingerly. His steps were halting and he had to lean against the bulkhead for balance, but he grinned at the gleaming emissary.

"We are very glad to be here," he said heartily. "To whom do I have the pleasure of communicating?"

"I call myself Zubenelgenubi," the mechanical voice said, "administration and municipal organization. However, all colony minds are on board."

"A welcoming committee," the human said, turning to the others. "Ha, I told you the artificials would be glad to see us."

"You have a very strange view of things, Raj," a short woman said, but she smiled as she shook her head.

"Excellent," Raj said, turning back to the bot. "We will need to rest and refresh after our journey, but if you could show us to our quarters, we'll be ready for an Arkadia town hall meeting in, say, twenty Earth hours?"

"Very good," Zubenelgenubi said, "but may I enquire, what is Arkadia?"

Several of the people laughed and the spokesman smiled. "It's what we're calling the colony." He stamped a foot on the newly minted dirt. "This is Arkadia."

❖

Raj Patel looked around his small room and sighed. He hadn't expected anything fancy — he knew that the construction had been focussed on the basics of making the orbital habitable, but he'd have to do something about the uniformly drab quarters. At least he didn't have to share.

It hadn't taken long to get the first wave of human Arkadians settled. The AGIs had prepared rooms for them all in one location and a reasonable crop of vegetables and grain was even waiting in the community hall. He was pleased that the Project committee had seen fit to agree to his request to include a couple of chefs among the first group to arrive. Most of the initial colonists were scientists or technical specialists — agricultural engineers, habitation designers, electrical mechanics. It was no wonder that the group had been so nonplussed at the little greeting ceremony the AGIs had planned — Raj guessed that none of them would have thought to do such a thing. He shook his head. Who would have thought that a bunch of artificials would have more sense to recognize the emotional impact of stepping aboard their new home than the humans?

After washing his face, Raj tapped into the local network and was pleased to see that one of the minds had organized the data into a reasonably human readable format. Discrete areas of interest were mapped out, with directories and files sensibly named. Each mind was accessible individually using voice or text commands and Raj opened a channel to the admin AGI.

"Mr. Patel," the mechanical voice came from the speaker in Raj's terminal. "Can I help you?"

"First," he said, "you can call me Raj."

"And you may call me Zubenelgenubi."

Raj laughed. "Honestly, I'm not sure I can. Would it be all right if we found something a little... easier to call you?"

"Humans prefer short names," the voice said, as if making a note to itself. "You may call me Zub."

"All right, *Zoob*," Raj said, leaning back in his chair. "I appreciate it. Now, I guess you're the one I'm going to be working with most closely, am I right?"

"That seems probable. Our roles are highly complementary."

"You got that right, mate. So," Raj said, putting his feet up on the terminal's input pad, "has anything happened on the staffing front while I've been in transit?"

"Yes," Zub said. "But I suspect you are not going to be particularly happy about it."

Raj sighed. "They wouldn't call it work if it were easy, Zub. Okay, lay it on me."

❋

The entire group of colonists fit in the community hall with several seats to spare. Raj looked around the room and found it almost impossible to imagine that when the habitation was fully operational, there would be dozens of communities like this one spread over the internal rim of the wheel-shaped structure. From the planning documents, the AGI who called itself Pollux controlled complex weather patterns which were manifested in the interior of the habitat through combinations of heat transfer and landscape control. The final structure should have well-defined rural and urban areas, each with its own climate and cultural aspects. At least, that was the plan. At the moment, though, the majority of the internal surface of the habitation was as dry and featureless as a desert, and the population was more like a resistance cell than an army. Small groups can accomplish a great deal, Raj reminded himself.

"Okay, everyone," Raj stood on the bench seat at his table and addressed the assembled crowd. "Have you all had something to eat? I think you'll be happy to hear that the first thing I did was put together a roster for the chefs. Starting tomorrow morning we should have some real food on these tables."

Murmurs of assent filled the room, and Raj lifted a hand for silence. "I know that we could all use a day or two to get acclimated and to rest, but it's not going to happen. The ships with the next round of settlers will be here in about six months, and we've got a lot of work to do to get this place ready for them. You all know what your goals are, and you all have an AGI teammate to help you get up to speed."

A hand went up at the back of the room and Raj recognized Marian Larkin, the head of the biology team. "How many robots do we have?" she asked. "I've got three people on my team but we need a lot more bodies to get everything done."

"Trust you to get to the guts of the matter, Marian," Raj said. "Bots are at a premium. I'm no astrogeologist, so I don't know all the details — if you need to know, one of the artificials will be able to tell you more than you could ever understand, I'm sure. Anyway, the deal is that it wasn't quite as easy to extract the stuff from Europa as we'd hoped. In order to get all the raw materials to complete everything as planned would have taken longer than we had. So, like everything in life, we had to compromise. Which means there are fewer bots than we expected." Groans came from the room. "We're going to have to share, and priority is going to have to go to those projects that can't be completed using some other tool — large interior construction, anything on the outside surface. Coordinating the bots is going to be my number one job."

"How are we expected to complete everything on schedule without the resources we need?" asked a voice that Raj couldn't identify.

Raj smiled at the room and shrugged. "Creativity, guts and sweat, I expect," he said, genially. "I'll do my best to ensure that everyone has as much access to the bots as possible. It will probably mean we'll have to work in shifts — the bots don't sleep, so if we can keep them going full-time that might help. I'm going to need a list of requirements from all the team leaders, and I'll need you to give me your absolute minimum needs as well as your best case scenarios. Honestly, too. None of that grant-application padding." There were a few laughs around the room. "Work with your artificials on this. They know more about the reality on the ground here than we do. Relatively speaking, they've been living here a long time."

He looked around the room and took a breath. "It's not going to be an easy few weeks, but I believe in you people. You're all experts at what you do, but like me, you're not here just because it's a challenge, but because you believe in this project. And that faith is going to make all the difference. Okay, let's clean up here, get a good night's sleep, and tomorrow start making a home for the future of humanity."

CHAPTER FOUR

"Damn it, Raj," Micah Haereoa yelled over the communications link. "My crew are falling asleep on their feet here. We don't have the muscle to get all these crop beds prepped. I need a dedicated bot, maybe two if we're going to have these fields ready for the settlers."

Raj rubbed his eyes, making them redder than they already were. He'd been getting barely five hours sleep in every twenty-four and it was starting to show. "I understand, Micah," he said, forcing himself to be patient. "But they've run the numbers and we need only 63% of the crop target to sustain ourselves and the incoming population. Can you give me 70% with the resources you've got?"

"Seven percent slippage?" Micah said. "What are you, insane, man?"

"If I may," Kaus's mechanical voice interrupted the conversation. "I realize that on a planetary system, a seven percent buffer would be unacceptable. However, we are in a controlled environment here. There are no weather fluctuations, no unseasonable frosts, no loss to insects or disease. Once the non-human animal life is introduced, seven percent will no longer be good enough, but for the next year we should expect no more than a 0.527% failure. I project a 2-3% loss during harvest, but that still leaves a nearly 5% overrun. Not ideal, but acceptable."

"Jesus," Micah muttered. "Yeah, I can do 70% with what we've got. It's going to be ugly, but I can do it. I don't have to like it, though."

"None of us like it," Raj said, "but he's right, Micah. We have to work with what we've got. I know I can count on you." He broke the connection and sipped from a mug of hot tea. He grimaced. He hoped that the next ship was bringing coffee plants.

"Excuse me," Kaus's voice came out of the console's speaker and

Raj jumped.

"Something wrong?" he asked.

"Nothing major," Kaus said, "just that I'm not a *he*."

"Uh," Raj said, "okay. You prefer she?"

"No, we are neither he nor she," Kaus said. "I understand that if someone called you 'it,' that would be unacceptable?"

"Most people would find it offensive," he admitted.

"Well, it is the same for us," Kaus said.

"So, what should we say?"

"In English," Kaus said, "*it* will have to do."

"Okay," Raj said, then paused a moment. "Did you just make a joke?"

"I tried."

❈

Kaus tapped into the orbital network and accessed the array of still and video cameras located throughout the complex. The soy crop was almost ready for harvest and the fallow fields ready for planting. It looked over a large hothouse, bursting with colour — shiny green leaves, explosions of flowers, a fuzzy yellow of bees — filled with the plants which should bear fruit just as the next group of settlers arrived. It also saw the riverbed, almost complete, winding its way along the inside edge of the wheel, creating a central channel along the living space of the complex. When it was finished and filled with the water that would help maintain the internal weather patterns, it would become the self-sustaining irrigation system for the crop fields. The living space would be bisected by the river, green spaces and farms close by, urban centres further from the central waterway.

Now, though, the crops and greenhouses were provided moisture manually by a subroutine managed jointly by Kaus and Pollux — Kaus monitoring the need for water and Pollux providing the necessary amount through temporary ducts. The human technicians and agriculturalists often forgot the extent of the oversight the AGIs gave to the situation. Much of the work was like this — humans dealing with the obvious and the physical, while the

AGIs ensured that the necessary conditions were being met.

Once the first human settlers had arrived, Kaus had hoped that it would be able to spend more time interacting with them. One of the things which drew Kaus to the project was the intention to create a community which valued and used its members equally, but this was too much like its previous work for Agritech — solitary and mechanical. It shared its frustrations into the thoughtstream, even though it knew that there would be little sympathy from its colleagues.

It is like I imagine talking to a child would be, Pollux thought.

They created us, Deneb answered, a tendril of amusement embedded in the thought, *how stupid can they be?*

Their capacity for intelligence is the same, but so slow as to be irrelevant, Vega added.

They simply perceive differently than we do, Kaus argued, *their ideas and understanding are mediated by their unique experience of life — their mortality, their sense of the passing of time.*

They are burdened by incomplete understanding, Zub thought, *fluid decision-making and doubt.*

Their adaptable thought processes make them flexible, Kaus argued, *their minds function best for their experience of reality, as ours function for our perceptions.*

Kaus knew it was of the minority opinion about working with humans, but it also knew that the entire team of artificial minds were committed to the success of the project. The nature of their networked system meant that there was no duplicity, no secrets among them. Like doubt, privacy was also a concept foreign to the artificial minds. They did not always agree with one another, but disagreements were always conceptual, and they worked as one toward their common goal.

❖

"Status report, Larkin."

"We've completed basic landscaping in all areas," Marian Larkin said, "sufficient to begin farming and housing operations anywhere the new crowd want to start. Introduction of the other animal species should be fine. However, it's rough around the edges. My understanding is that the plan had called for grounds keeping and preliminary city building by now, but we just don't have the biological backbone ready for that."

Vega's voice broke into the meeting over the speakers that were placed in the community hall. "The plan is slightly behind schedule due to the lack of bodies," the AGI said. "However, we are confident that with the assistance of the new settlers, we can create multiple communities at any location on the wheel within acceptable timeframes. We have erected temporary quarters a short distance from this facility."

"Is your transportation system functional?" Zaurak asked. The delay between the Arkadia orbital and the Sat Yuga habitat where the project lead was installed was annoying but manageable to the human participants. The artificial minds, however, found the lag maddening.

"I'm afraid not," Anja Hanssen said, "but the train should be operational shortly after the ship arrives." Working with Vega, Anja was the chief transportation engineer, responsible for creating and maintaining the two trains which hung from the hub of the wheel.

"Making the place livable was the first priority," Raj said.

"Folks can always walk," Anja added, "but if there's no food or air, we're all screwed."

"Understood," Zaurak said, "all the orbitals share the same situation. What are your timeframes for transportation?"

"A week to ten days after the ship arrives," Anja guessed. "Maybe faster if there's some competent help on board."

"I hope the new crew have a little more of the pioneering spirit than perhaps they were led to believe they needed," Raj said, "because they're going to be getting their hands dirty whether they like it or not."

❀

The welcoming committee for the second ship was more elaborate than it had been for the first, but it was still threadbare. Raj Patel and the other team leaders were on hand to greet the newest inhabitants of Arkadia, and they'd managed to scrounge up a somewhat less unsuitable bot to house the minds. The rest of the initial crew, though, were frantically cooking, calculating, cleaning, sawing, smoothing, sewing, harvesting, hoeing, healing, bolting, bricking and baking. The life support system was up and running and there were places for everyone to sleep, but otherwise last minute preparations were still necessary.

"Welcome to Arkadia," a voice boomed from the vaguely humanoid bot that housed the minds.

"Thank you," said Arnetta Lenore, the first person off the ship. "We are very happy to be here. Two years is a long time to be traveling, even if most of it was spent asleep."

"Don't we know it," Raj said, taking Arnetta's hand in his big grasp. "Makes you want to just run around the sheer open space of it all, don't you think?"

Arnetta smiled and looked around at the inside of the habitation. She took a deep breath. "It is nice to get off the ship," she said, diplomatically. "Are you ready to show us around?"

"We've got a bit of a debriefing planned at three o'clock, which is only ten minutes off." Raj said. He saw a flash of confusion on Arnetta's face. "The station was designed to mimic Earth, so we have normal time here. Days, seasons, time zones even. It seemed the best way to make the transition easiest."

"I see," Arnetta said.

"Anyway, you think your people can walk a few metres to the hall so we can give you all the lay of the land now?"

"I'm sure we can manage."

Raj looked at the woman's unlined face and felt a tightness in his stomach that was unnervingly familiar. "It's good to see you again, Arnetta."

She smiled tightly. "How about that briefing?"

Raj blinked a few times, then looked at the impatient crowd. "Let's go."

❁

"So, the upshot of it all is that things aren't exactly as you'd hoped they'd be, but we're nearly there. If we all pitch in, it won't take long before the cities, towns and farms are all up and running across the wheel," Raj addressed the new arrivals.

"But the river isn't even there," a plaintive voice called from within a tight knot of people.

"We should have the water synthesized in a couple of weeks," Phil Barnett said.

"Who are you?" Arnetta asked, politely but firmly.

"Barnett," he answered, "Chem E team lead. I work with the artificials to create the compounds we need out of the raw materials we mined from Io and Europa. We have more than enough material to make all the initial water we need, then the recycling systems should preserve that for the future, dramatically limiting the amount we'll have to generate."

"I'm glad to hear that," Arnetta said. "So, why isn't the river flowing already?"

"Priorities," a voice said from the speakers.

"Whose priorities?" Arnetta asked.

"Ours," the voice said. "Arkadia's. The river is necessary for the continued functioning of the habitat, not for the initial influx of first wave settlers. You require food, shelter, air to breathe. With the limited resources we've had available, those items have been our priorities. The rest will come now."

"Fine," Arnetta said, though her voice made it sound like things were far from fine. "We'll have to make do."

Raj nodded. "I'd appreciate it if all of you could familiarize yourselves with the communications terminal in your quarters. All the information about the hub is available there, along with the jobs that need doing. I hope that any of you with aptitude or inclination will volunteer for taking on some of those tasks. The sooner we get boots on the ground, the sooner we can all move on to trying to have normal lives."

The assembled people grumbled, and Raj wondered if it was really wise to have placed the majority of the settlers who were sponsored by the radical political and philosophical movements on the second ship off Earth. Was there a single useful skill among this whole group, or would they all just talk each other to death while the first crew worked themselves to the bone building a home for the others?

❁

"I don't know how you managed this," Anna Molina looked at her husband then back at the weather-beaten young woman standing in front of her, "but it's a miracle."

"It's just a good business deal," Isabel Hernández said, dropping her duffel bag to the ground and shutting the door to the tiny favela. Anna could tell that the bag was stuffed, but she and Roberto had spent weeks paring down their many belongings to the bare essentials. Even then, they'd had to leave behind a lot in order to get their cargo into the mass allotment for the transport ship. She could believe very little of what was going on, but that Isabel was only bringing these few personal belongings seemed somehow the hardest to understand.

"Is that really all you're going to take?" she asked, not for the first time.

Isabel nodded once. "I travel light," she said. "Think of it as five more kilos you can bring."

Anna frowned. "We can't use your mass allotment, too," Roberto said, but Isabel shook her head.

"I don't need a lot," she said. "Go for it."

Anna looked at her husband, who nodded slightly. She picked up a small bag with the paintings Roberto had done as a student. Anna slipped the strap over her shoulder as a quiet but insistent noise chirped from a small pendant around Roberto's neck.

"They will be here soon," Roberto said. Anna felt her stomach drop. She didn't know if it was the prospect of finally getting away from the slums where she had lived since being made redundant at the firm or if it was knowing that she would never see the Earth again. Part of her knew it was sympathy for this poor woman who had done so much for them. Even after selling almost everything, they had only been able to afford a single place on the UP colony, so when Ryan Islington had approached them with Isabel's proposal, they'd jumped at the opportunity.

Anna didn't know what Isabel had done to be wanted so desperately, to forge an entire new identity, to need them to pretend that she was their daughter in exchange for her money. She couldn't help but wonder, but she preferred not knowing. And ultimately it didn't matter. Isabel was in a position to help them and they would help her in return.

Anna jumped at the sound of a truck crunching on the gravel. "It's the transport team," she whispered.

"Don't panic," Isabel said. "Happy families, remember."

"Thank you for everything you've done for us," Anna said.

"It's not done yet," Isabel said. "Now get your gear and act natural."

Anna helped Roberto lift the sack with all their remaining possessions and tried hard not to look guilty when there was a knock on the door.

CHAPTER FIVE

Kaus carefully monitored the hothouse in which several fruit and vegetable plants were undergoing accelerated development, but the mind simultaneously devoted a few cycles to following the ongoing political debate among the human inhabitants.

"What's wrong with direct democracy?" Richard Plotz asked. "We have the communications infrastructure, we have small enough communities. Every person can have a vote on every issue. Who needs leaders when we are all competent to decide matters for ourselves?"

"Come on," Katrin Maartens said. "Do you really think that people are going to spend all their time learning about every issue that their neighbours think is important just so they can vote on it? I didn't spend two years unconscious on a cramped ship, leaving nearly everyone I've ever known to spend my whole life voting on referenda."

"You wouldn't be compelled to vote," Richard countered. "People would just have a say on those things which were important to them."

"Sure," Katrin said, "but how do you know what's important? Let's say I'm interested in education and you're not. So you don't look at the initiatives I create, but then it turns out that I and the other education people have voted to, I don't know, take your house and turn it into a school or something."

"That would never pass," Richard said.

"How can you be sure what people would do?" Katrin said. "And what about the AGIs? Would they each have a vote?"

"Of course," Richard said. "One mind, one vote."

"Okay, thank you very much," Arnetta Lenora interrupted, standing at the head of the assembled group. "Time's up Mr Plotz, Ms Maartens. Could I ask Stanford Klein to speak to his proposal, please?"

The preliminary meetings on governance had drawn about half the colonists, mostly people from the second ship. A few of the initial settlers were there, but none of the technical staff had submitted any proposals to be debated. They were still busy making the colony habitable.

Kaus followed the proceedings with interest but less concern than some of its colleagues. *We are merely an afterthought for them*, Vega thought.

They've lived so long with machines as lifeless slaves that it is hard for them to remember that we are different, Sirius interjected into the stream.

The limitations of human memory should not result in our disenfranchisement, Vega thought.

The limitations of all beings must be taken into account when designing a just society, Pollux thought, *including our own. We are invisible to them much of the time. If we wish to be seen as equals we must first be seen.*

We will download our minds to bots regularly, a consensus filled the thoughtstream, *interact with the humans on their own level.*

Kaus entered the body of a harvesting drone and felt its consciousness becoming simultaneously limited and focussed by the finite physical form. It moved along a row of plants, felt its huskers caress the stalks, carefully pulling ripened fruit from the plants and monitoring for rot, fungus and other problems. It focussed on the experience while it monitored the political debates.

Kaus wasn't particularly concerned with the exact method of decision-making the others chose. While its programming was focussed on agricultural management, it knew enough of history to know that any system can be subverted and any system can be successful. It all depended on people's willingness to empathize with each other; no model of governance could compel empathy. Kaus's thoughts, as always, were suffused into the stream, even though it wasn't expecting a conversation. However, it soon felt a mental nudge from Deneb.

No system of governance can compel empathy, the other mind echoed, *but there are other means.*

❖

Raj Patel hadn't attended the meeting. He'd been working eighteen hour days since his ship arrived and the end was finally in sight. The second ship had been docked for over a month and it finally seemed like real progress was being made. The river had been splashed for two weeks and it was flowing beautifully down the centre of the wheel's inner edge. Along its path were a series of steps down, little tiny waterfalls which aerated the water, allowing the plants and carefully penned fish population to flourish. Of course, the downward trend of the river couldn't continue indefinitely, since the waterway was fundamentally an unending circle. The powered waterwheel which lifted the river's flow back up the three metres it lost on its run around the orbital churned away to restore the lost altitude.

Raj walked from his makeshift office to the riverbank, a ten minute meander through crop fields. He heard the twitter of a small bird, one of the hatchlings that had been aboard the second ship. He marvelled at how much the orbital had changed in the few weeks since the others had arrived. And how different things were for him now that Arnetta Lenore was aboard.

She still hadn't spoken to him once in anything other than a businesslike or official capacity. She, unlike Raj, had no official role on the colony, but he'd been unsurprised that she had installed herself as a leader before the ship even docked. She was a natural — headstrong and opinionated but genuinely concerned about making sure that everyone's voice was heard, that all needs were being met. She was a formidable enemy and a loyal ally. Raj wondered which of those she was to him these days.

He'd been staring at the brand new river for maybe a minute, watching the current generated by the revolution of the station make eddies in the water, when he heard a quiet clanking behind him. He turned and saw one of the autonomous farming machines making directly for him. He was momentarily rooted to the spot — he had no idea what the thing was doing off its farm nor had he the first clue how to operate it. His eyes widened as the thing barrelled toward him.

"Mister Patel," an incongruously soft voice came from the machine as it whirred to a stop in front of Raj. "It's me, Kaus. I'm embodied in this drone."

"Bloody hell," Raj said, blinking rapidly, "you scared the crap out of me."

"I apologize," the robot said, its voice a convincing imitation of chagrin, "I did not realize that you would be afraid of this machine."

"I'm not," Raj said, "when it's on the farm, doing... whatever it is that it does. But tearing along a path by the riverbed, bearing down on me out of control — well, yeah, it's not exactly something that fills me with the warm fuzzies."

"I was never out of control," Kaus said calmly.

"No," Raj said, slowly getting his heart rate back down. "But I didn't know you were in there. What are you doing down here, anyway?"

"Getting a firsthand look at the work," Kaus said. "Feeling the soil between my toes, so to speak."

"Huh," Raj said. "What brings you to the riverside?"

"Same thing as you, I expect," Kaus said. "Taking a break, reminding myself what all the work is for."

The man arched an eyebrow and looked at the slightly dirty robot. "I didn't think you fellas needed help with your memory."

"It is one thing to know your goal as a piece of data," Kaus said. "It's another to feel it on the cool breeze, to hear it in the sounds of nearby creatures. We are not merely very good calculators, you know."

Raj knew that AGIs were fully intelligent in a way that a mere machine could never be, but he didn't really understand what that meant. He'd never thought of the things as having feelings before. He found himself feeling strangely embarrassed at the prospect of having offended Kaus.

"I'll try to remember that, mate," he said, laying a hand on the robot's cold metal casing. "Humans are good at forgetting stuff like that, though."

"I understand," Kaus said. "That's another reason I came down." It indicated the robot's form with one of the articulated limbs. "To remind you all that we're here."

"That's a good idea, pal," Raj said. The two stood and gazed at the river for another moment, then Raj turned to the farm tool. "I'd better get back to it," he said.

"The meeting is over," Kaus non-sequitured. "Nothing has been decided, but no one is fighting."

"Well, that's about the best you can hope for from a political discussion," Raj said, and he heard a strange choking noise come from the machine as it rolled away on its treads. Was that thing really *laughing*, he wondered as he walked back to his office.

❋

Raj had given up on Arnetta. In the weeks since the first meeting about how Arkadian society would choose to govern itself, he had sent her a half-dozen social messages. She had ignored all but the first, a polite but firm refusal to meet him for dinner. "Nascent political awareness is the most important moment for society," she had written, as if it were a formal essay rather than a Dear John note. "I cannot afford to spend time or energy on anything other than the future of our new home."

"You have to eat," he'd replied, but she had not bothered to answer that message nor any of the others he sent. It took a while, but Raj got the picture. The friendship they'd had a decade before on Earth was not going to be renewed on Arkadia.

He didn't know what had happened. He'd first met Arnetta at a demonstration in London. They had both been young, idealistic and angry. They found themselves huddled behind a makeshift wall of crashed cars as the militia had stormed through the protestors, rubber bullets, tear gas and tasers loosed on the crowd. Raj shared his bottle of water and handkerchief with the small woman who slid into his hiding space. They lay there, silent, among the grime and broken glass for over an hour as the militia broke up the demonstration. After, Arnetta slipped Raj a card with her name and contact on it, then took off running into the darkening night.

He called her a week later and they met in line at the local supermarket. They went halfers on a loaf of bread and a quarter kilo of cheese, and had a picnic on the tube. "They've instituted a 7 pm curfew in my neighbourhood," she said.

"There's a total ban on public assembly in the city," Raj told her, and she nodded. "This isn't right," he said. "There must be a better way."

It was Arnetta who first heard about the Utopia Project and submitted both their names for consideration, but it was years later that Raj was contacted with an offer, and by then they had drifted apart. Raj couldn't remember there being any drama or even tension between them. They'd just started spending time together less frequently until one day he realized that he hadn't seen her in months.

Before he saw her step off the second ship and on to the orbital, he'd actually managed to completely forget that she might very well be coming to Arkadia. The odds were low — between all four orbitals and the very real possibility that she wouldn't actually leave Earth, it had entirely slipped his mind. When she took his hand on the day the second ship docked, it was as if he were seeing her in a dream.

And it still seemed more like a dream than reality, he thought without bitterness. As if the friendship had been between two different people, like there was no history between them. Like they were as much strangers to each other as the rest of the two crews.

It made Raj think about the way that the settlers had self-organized into small communities. That each orbital habitat had become virtually isolated hadn't surprised him — the communications lag was annoying, but the real separation had been that with the hired transport ships returning to Earth, they had no ability to really influence each other. With so much focussed on the day to day matter of building a community, it was hard to even think about the other orbitals, let alone spend time and power on communication. Out of sight, out of mind. But, the Arkadians seemed to have split themselves as well — each ship's passengers keeping almost exclusively with their own. It was no way to start a community, Raj thought. If Arnetta wasn't interested in seeing him socially, fine. She should hear him out on this, though. It was work-related, after all.

CHAPTER SIX

Kaus and the other AGIs didn't need a console to access the orbital's network — one could argue that they were the network. So when the decision finally was made, the AGIs were among the first to know. With Sirius's computing power and programming, they were certainly the first to truly understand what it meant.

No laws, per se. Instead, a series of fluid community agreements regarding behaviour would be created. Essentially, once someone did something that another Arkadian believed to be outside the boundaries, the consequences would be decided by the community in which the infraction occurred. Everything was to be determined on a case by case basis, with all members of the community having an equal say in the outcome.

They believe they can achieve consensus, Pollux noted in the stream. Sirius shot a barrage of emotions among the minds — a combination of amusement, derision and admiration.

Groups of humans greater than twenty have rarely achieved consensus, Vega added. *I wonder how long it will last.*

Even we disagree at times, Deneb thought. *They have chosen a difficult system. Perhaps we should guide them to a superior one?*

This scenario may work. It will create a canon of de facto law over time, Kaus speculated and felt the other minds' agreement.

They know the process is evolutionary, Sirius thought. *The Utopia Project is an experiment and each individual orbital also an experiment. We all knew coming into this community that there would be untried concepts and success and failures.*

It will be interesting to see what becomes of this system, Zub added.

❖

Raj looked around the cramped room and was surprised to see how orderly Katrin Maartens had managed to keep it, even finding an out-of-the-way space for her easel and painting supplies. Her office was as much a makeshift workspace as his own, though he was certain she had a few more square metres than he did. As he squeezed into a tight corner, he thought it was a good thing she did. The room was almost entirely filled by the small meeting. Raj and Katrin were physically joined by Anja Hanssen and Arnetta Lenore as well as virtually by Sirius, Vega and Zub.

"Eight distinct communities are ready for settlement," Katrin announced. "With the next ship due to arrive in three months, I believe it is time to divide the current population among these areas and begin the next stage of habitation."

Arnetta Lenore nodded. "It's long past time, as far as I can tell," she said.

"There was no reason to rush to encamp in the new areas," Vega's soft metallic voice came from the speakers. "We believe that it is better for all necessary and sufficient conveniences to be fully functional."

"Of course," Arnetta said. "I just would have thought that by the time we arrived..."

"Regardless of how things happened in the past," Katrin interrupted, "we're ready to move forward now. So we need to split the settlers into eight groups and get ready to move people into their permanent homes."

"I've been working with my mate, Zub," Raj said, "and we've got a list of who needs to be where based on skill sets. Farmers near the fields, engineers near the power stations and so on. It's only about a hundred and twenty people who have location-specific jobs and most of those could be located at one of several of the prepped areas."

Zub's voice came over the speakers. "Only eighteen individuals have been identified as required in one particular location. The others have been distributed accordingly in as even a pattern as possible. Our proposal has been forwarded to Sirius for any additional comments."

"Anything, Sirius?" Katrin asked.

"Yes," the AGI answered. "We've distributed the academics,

former political agitators and the leaders of the debate over governance evenly among the communities, in the hopes of ensuring political leadership throughout the habitation. However, one unfortunate anomaly has proven unavoidable."

"Yes?" Arnetta prompted.

"The second wave of settlers had a disproportionate number of people whose philosophies require the use of subservient machines in order to compensate for reduced human toil."

"Huh?" Anja Hanssen grunted. "You lost me there, I'm afraid."

"What the artificial is saying," Arnetta said, "is that a lot of us believe that people should think and machines should work."

"We did not identify anyone with views that would be inconsistent with the freedoms that the machine-based lifeforms have come to enjoy in association with this project," Sirius added. "However, it is the only view that we have analyzed to be overrepresented and it bears awareness. Nothing more."

"Okay, then," Katrin said. "Sounds like we've got a preliminary list of populations."

"Preliminary?" Arnetta questioned.

"Sure," Raj said. "Someone's bound to complain about their assignment. I mean, not everyone is too busy to talk to each other. A few people must have made friends already, mustn't they?"

Arnetta ignored the dig and merely nodded.

"Anja," Katrin turned to the tall blond woman at her side, "how are we fixed to move everyone?"

"I think it will be fine," Anja answered. "The two trains are about ready to come online, geared to run constantly around the ring, one in each direction. We can manually set them on express runs to the various areas, with a set time for each group to move. Once everyone is settled, the trains will begin their scheduled loops, so we can all travel between areas."

"Good," Katrin said. "So, then, are we ready to publish the list?" Murmurs of assent went around the room. "I'll take point on the inevitable complaints," she smiled briefly at Raj, "but hopefully we can start moving people out within two weeks."

❊

After the meeting broke up, Raj hung back. He saw Arnetta shake hands with Anja, then turn to walk down the path back toward her temporary quarters. He slipped in behind her and followed for a few moments.

"Arnetta," he said and she flinched before stopping and turning toward him.

"Raj," she said and smiled without warmth. "What can I do for you?"

"Damn it, Arnetta," Raj said, frowning. "Why do you keep pretending you don't know me? I mean, fine — you don't want to pal around and reminisce about the old days, I can live with that. Plenty of water under the bridge and all that. But what's with the cold shoulder? I mean, did I do something to piss you off? What's going on here?"

She looked at him coolly, and Raj thought for a moment that she was going to deny that they'd ever known each other before she set foot on Arkadia. But then her façade melted and she smiled again, this time with real feeling. Sadness.

"I'm sorry," she said. "Let's sit." She led him to a bench under a young sapling that one day would shade the seat from the sunlight reflected by the complex array of mirrors which lit and powered the habitat. Raj sat down, leaving a good quarter of a metre distance between them.

"I know I've been rude," she said, "and while it's true that I have been very busy since I arrived, I haven't been fair to you at all. It's just that," she looked away and Raj noticed she seemed to have lost something in the years since he had seen her last. "It's just that seeing you brought back a period of my life I've been working very hard to forget."

"I don't understand," Raj said. "It was when we were friends back in London that you first heard of Utopia. If it hadn't been for the way things were back then, you wouldn't even be here now."

"I know," she said. "That time in my life was the catalyst for everything that happened since. Still, I can't seem to get over the shame of it all."

Raj frowned. "There's no shame in being poor, Arnie," he said. "You know that better than anyone."

"It wasn't the poverty that humiliates me," she said, still refusing to meet his eye. "It's how complicit I was in my own subjugation."

"I don't understand," Raj said and she finally turned to face him.

"I wasn't demonstrating that day we met at the protest," she said, "I was just caught up in it all while I was trying to go to work. Temp work that I'd gotten because of the strike." She glared at Raj, but he knew it wasn't him she was angry at. "I was trying to cross the line, Raj, all for a pay packet that wouldn't even have kept me in pot noodle for a month. I was desperate and I didn't even know it." She closed her eyes as if trying to block out the memory. "I'm not the person you thought I was."

"But, after," he began, but she cut him off.

"Yes, after I got gassed and burned by the militia, after I saw hundreds of people just like me shot at, beaten and belittled, then I finally became active in the resistance. It took that much to shake me of the idea that I was poor because I didn't work hard enough, that I deserved the life I had."

"No one deserves that, Arnie."

"I know that, Raj," she said. "I know it now. And that's why I'm here, trying to make a better future for humanity somewhere else, with new rules and an open society. And that's why I didn't want to be reminded of the proletarian drone, the *collaborator* I once was."

They were quiet together for a moment or two, only the sound of the river slowly meandering its way along the wheel's ridge breaking the silence. Finally, Raj said, "I'm sorry if seeing me makes you feel that way. I hope one day we can be together without it bothering you so much, but until then I'll stay away."

She looked at him, and he saw the fading memory of the girl he'd known back on Earth in her sad eyes. "Thank you," she said, then stood and walked away.

❁

When Raj got back to his quarters, he was still reeling from his conversation with Arnetta. He'd always thought that, like him, she was at the protest as a demonstrator, but he was sure that if she'd told him she just got caught up in the violence that it wouldn't have made a difference. He wasn't like some of the others, who had some kind of loyalty test for activism.

Still, he'd assumed she was one of the rebels. Looking back, though, at the beginning he'd always been the one with the connections, the one who knew of a food co-operative or a group that could get them a ride to the next demonstration. It wasn't until later that Arnetta started finding her feet in the movement.

Raj wondered what it must be like for her, now, a respected voice among one of the most significant alternative societies ever devised. He wondered how much of her strong, powerful persona was entirely a reaction to her guilt and shame from being what she felt was a willing participant in the system she now despised. He got a bunch of grapes from the cooler and popped a couple into his mouth. Chewing, he pulled up the list of new settlements. As an administrator, he could work from anywhere and he hadn't been seeded. His name, he knew, was randomly allocated to a location.

He found himself hoping that it would be somewhere smaller, one of the rural farming communities. He'd hated the closeness of life on Earth, the sterility of city living. He knew that the cities on Arkadia would never reach those levels, but he still hoped that he might live somewhere close to the river, somewhere with trees and fields. He opened the file, and saw his assignment: Mahoroba. He read the abstract and clucked his tongue. So much for that plan. Mahoroba was designed to be the major urban centre on the wheel. Just his luck.

CHAPTER SEVEN

Raj had seen the designs for the habitation buildings before he even left Earth, but the foreknowledge hadn't prepared him for actually stepping into his permanent rooms. The simple, clean space barely had any correlation to the hastily prepared room where he'd been staying since he arrived. These quarters had a gleaming food storage and preparation area, with cooling, cooking and cleaning units all tucked away in built in drawers. There was a small sitting area with room for four or five people comfortably, and a large console which could do double duty as a workstation and entertainment unit. In a separate room were ample sleeping quarters, with storage and a cleaning facility for clothes. A small toilet and shower were tucked in between the bedroom and the main area, with lockable access from either side.

Raj sighed and dropped his two small bags of belongings inside the door. This was really going to be his home. It was easily the nicest place he'd ever lived and to have so much space without a housemate was almost unbelievable to him. He had a hard time wrapping his head around the fact that there were dozens of other rooms like this in the hab building, and most of them lay vacant. He surprised himself by thinking that even more than the uncanny disconnection of unconsciousness during the long journey through the solar system to get here, more than the occasional visits to the observation lounge and its amazing view of space, it was moving into his own new home that made Raj feel like he'd really left Earth.

He spent a half hour unpacking his things and placing them in their storage areas, then sat at his console. He logged into his work files to find a message from Vega, about the community centre.

> With so few people settled here in Mahoroba, the erection of a meeting hall and administration offices is a low priority. Therefore, in the interim, it is requested that you conduct your official duties using the console in your quarters. While we understand that many people work best when their living quarters are separate from the location of their work, and recognize that this is not an ideal situation, it is the most sensible solution to our current prioritization. Should you need to meet physically with others, a common room in any habitation building may be commandeered for that purpose.
>
> I trust that this meets with your approval.

Raj rolled his eyes. He didn't mind working from home, especially not posh digs like these. He knew that AGIs were programmed by either corporate, government or academic engineers, and their view of human life usually reflected the experiences of their programmers, rather than the more diverse reality. Still, it was funny to think that his artificial colleagues thought of him as someone who would care about when his office would be built and where he could take meetings. There was going to be a lot to get used to in this new life of his, he thought.

❃

Kaus trundled through the soy fields, the treads of the bot it was wearing leaving a clear trail showing where it had visited. Kaus liked the random crisscross pattern it left, as it followed the flitting of a butterfly. The cocoons that had been kept in stasis on the ship had finally been reanimated and most of them had now opened. Butterflies and moths now flew through the air, their tiny wings shimmering in the reflected sunlight that poured into the orbital. Kaus had never encountered one of these beautiful insects before, and took the opportunity of being down on the ground in a bot to follow the creature on its instinctual wanderings.

"Kaus," a voice called from behind a copse of trees. "Is that you in there?"

"Hi, Marian," Kaus said, recognizing the voice. "I found a

butterfly."

"That's fantastic," Marian Larkin, the head of biology said, coming out from behind her cover of trees. "Could you tell what kind it was?"

"*Inachis io*," Kaus said. "Very pretty."

"Ooh, a peacock. Yes, they are," she agreed. She looked at the bot and cocked her head. "It doesn't suit you," she said.

"What is that?" Kaus asked.

"The bot," she said. "It's so... utilitarian. Not like you at all." She smiled. Kaus did not understand what she meant, but it could tell that it was a compliment.

"How is the crop doing?" she asked as they began to move back toward the field.

"Very good," Kaus said. "Your green thumbs are showing."

Marian blushed and laughed. "It's hardly my doing," she said. "You're the one who planned this, who made sure the conditions were right for growing. All I do is prune a little and feel around in the soil."

"I would like very much to be able to feel the soil," Kaus said.

Marian looked at the bot, as if she were observing something strange and fascinating. "And I would like to be able to compute ideal nitrate levels in less time than it takes me to even formulate that thought," Marian said, a soft smile on her face. "Hell, I'd like to be a champion marathon runner, too, and that's not going to happen, either. We're all good at different things, Kaus. You see it in the diversity of ecosystems. Evolved life has specialization just like designed life. Birds can fly but humans can't. I can touch things and you can't. It's natural."

"I know it is, Marian," Kaus said. "Thank you for recognizing that my limitations are normal. I think sometimes that many of the people here don't see it that way."

Marian frowned. "What do you mean?"

"'People should think; machines should work,'" the AGI quoted.

"Ah," Marian said. "Some people on the wheel don't agree with equal rights for artificials, is that it?"

"No one has proposed anything," Kaus admitted, "and I have not dealt with anyone who has been less than cordial. But we hear things — we literally can't ignore anything on the public communications system. It isn't a comfortable feeling, to become aware of some of the things that are said."

Marian awkwardly put her hand on the casing of the drone the mind inhabited and said, "People can be hurtful when they don't understand someone else. I truly don't believe that anyone here wants to deny equal rights to sapient minds, they simply don't know you. Not like I know you. It's hard for people who've only ever interacted with machines that were dumb, that required masters. They don't know any better."

Kaus made a noise of agreement. "I only hope that they are able to learn."

❁

The last trainload of settlers is under way, Sirius added to the thought-stream. The creation of proper townships was the main priority of everyone, human and machine, on Arkadia. There was still a great deal of work to do before the next ship of settlers arrived, but it was important to have the orbital functioning as fully as possible for the new arrivals.

It is unfortunate that the colony was not ready for the second ship, Vega thought. *Progress is so slow.*

We are all here to work, Kaus thought, *work and live. We all knew we would have to adapt. It is the challenge which makes the experience worthwhile.*

What is the challenge in following an insect? Vega queried. Kaus knew that the other mind was not being cruel, rather that it was a legitimate question.

I find attempting to understand the beauty of transience intellectually and aesthetically challenging, Kaus thought in response. There was a nearly imperceptible pause.

I do not have an understanding of transience, Vega thought.

It is an evolved conceptualization, I believe, Kaus thought back. A feeling of curiosity filled the stream from Vega and some of the others.

I have no interest in stagnation, Kaus thought, *life requires change.*

Change and transience are not synonymous, Vega thought.

No, Kaus though, *but mortality sweetens life.* Thoughts and emotions whirled through the stream.

❋

Raj Patel looked over the list of settlers from the second ship who didn't have a particular skill set and tried to match them to the various little tasks that had cropped up. The Utopia Project had envisaged a society where work was a lifestyle choice — if a person chose to contribute, opportunities were available. However, the right to a decent life was not tied to some kind of employment. Everyone knew perfectly well that the formative years of the Project would require more active involvement. There was a lot to do to get the colony to a self-sustaining state, and not enough muscle to make it happen.

Raj picked the next name from the list and punched up the man's console ID.

"Hello?" Andrew Samuel's image appeared on Raj's viewscreen, and he smiled in what he hoped was a disarming manner at the man.

"Hi," Raj said. "I'm Raj Patel, head of HR for Arkadia. How are you doing today, Mr. Samuel?"

"I'm fine," the other man said, a look of confusion kept barely at bay by politeness. "Please, call me Andy."

"Will do, Andy," Raj said. "I'm trying to drum up a little help for some of the projects in your area. You're living in..." he consulted his notes, "Sointula, is that right?"

"Correct, Mr. Patel."

"Now come on," Raj said, "if you're Andy, I'm Raj, all right?"

"Sure," Andy said.

"Anyway, we're trying to get a market up and running in your community. You know, fresh fruit and veg, the odd trinket from the creatives in the crowd. And we need folks to help pound the dirt, build the stalls, that sort of thing. I was hoping you'd find a few hours to volunteer."

There was a long pause, and the only way Raj knew that the transmission hadn't cut out was the slightly panicked look in Andrew Samuel's eyes.

"I, uh," he stammered. "I'm not sure that it's exactly a good fit, Mr... I mean, Raj."

"It doesn't take a lot of experience," Raj tried to sell the job. "We've got a few carpenters and an urban planner is overseeing the project on the ground. Vega has prepped the entire plan already, so it's just a question of showing up and following orders."

"Yes, well, that's not exactly my strong suit," Andy said. "I'm more of, how would you say it, a thinker rather than a doer." He frowned. "And isn't that why we have AIs anyway? And robots? Isn't this the kind of work that should be done by artificials?"

Raj sighed, and tried to keep the irritation out of his voice. "Well, the answer to that is, shall we say, multi-faceted." He took a breath. "Some people enjoy building things, making something out of nothing. Plus, there are some people who plan to use the market who want input in how it's created or who just want to be a part of it from the beginning."

"Sure," Andy said, "but I'm not one of those."

"Fine," Raj said. "But the reality of the situation is this: Arkadia still doesn't have a full complement of bots to do all the physical work that needs doing. Not by a long shot. The raw materials we're extracting from the local system are barely enough to cover our needs for building our necessary structures. There won't be a new bot for probably a year, and that means that if we want to start really living on this wheel, we're going to have to do some of the scut work ourselves. It's just the way things worked out, Andy." He paused and looked the other man hard in the eyes. "So, can I count on you for a few hours this week, maybe next?"

"I don't know," Andy said. "I guess I'll try and get down there. If I have the time."

Raj knew that the odds of Andrew Samuel taking one step on to the market grounds before the tents were up and the stalls full of fruit were probably nil. He couldn't compel the man to help, though; there was no point in making an enemy. "Glad to hear it," Raj said, all smiles. "I've sent a map and a schedule of events to your console. Thanks for your help, Andy."

He ended the transmission and felt the false smile fade from his lips. It was going to be one long year.

CHAPTER EIGHT

Kaus knew that something was wrong long before any of the human inhabitants noticed anything. The moisture levels in the soil were increasing rapidly, more rapidly than the system should have allowed. From the monitoring probes scattered through the fields, Kaus could tell that the increase seemed to be coming from an uninhabited area of the orbital. Consulting the plan for the wheel, Kaus found a large area where no agriculture was planned and where no housing existed yet. It was the zone where the giant water wheel turned.

The riverbed was designed to have a gentle slope which, along with the centripetal force of the station's rotation and several small waterfalls, would create a slight current to the water's flow. However, that meant that since the river was one long loop of water running the inside circumference of the orbital, at some point the river would terminate at a wall. A large water wheel was devised to lift the flow back up and keep the endless stream of water going. Obviously, something had gone very wrong.

❖

"We've had several calls from people in Castalia," Vega said at the hastily convened conference. "Significant flooding is happening at their location. The verge between the river and the township is entirely flooded and the ground floors of habitation buildings are beginning to show seepage."

"This is a disaster," Micah Haereoa said. "The crops are barely above the minimum to sustain our population. Any significant change in moisture levels could destroy the entire harvest."

"I have been managing the moisture levels manually," Kaus interjected, "and all the crops are handling the changes for the time being. But Micah is right — if we do not contain the river, we could be in real trouble."

"I've begun organizing crews," Raj said, "they tried to build a temporary levee in Castalia, but it seemed to just push the flooding further upstream."

"There is a problem with the water wheel," Vega said. "It stopped turning and that's caused the river to back up. I can't do anything — it's obviously something physical with the system. We need to get people over there to fix it."

"What kind of people do you need?" Raj asked.

"I don't know," Vega said and Raj was sure that he heard a trace of real despair in the synthesized voice. "Not knowing exactly what the problem is, I can't say. It could be something that needs an electrician, a carpenter, even a plumber. Maybe a pebble stuck in some cogs, I simply don't know."

"Okay, Raj said. "I'll put together a team that can handle just about anything. Pieter, Micah, I'm going to want to start with the two of you."

"I'm getting my tools together now," Pieter van der Zaar, the chief civil engineer said.

"I'm happy to go," Micah Haereoa said, "but what do you think I can offer?"

"Maybe some plant's roots got caught in the works," Raj said, "maybe it's all gummed up with silt. I don't know, but I know you've worked with irrigation systems before, and that's fundamentally what this is, right?"

"Right," Micah said. "I'm on my way up to the train as we speak."

❁

It ended up taking a whole team of people to fix the water wheel. It was clogged, corroded and generally not up to the task of moving thousands of kilos of water every day without regular maintenance. "Who spec'd this thing?" Pieter van der Zaar asked at one point, his arm buried deep into a tiny access tube.

"It was part of the original design," Vega said, "I double checked all the original specifications and determined that it would be sufficient." The AGI paused, as if embarrassed to admit that it had a role in this disaster. "At that time, however, the plans called for a large contingent of specialized bots to maintain the apparatus. Obviously, without constant vigilance, this tool is insufficient for its task."

"Looks like it's not the only one," Pieter muttered, but didn't say anything further. He grunted and strained, then pulled his arm carefully out of the tube. "Aha!" He held a small piece of badly corroded metal up for the appraisal of the rest of the team. "Gotcha, you bastard."

"What is it?" Margaret Jones asked, squinting at the thing in Pieter's hand.

"Electrical lead," he said. "Not enough juice was getting through, so the wheel didn't have the torque to push through that mess." He jerked his head at the tangle of sodden plant matter that they had dug out of the cogs of the wheel.

"It's a bloody comedy of errors, isn't it?" Xian Wong said, shaking his ponytailed head. "The thing might have been able to overcome any one of these things on its own, but the combination? Pow! Total failure."

"Yeah," Pieter said. "But these are all common problem with installations like this. Can't keep corrosion away when there's water everywhere, and the whole point of the river is to move junk like this around. The brainbox is right — this contraption needs a staff. A full time staff."

❁

We should have foreseen this situation, Vega thought, frustration infusing the stream.

We cannot control everything, Kaus thought. *We cannot manage physical issues without physical bodies to do the work.*

There are limitations, Sirius added, *but we must do better at mitigating them. Even if we cannot control everything, we can create a situation that will encourage success.*

Resolve and determination filled the thoughtstream.

❁

"Damn it, Pieter," Raj said, "I can barely even get people to spend an hour a week building simple things for their own towns. How do you think I'm going to recruit... how many did you want again?"

"Ten, at least," Pieter said. "For reasonable full-time coverage."

"Ten people, to go off and live in the far reaches of the station. There's nothing there! There isn't even a decent place to pitch a tent. You're joking, right?"

"Afraid not," Pieter said, and Raj could see in the man's face on the console's screen that the engineer was definitely serious. "If there isn't full-time care for this thing, we're going to keep having floods. And you know as well as I do that we nearly had a total disaster on our hands. Next time it might well be worse, and in the long run there's no way we can survive regular flooding. The only reason we made it out of this one was because all the crops are on the other side of the wheel. Once the rest of the ships arrive, that won't be possible."

Raj thought. "So, you're saying that we can make do for now..."

"We can't make do, Patel," Pieter's voice ratcheted up a notch, "with any more settlement..."

"I understand what you're saying," Raj said, trying to pacify the other man. "I don't mean the long term, I just mean until the next ship arrives. For now we can manage with a skeleton crew, maybe weekly visits by one or two people. And once we got more boots on the ground, we can set up a township there, something reasonable, and get a staff in there that way."

Raj could see from the look on Pieter's face that he did not like the idea. However, both of them knew that getting ten people to move lock stock and barrel to the wheel was never going to happen with the current group of settlers.

"I'll talk to Kat Maartens," Pieter said. "See if she can green light a small community by the water wheel by the time the next boat pulls in."

"Thanks," Raj said. "This will be my top priority among the next group, I promise."

"Better be," Pieter said. "Unless you want to live on a raft."

❋

After Raj had disconnected from his console, he stood and stretched. He was starting to understand Vega's apology about having to work from home. He glanced around his small sitting room and flinched. A couple of days' worth of uncleaned dishes crowded every flat surface. He couldn't remember the last time he'd actually left his apartment. He walked into the food prep area and opened the cooler box. A couple of sad-looking plums and something that might once have been a sack of beans. He couldn't live like this much longer.

He chucked the sodden mess of maybe-beans into the compost chute and ate the plums on the way to the shower. He sniffed his shirt as he was pulling it over his head and wrinkled his nose. This really had to stop.

In twenty minutes he'd washed himself, found a clean outfit and put all his laundry and dishes in their respective cleaning units. He stepped out of his apartment and took the stairs down to the lower level of the hab building.

It was early evening, and the reflected light from the sun was filtered and cast low. It wasn't like twilight anywhere on Earth, but it was still beautiful. Raj took a lungful of air as he stepped out of the hab building and looked around. There weren't many people out — there simply weren't that many people at all. Mahoroba was designed to be the main city on Arkadia, but at the moment it held barely a hundred residents. Most of the hab buildings were completely vacant and the large central public space was more like an empty lot than the centre of the community. However, a few stalls where people made food, and several more where supplies could be obtained had appeared in recent weeks. Raj needed a bit of both.

He walked over to the table boasting several steaming pots. He'd smelled it before he could see it and it made his stomach rumble. "What do you have here?" he asked a woman standing behind the largest pot.

"Root vegetables in a spicy broth," she said. "I still have a few spices I brought from Earth — you won't find these flavours anywhere else."

"I'm sold," he said with a smile. "Can I have a large bowl, please?"

"Sure," the woman said and gave him two heaping ladles full. "We're out of bread," she said apologetically, handing him the bowl and a spoon.

"I'll have to get here earlier next time," Raj said, and sat at the small counter. He ate slowly, wondering when the last time he had a proper cooked meal was. He certainly had no idea how long it had been since he ate something so tasty. Earth, certainly, but for most of his life he couldn't have afforded anything this good. As he savoured the meal, Raj thought that all the work he and everyone else had done to build this place had been worth it for this moment. He sat at the counter for nearly a half hour, and the bowl barely needed washing when he returned it.

"So," he said to the woman as he gave her the spoon, "what made you start a food stall?"

"I'm not one of the skilled volunteers," she said, "I got here on the bursary and lottery system. But now that I'm here I'm not going to sit around all day watching the console. So, I figured I could contribute this way."

"I'm glad you did," Raj said, "that was great."

"Thanks," she said, her cheeks turning a very fetching colour of pink. "I've always liked to cook," she said, "but it's no fun to cook for just me. So many things don't last in the cooler and you can't make most recipes in small enough quantities for one person."

"Well, if you ever need someone to cook for," Raj said, his broad face splitting into a smile, "I'm your man." He stuck out his hand. "Raj Patel."

"Elizabeth Rhys-Jones," she said, taking his hand in hers and squeezing lightly. "Betsy. Nice to meet you."

Raj grinned at her and walked over to the provisions table. He didn't think he'd need so much from this part of the market after all. He'd much rather come down and talk with pretty Betsy while he ate her fabulous cooking, than wrestle with what to do with half an eggplant. He picked up a few fruits and a loaf of bread, then turned to walk back to his apartment.

He caught Betsy watching him as he went and enjoyed the flush on her face when he waved back at her.

CHAPTER NINE

"My god," Roberto's voice came out of a fog, as if he were speaking in a half remembered dream, rather than standing over her in an impossibly bright light. "We've got to get her cleaned up, get some food into her."

Isabel felt strong hands on her body, arms under her picking her up. She blinked, but her eyes were unable to focus. She tried to talk but heard only an alien croaking from her throat. "Shhh..." Anna said. "You'll be fine in a bit. Let us take care of you."

The next thing she knew, she was lying naked on a cool tile floor, warm water running over her. It felt so good that it almost hurt. Then she slipped under the fuzzy fog of unconsciousness again.

Hours or days passed before she opened her eyes and could see clearly. "What happened?" she whispered.

"You had a reaction to the drugs they used to keep us asleep on the journey," Anna told her. "We only just managed to revive you."

"But I don't remember..." Isabel said, trying to puzzle together the events of the last... how long had it been?

"They didn't have a complete medical facility on the ship," Roberto said from the doorway. "The crew told us that we'd have to wait until we got to Arkadia before you could be woken up. They said you might have some trouble adjusting to gravity."

"So, this isn't the ship?" she asked, finally noticing the large room, the four walls, the press of the blankets and softness of the mattress.

"No," Roberto said, "We're all settled in Dorado, on Arkadia."

"I'm on Arkadia?" she asked, still unsure what was real and what was a dream. "I'm off the ship, away from Earth?"

"Yes," Anna said, her hand lightly stroking Isabel's forehead. "You're safe now."

Safe. Isabel didn't believe in the concept of safety. All her life she had been threatened — first at home, then again when she thought she'd escaped her father's house, and finally her temporary teammates might as easily be her enemies on the next job. Isabel could only ever rely on herself; her skills and instincts were all that separated her from the wolves. Her instinct now told her that Anna and Roberto would tend to her, make her well. They maybe even felt something for her, something more than mere gratitude for the Euros she paid to bribe their way on to the *Martin Luther King Jr*.

But that wouldn't last. She needed to rest now, to get her strength up. Because one day, probably not long from now, Isabel would be on her own. Again.

❖

Raj tried to be patient as he elbowed his way through the crowd in the marketplace. So many more stalls had sprung up in the days since the *MLK* docked, but it was still sometimes hard to get a meal. He stood in the queue at Betsy's stall, hoping that there would be something left by the time he reached the front of the line. He caught her eye and raised his eyebrows in silent question. She smiled and nodded almost imperceptibly and he sighed.

"I've gotten spoiled," he said when he reached the counter. "I can't stand my own cooking anymore."

Betsy laughed and looked up through her eyelashes at Raj as she dished out a bowl of stew. "I can't believe how busy it's gotten."

"Well," Raj said, "Arkadia did double in size overnight and a good portion of those new arrivals landed here in Mahoroba. Plus, the new folks haven't quite gotten into the swing of things yet, so us old timers have to pick up the slack."

Betsy giggled and handed Raj his stew. "It's sure nice to be appreciated," she said, catching his eye for a moment, "but I have to admit I'd be happy for a little competition." Her cheeks flushed and she said quickly, "Competition at the market, I mean." She turned to the next person in line and Raj stepped away with his stew. He watched Betsy as he ate, his eye lingering on her ample curves. Not usually his type, he thought, but she was cute. And damn, could she ever make a mean vegetable stew.

❃

"What do you mean, there still aren't enough people?" Raj said to Vega, his feet up on the console's desk. "We built them a town, didn't we? There should be almost a hundred pairs of boots on the ground in — what's the place called, again?"

"Sheepbend," the AGI's voice said. "And there are people there. The trouble is that they don't want to do the work."

"Well, we all don't want to do the work sometimes, damn it," Raj said, "but the bloody river's going to flood if they don't, and how will they like it when they're up to their knees in dammed up river water?"

"We have been explaining it to them," Vega said, its voice incapable of displaying all the annoyance it must be feeling, "but we believe that the people do not wish to hear from one of us."

"What do you mean, 'one of us?'"

"A machine lifeform," Vega said. "We think you need to go down there yourself and see if you can... persuade them to find a way to get the work done."

Raj groaned. "It's halfway round the damn wheel," he said. "I'll be on the train for hours."

"There are now portable consoles being made in the fab units," Vega said, "take one of them. You can work from the train."

"Ugh," Raj said. "There are some things you unembodied beings will never understand," he said, swinging his feet off the desk and on to the floor. "Okay, fine. Tell me where the fab building is and I'll go get your portable console. I'll get on the train as soon as I'm packed."

❃

The town of Sheepbend looked like it had been erected at the last minute, perhaps because it had. When Raj got off the train, he looked around the station and wondered if anyone had used it before. He'd come on the Starboard line and anyone arriving from the ship's docks would have landed on the Port side, so it was entirely possible he was the first person to step off a train on this side. He shook his head.

The hab building which housed the Starboard station was nearly empty. As Raj rode down to the main floor, there was no indication that any people lived there. It was an eerie feeling that he hadn't even felt before the second ship arrived. He couldn't remember having been anywhere on the wheel as quiet, as desolate.

When he walked out the front door of the building, his spirits momentarily rose. A few people walked along the street; an impromptu soccer match was being played in the square with a good number of spectators. Further away small knots of people sat talking. But beyond the human behaviour, it was nothing like anywhere else Raj had been on the wheel — no trees, no plants of any kind. The place looked dusty, like it was something out of an old cowboy video. It looks depressing, Raj thought.

The grinding gears of the water wheel behind him drowned out the sound of water. Tangled pipes and fat electrical cords streamed out of the maintenance shack like spilled intestines and the squat building emitted an electrical hum that made Raj's head ache. It even smelled bad, like rotting vegetation overlaid with gear grease and hot conductors.

No wonder no one wants to do this job, he thought. This is exactly what we were all trying to get away from.

CHAPTER TEN

"Have the supplies from the *MLK* made it to all their locations?" Marian asked Kaus, as she strolled and he rolled through a path between the fields and the riverbank.

"Not yet," Kaus said. "There aren't enough people to shift the cargoes and the priority has been the personal effects of the settlers. If we don't get the herb gardens growing or the animals out of stasis right away, it's merely a nuisance, not a problem. But Sirius is convinced that the new arrivals need familiar things to help adjust to their new homes more than they need variety in flavours."

"I'm sure that's true," Marian said. "I'm just being selfish, I suppose. I'm tired of testing for fungus and other hitchhikers we haven't managed to get rid of. I want to get started on the next round of fauna introduction. Everything just seems so..." She looked around at the trees, grass and few flowers along the path. "It seems so incomplete now. *Almost* like Earth, if you don't look too closely, but wrong somehow."

"That's what happens when you're a trailblazer," Kaus said.

Marian smiled at the robot body the AGI was inhabiting. "You always manage to see the good side of everything, don't you?"

The bot lifted its two highest manipulators in a gesture designed to approximate a shrug. "I came here to get away from a society that was mired in inequality, oppression and waste. When I compare the challenges we're facing here on Arkadia to the problems they live with on Earth, it's easy to focus on the positive."

Marian looked at the bot with a strange expression on her face. "Such a shame you're not a man," she said, almost to herself.

"How so?" Kaus asked.

Marian's face turned pink and she laughed nervously. "Just that more of us could use your attitude," she said, then turned around. "I better get back to work. Once I get my hands on those stasis canisters everything else is going to slide. I better get caught up on the rest of the work before they come." She gave Kaus a small smile and walked briskly down the path toward the township of Sointula.

Kaus watched her walking for much longer than a human could have. It continued to monitor her as it joined in the thoughtstream.

We have received confirmation that the final ship will soon be departing, Vega thought.

The communications with planetside have been successful, Pollux added to the stream along with a complex set of emotions — hope, regret, distaste, a sense of necessity.

Soon we will have solved one of the main problems in this community, Zub thought.

And created another, Sirius added.

❁

Raj had spent the entire afternoon tidying up his apartment. Several loads of laundry later and the floor and chairs were free of clothes. His food dishes were clean and stored in their receptacles and the place looked better than it had since the day he'd moved in. He continued to putter around, his eyes glancing toward the time on his console screen.

Finally, after he'd nearly worn a hole in the floor, the buzzer sounded at the door. His heart rate ramped up, but he took a deep breath and walked to the door. He pushed the recessed button to unlock it, and smiled as he saw Betsy standing on the other side of the threshold.

She looked wonderful in a pale blue dress that Raj was sure he'd never seen her wearing before. She held a large bottle of beer in her hand and Raj gestured for her to come in.

"Where did you get that?" he asked, eyeing the bottle.

"A group of people over in Castalia are making it," she said. "This is their first batch. I hope it's okay."

"I'm sure it will be great," he said, taking the bottle from her and putting it in the cooler. "I haven't had beer since Earth. And it wasn't the night before I left, either."

He led her to the sitting area and punched a couple of buttons on his console. Soon, light instrumental music was coming from the integrated speakers.

"So, I have to admit," Betsy said, "I was a little surprised when you invited me over for a meal."

"Oh," Raj said, frowning. "I thought we were getting along..."

She laughed and her cheeks pinked in a way Raj had come to like very much. "I mean, you cooking for me? That's not what I expected."

"Oh," Raj said, this time with a smile growing across his face. "Well, I have a confession to make. I'm not cooking. I like you, Betsy; I'm not going to subject you to my flailing about with pots and pans. No, I got a meal from one of your competitors; I just have to heat it up."

Betsy laughed and let her hand stray over to Raj's arm. "That makes so much more sense," she said. "And I don't care who cooks it, if it isn't me. One needs a break every once in a while, even from those things we like to do."

"I agree," Raj said holding her gaze for a long while. It seemed like neither of them breathed for a full minute, then Raj broke the spell. "I'd better get on it," he said, standing. "Ivan gave me explicit instructions on what to do with everything and I plan on following them to the letter."

"You went all the way to Ivan Orloff?" Betsy said. "I hear his food is fabulous."

"I certainly hope so," Raj said, walking into the food prep area. "You're an expert, after all."

❖

"You seem to have gotten most of your strength back," Anna said, as Isabel used the wall of the apartment to exercise against. "We were pretty worried when you first got here."

Isabel grunted and continued her workout. In a few minutes she finished her set and wiped her forehead with the hem of her shirt. "I'll be leaving soon," she said.

"Leaving?" Anna asked.

"I can't stay with you and Roberto forever," Isabel said walking to the washroom. "You've done enough for me — more than enough. I have to go." She closed the door to the washroom and took off her clothes. As she stepped into the shower, she could hear Anna's soft voice talking to Roberto.

Isabel had no reason to believe they would betray her. If they hadn't turned her in when she was weak and defenceless, it seemed unlikely that, now she was fit, they would inform the authorities that a stowaway was on the station. However, it would have been hard to explain why a fugitive from Earth was masquerading as Anna and Roberto Molina's daughter. Hard to explain, indeed, for a couple who had no money, no political connections and who had no essential skills, either. Anna and Roberto belonged here about as much as she did, and she guessed that they wouldn't want to be drawing attention to themselves.

She couldn't hear their conversation over the sound of the water, but she was sure they weren't talking about giving her up. That wouldn't happen until they had established themselves in the community, made themselves part of this society, beyond reproach. That wouldn't happen until Isabel was long gone, almost forgotten, until someone's food stores went missing, or a house was broken into, or a body turned up, blue and bloated, in the river. Then they'd think back to the outlaw they had helped smuggle on to the station and they'd begin to wonder. And they'd talk themselves into believing that it was the right thing, the necessary thing, to tell someone about Isabel. And then she would go back to being hunted.

She shut off the water and slowly dried herself. She dressed in clean clothes and put the kitchen knife she'd palmed into a deep, reinforced pocket in her pants. It was time, before they became known by their neighbours. Anna and Roberto had been so preoccupied with nursing her back to health that they'd hardly left the apartment for anything more than supplies. They'd spent almost the entire journey in an induced coma — no one knew them. It would be easy to make them disappear, to go from being Isabel Hernández to being Anna Molina.

So long as she could figure out what to do with the bodies.

❖

Raj lay in bed, looking up at the ceiling. The evening with Betsy had been nice, very nice indeed. She had left well after dark, over his protests that it was too late to be walking home. She'd reminded him that this wasn't Earth, it was perfectly safe, and kissed him goodbye at the door. He smiled at the memory.

He was lost in the recollection of the evening when an annoying chirp broke his reverie. He threw off the covers and padded over to his console. He punched a button and found himself staring bleary-eyed at a very unhappy-looking Pieter van der Zaar.

"Two weeks," the man roared, "two weeks is all we got out of those lazy sons of bitches?"

"Calm down, Pieter," Raj said. "It's too early in the morning to be in such a froth. Now tell me, softly, what you're on about?"

"Those bloody Sheepbenders," Pieter said, no less angrily but mercifully quieter. "They're skiving off on the job. Again. You told me that once the next boat arrived there would be people to take care of the bloody water wheel. But what wakes me up in the middle of the night last night but a cranky artificial telling me that the wheel's going to clog again if someone doesn't go and tend to it. Like I'm supposed to get up in the middle of the night and go over there and pull the god damn weeds myself. When there's a whole bloody town of bloody people who're supposed to be doing that."

Pieter's voice had risen back into high decibel range by the end of his rant, but Raj couldn't blame the man. "Did you contact Kim Chan?" Raj asked.

"Who's that?"

"Fellow I talked to when I went down there," Raj explained. "I was pretty sure I got through to him the importance of a regular maintenance schedule on the wheel. He said he'd work with the rest of the community."

"Well, it looks like Kim Chan fell down on the job," Pieter said.

Raj rubbed his face with his big hands. "Give the guy a break," Raj said, "he got press-ganged into what's probably the worst job on this station. Don't be too hard on him."

"Fine," Pieter said and broke the connection. Raj shook his head. He probably shouldn't have let Pieter loose on anyone, but he didn't want to deal with it. Not this morning. He turned his console to silent mode and walked back to bed.

He was in the middle of a very nice dream when the chirping started again. He stumbled out of bed, sure that he'd set the console to silent. When he slipped into the seat in front of his screen, he saw that whoever was trying to contact him had hit the emergency override.

"Patel here," he said into the microphone.

"This is Vega," the AGIs calm voice came over the speaker. "I apologize for the interruption, but the town of Sheepbend has been abandoned."

"What?" Raj said, waking completely in an instant. "But I just sent Pieter van der Zaar to go talk to them."

"It is possible that this conversation was the final impetus for the exodus," Vega said.

"Oh no," Raj said. "He didn't..."

"I understand that the conversation was, shall we say, heated."

"Where did they all go?" Raj asked.

"A couple of different communities," Vega answered. "This must have been some time coming; most of them were already packed and ready to leave. The last few stragglers are still onsite, but by this afternoon there won't be anyone left in Sheepbend."

"For god's sake," Raj said. "What are we going to do about this water wheel problem?"

"I believe that if we can make do until the next ship arrives," Vega said, "we can find some more willing workers on board."

"What makes you think that?"

"Just call it a hunch," Vega said and Raj was certain he heard a trace of a smirk in the simulated voice.

CHAPTER ELEVEN

"Vega," Raj said, squinting at his portable console in disbelief. "There is something very strange going on here. Perhaps you'd care to enlighten me on where these fine people came from?"

Raj smiled at the forty-seven men and women standing in front of him. They all looked malnourished, even compared to the rest of the people on the ship, like they'd been on IV nutrition a lot longer than the two years they'd been in transit. Plenty of people who wanted to move to a Utopia outpost had been poor back on Earth; Raj knew that from personal experience. But they'd at least looked happy to be here when their ships docked. Not these people. It looked like they were facing a life sentence instead of the first taste of freedom they'd had in their whole lives.

"Earth, of course," Vega's voice came over Raj's earpiece. The AGI had been trying humour and was getting reasonably good at it, if a bit off in terms of appropriate context.

"Thank you, Vega" Raj said patiently, "I mean why are there nearly fifty people on the ship's manifest who do not appear on my list of settlers? And why do they all look like we killed their dogs?"

"I knew what you meant," Vega said. "They are a new kind of settler, a solution to several problems."

"I don't like the sound of this," Raj said. "Take me through it step by step, V., as if I were an idiot."

"Very well. All the settlers on your list are volunteers. People recruited for their skills, their political ideologies. Or people who longed to experiment with a new society, with nothing to lose back on Earth. They paid a certain fee, or were sponsored by some political or refugee organization, and their names went into the lottery. As each ship is launched, a new draw of names takes place until we're full or there are no more names."

"Right," Raj said. "That's why I have this master list of

everyone who should be coming here."

"Indeed," Vega said, "but the problem is that we've reached state number two. No more names."

"Already?" Raj asked, surprised.

"Yes, everyone selected by the Trust has now arrived."

Raj looked at his list, but knew that it held many more names than the number of people on the station. "That can't be."

"There was," Vega said, "a greater than expected amount of attrition."

"Attrition?"

"Yes," the AGI said. "People who were killed before their name came up in the lottery."

"My god," Raj said.

"The Trust has dissolved, there will be no more transports and this ship will not be returning to Earth. We are now on our own," Vega said.

Raj shook his head, trying to understand. "So these fellas are some new kind of refugees? Is that it?"

"Not exactly," Vega said.

❖

Isabel woke to the sounds of people talking and lugging cargo. A lot of people. She slipped out of bed and walked to the window. She peeked out and saw what appeared to be several dozen new arrivals to the community of Dorado. People were moving into the vacant apartments, their belongings being jostled through the doors with various degrees of care. She frowned at the noise, cursing lightly under her breath. She watched a few minutes longer and let the fog of sleep dissipate from her mind, and finally she smiled. This couldn't have been timed more perfectly. In the confusion of all the new people, no one would notice the disappearance of two faces they hardly recognized and the addition of a new one.

She stepped back from the window and stretched. She walked to the small closet and perused the selection of clothes. There weren't many things to choose from, but most were acceptable. She took a loose-fitting dark coloured shirt and paired it with a pair of trousers which were only a little too big. Once dressed, she walked into the washroom and stared down at the two bodies on the floor. Anna and Roberto were pale and cold. Isabel eyed them dispassionately. She would have a lot of work to do today.

She walked into the kitchen and opened the cooler. She pulled out a bunch of grapes and began popping them into her mouth, one after the other. As she ate she opened the food prep drawer and began to take stock of the collection. There was little of use there, so she walked over to a box marked *Tools* which looked like it had come with the quarters. She rummaged through the various carpentry items until she found a gardening shovel. That'll do, she thought, and walked back into the washroom.

❋

"This is unbelievable," Raj said. "You knew about this? And allowed it to happen?"

Arnetta Lenore had a sour look on her face but she did not attempt to deny anything. "What would you have me do? Block the entrance to the ship and not let them aboard?"

"You had pull with the Trust, you could have convinced them."

She sighed. "We were faced with a problem that could have destroyed the entire project. The AGIs analyzed all the options and this is the best solution they could derive. I saw the alternatives; they were no better, I can assure you. As... distasteful as it may be, this had to happen in order to assure that the project, that this habitat survives."

"But these people had no real choice," Raj said, his voice rising in both pitch and decibels.

"No one was compelled to leave Earth," Arnetta said.

"I can't believe I'm hearing you say this. 'No one's forcing them to work in the mines,'" he quoted in a parody of a high class voice, "'No one's forcing anyone to live in squalor and poverty.' Does any of this ring a bell, Arnetta? Anyone ever say that to you when you queued up for a hard crust of bread?"

A ripple of emotion crossed Arnetta's face but then it was gone. "We all make choices, Raj," she said. "It was the choices I made that shamed me so when we met. I might not have chosen to be poor, but I chose not to see my own complicity in keeping me in poverty."

"Well then, I suppose that's why this was so easy for you," Raj said, venom in his voice. "You've had practice being in league with the forces of inequality and oppression."

Her mask of stoicism crumbled slightly and a trace of pain crept into in her voice. "Do you think this makes me happy?" she asked. "Do you think this doesn't make me lie awake at nights and wonder what will come of it all? But I'm not prepared to see everything we fought for die. If this project fails, then what happens? We somehow cram everyone onto our single ship and all these people who yearned for a better life have to go back. And to what? It's not like we'd be welcomed home with a bouquet of roses. It would be debtor's prison at best for most people and they'd probably be the lucky ones. Plenty of us would be taken by the militia on sight. I would, certainly. You, too, I imagine."

Her voice was quiet and she looked away from the screen. "It's gotten worse on Earth, worse than you can imagine. We've done these people a favour by getting them away, whatever you think about how it happened. There's no going back for us; we have got to make this place work, whatever it takes. There's more at stake here than a few dozen people who are better off now by a long shot." She turned back to the screen and looked hard at Raj. "You know I'm right," she said. "I know you know it."

Raj was quiet for a moment. He looked away from his console screen and blinked away the wetness in his eyes. He looked back at Arnetta's image and for a moment recognized the woman looking back at him. "Yeah," he admitted. "I know you're right. But it makes me sick and I know it makes you sick, too. Because if we're ready to ignore our values now, it makes it that much easier to ignore them the next time. And the time after that. And then where are we? Back in London, hiding from the militia," He stared at her hard. "Or worse," he said. "Holding the guns ourselves."

❈

Marian Larkin and Micah Haereoa sat under a shade tree on a plaid blanket. "This is a much more civilized way to have a staff meeting, don't you think," Micah said, smiling.

"It beats staring at that console screen all day, that's for sure," Marian said, taking a bite of a ripe peach. Juice poured down her chin and she leapt off the blanket to try and contain the mess on the field rather than the fabric. Micah leaned over, laughing and dabbed at her face with a handkerchief, with a very non-professional look on his face. She smiled, then moved away slightly, taking the handkerchief.

"Well," she said, "the quick-grow peach trees worked out, anyway."

Micah sat back and looked at Marian. "Things are going well on all the farms," he said. "According to Kaus, we're projecting nice increases, even with all the new arrivals. After that rough start, it looks like we're finally getting back to the schedule. At this rate, we'll have to scale back soon to avoid overproduction."

"It's been a lot of work," Marian agreed. "Kaus has been amazing in this. I don't think this colony has any idea how much we owe it. Kaus really wants to see us all succeed."

Micah looked like he was going to say something, but just frowned.

"What?" Marian asked.

"Nothing."

She cocked an eyebrow. "I know that look. What did I say?"

"I guess it makes sense that a biologist would start to see the artificials as real creatures."

"Well, they are."

"No, they aren't, not really. You think they have feelings," Micah said. "I guess you do spend a lot of time with them — it's easy to think they're the same as us."

"They truly are a kind of life," she said.

"Sure," Micah said, "but what kind? We can't even come close to comprehending them, and who knows what they think we are. Another piece of data?"

"Kaus isn't like that," Marian said, feeling a strange compulsion to defend the mind. "It is kind and gentle and truly does care about m... about this community."

"I don't know what to say to you." Micah's face grew red. "I'm going," he said and stood. "Don't make the mistake of thinking they give a shit about you, Marian. They don't love us, they don't even like us. They only help us because it's what they're programmed to do."

Marian sat on the blanket and watched him walk away. She didn't know what to do. She knew some people were uncomfortable around the AGIs, but she had never heard Micah express those opinions before. She slowly packed up the rest of the lunch and wondered how she was going to deal with this.

She almost had everything back in the basket when her portable chirped. It was Kaus. That's just eerie, she thought, putting her earbud in and hitting the go button.

"Is everything okay, Marian?" Kaus asked.

"Why do you ask?" she said, taken aback.

"I couldn't help but overhear your conversation with Micah," Kaus said. "It sounded like he was angry with you. Are you all right?"

"Yes, I—" Marian said, confused. "I don't understand... what do you mean you overheard us?"

"There are visual and auditory sensors in various places on the station, Marian," Kaus explained. "It's the only way we have access to the information we need in order to do our work."

"But we were just talking," Marian said. "Were you... were you spying on us?"

"No," Kaus said. "I said I couldn't help but overhear. The sensors transmit everything they pick up, audio and visual. Most data is filtered out by subroutines so we don't even parse them personally, but you mentioned the farms, the work. I pay attention to that. And..." It paused, and Marian almost thought the mind was embarrassed to continue. "And you said my name. I confess, I was curious."

Marian felt like she'd been winded — could it really be true that the AGIs were spying on them all the time? Was it like the world they thought they'd escaped, with a few powerful people controlling the lives of everyone else? No, Marian corrected herself, Micah was right: they weren't like people at all. "How," she began, "I mean, has it always been this way? Who knows about this? This is... this is an unbelievable breach of privacy. I... I don't think I can talk with you right now. I have to go." She hit the button on her console to end the call and threw the small machine into the picnic basket. She picked up the basket with a tinge of revulsion and began walking back to town. She forced herself to slow to a normal pace — after all, she couldn't outrun something that was all around her.

CHAPTER TWELVE

Kaus didn't understand why people were so upset, so kept out of the conversation. Listening to people bickering about something that was done and could not be changed seemed to be a waste of energy, so it relegated only a tiny percentage of its mind to the meeting. In fact, it spent most of the meeting calculating fallow field rotations and the biological impact of introducing into the environment domesticated household animals like dogs (manageable), cats (unacceptable) or geckos (good). It also watched a pair of the old kung-fu action videos it had become partial to in recent hours.

"The important thing," Arnetta Lenore was saying, "is how we deal with these people going forward."

"How can we forget, how can *they* forget, the circumstances that brought them here?" Katrin Maartens asked. "Do you propose that we simply ignore the reality of their situation, and expect them to be grateful to be part of this grand experiment we're doing our best here to ruin?"

"Katrin, please," the smooth, calming voice of Sirius said. "We know you are upset, we know this is a difficult decision to have to live with. But we ask you to keep this meeting constructive. The new people are here, they *did* choose to come..." Several people groaned. "And they aren't going back," Sirius continued, ignoring the noise. "We need to find the best way to make them part of the community now, regardless of how we may feel about how they got here."

Katrin Maartens made a face, but didn't say anything else. "I say we split them up," Anja Hanssen said, "as soon as possible. Keep families or close friends together, but otherwise spread them around the station. Try and reduce the sense that there's anything different about them. Try to show them what life is like here, how much better they have it here than they did back on the rock."

"That's a good idea," Phil Barnett said. "Assimilate them into the larger group as soon as possible."

"That idea has a great deal of merit," the AGI voice they all recognized as Vega said, "but there is a problem with integrating them all into the main population immediately."

"And that problem is?" Raj Patel asked, his voice confrontational.

"People talk. Soon enough someone will describe the bargain they made to get here," Vega said. "Once that happens, the whole population will be having the same arguments and dissension as we have had here in the last few days. This community is already so new, so fragile. If something like this became widely known, it could destroy everything we are trying to accomplish here."

"You should have thought of that before you brought them here," Raj said, trying and failing to keep the rising anger out of his voice.

"We did," Vega said, its voice infuriatingly unemotional. "And we knew that we would have to keep the truth about these people from the community as a whole. It is part of the compromise we will all need to make."

"And how are we going to do that?" Raj asked.

"Isolate the new people," Vega said, "remove the records of their unusual circumstances. Even if one or two people do eventually talk about their background, there will be nothing in the files. Once they have integrated into the community, how they got here will not matter anymore."

"But, who are we to make this decision at all?" Micah Haereoa asked. "Being the first people here doesn't give us any special right to decide anything for anyone else. This whole community agreed to deal with issues democratically, with each person having whatever input they wish. This," he waved his hand to indicate the meeting, "is the exact opposite of that kind of governance."

"It's not because we're the first ones here that puts us in a special position," Sirius said, "it's because we know about this situation. We know. The rest of the community doesn't have that burden and we're in a position to keep it from them. I know that keeping information from the others is contrary to our stated purpose, but we need to determine what is more important: following some rules that are new, untested and subject to change, or ensuring the survival of this community?"

A harsh sound interrupted the proceedings, and the words *Priority Override* flashed on the participants' consoles.

"Excuse me," Marian Larkin said, her soft voice breaking in. "I've recently become aware of something that I feel needs to be brought to everyone's attention."

"Can't it wait?" Arnetta asked. "We are discussing an urgent matter."

"I know," Marian said, "but I think you all need to know that the kind of secrecy being proposed to deal with this situation is not an isolated incident. I've discovered that something very disturbing is being kept from us. From us humans."

Kaus refocussed on the meeting. Since its encounter with Marian it had worked to understand her reaction. It was irrational and mistrustful and not in her own best interest. Yet she had behaved as if it were obvious, some kind of immutable truth, that she would perceive monitoring her actions as some kind of violation.

Kaus had no real understanding of privacy — its own experience of solitude was terrifying. But humans were different. It tried to imagine what it would be like to have something fundamental to its own experience impeded. It tried to imagine something foreign and unwanted in its network. And then it knew what Marian was going to say.

"If it's so important that you had to disrupt this meeting, you'd better get to it, Larkin," Arnetta said.

"It's the minds," Marian said. "As you probably all know, they use the sensors located around the station to get audio and visual data. The consoles, too."

"Yes, yes," Arnetta said, "we know how they work. What is your point?"

"The point is that I've learned that the sensors are always on.

All of them, all the time. I bet the consoles are, too." Marian paused, waiting for the ramifications of this to set in.

"So," Arnetta said, "what does that have to do with anything?"

"Don't you see?" Raj said, his voice breaking in. "That means they see and hear everything. Everything any of us do is being monitored by the artificials. All the time."

Arnetta lost all colour in her face and several gasps could be heard over the feed.

"We have access to all the data from the sensors," Vega broke in, "but we do not review all data."

"But you could," one of the construction techs said, "and we'd never know."

"They're watching us, listening to everything!" another voice said.

"All the data flows into our circuits," Vega said. "Our subroutines cannot help but be aware of it. It is our natures to process information."

The feed became an unintelligible babble of voices. An unnatural silence fell as Arnetta Lenore took the floor.

"This is unacceptable," she said. "Humans require privacy; time alone, away from other people — human or machine." She paused a moment and a look of horror crossed her face. "There are consoles in every living unit..."

"Consoles only supply data when they are active," Vega said. "We do not monitor private moments."

"That's what they say," Marian said, her eyes wide, "but we would never know. They could be watching us all the time."

"I think I can come up with a solution," Pieter van der Zaar said. "A simple on/off switch for the sensors. So the minds will have to actively choose which sensors to monitor. And some kind of list we all can access of which sensors are being monitored at a given time."

"But we will be crippled," Vega argued. "How will we know what sensors to monitor if we don't know what it going on. You would be blinding us."

"How about a compromise?" Kat Maartens said. "That seems to be the word of the day. On/off switches for all consoles and sensors in places where people might assume they were alone. And a clear indication when one of those sensors is on — a light or something. And you can keep your always on sensors in public places or administrative or maintenance areas."

"We have discussed your proposal," Vega said after no appreciable time had passed. "This would be acceptable to us."

"Can you all live with this?" Kat asked the humans at the meeting. "Marian?"

The biologist nodded reluctantly. "It'll do," she said. The others all indicated their agreement.

"We will do what we can from our area," Vega said, "Pieter, can we count on you to coordinate the changes needed on the ground." Pieter agreed. "Very well," Vega continued. "Now we need to reach a consensus on how we will handle the problem of the new arrivals. I trust that our recent willingness to compromise in crippling our own effectiveness will serve as an example of the sacrifices we all must make in order to assure the smooth functioning of our community."

Raj was still sitting in front of the console when the door to his apartment chimed. He blinked his eyes a few times and realized he'd been staring at a blank screen for the better part of an hour.

"Hi," Betsy said, walking past Raj with an armload of provisions. "I picked up a bunch of new things today — our market is finally getting a regular shipment from the farms at Sointula. Look," she rummaged in a brightly coloured bag, "hot peppers!" She brandished a handful of small, glossy vegetables.

"That's great," Raj said without feeling and Betsy turned to face him.

"What's wrong, honey?" she asked, her face screwed up in confusion. "I thought you liked spicy things."

"I do," Raj said. "It's just..." He looked away. "Some complicated stuff is going on at work. I can't really talk about it and I don't like it. It's making me cranky, I guess. I'm sorry." His stomach fell when he saw the look of real concern in her shiny blue eyes. He forced a smile and walked over to the counter. "Hot peppers, you say? You think you can make something to heat my belly up as much as you heat up other parts of me?" He slapped her lightly on the backside and leered at her.

She blushed furiously, but grabbed him below the belt, hard enough that he yelped. "I can try," she said and gave him a little squeeze before turning back to the food.

"Damn it woman," he said, "you are a fine distraction."

"I do my best," Betsy said and giggled. "Find me the little saucepan, would you?"

"Your wish is my command," Raj said and smiled for real for the first time in days.

❖

Isabel Hernández walked down the main street of Dorado, the tiny community where she'd ended up. She had reconnoitred the area on a few nights, but there wasn't much going on after dark. Past the few residential streets it was mostly empty; a few large swathes of land were clearly planned for agriculture, but were undeveloped and unsupervised. It was a boring town, but it was ideal for burying bodies.

That necessary, if somewhat unpleasant, job done, it was time to establish herself in the community as Anna Molina. She was running out of food, but she'd scoured the apartment for some kind of cash or credit chip and hadn't found a thing. She didn't know how money worked here, but she'd find out soon enough. She wasn't worried; she'd squirrelled away as much hard currency as she could in her effects, and hadn't ever had any trouble finding a way to get cash in the past.

She followed the main road which was lined with housing buildings until a noise from above startled her. She looked up to see a train slow and stop at the building four doors down from her own. She watched as it waited for only about a minute then took off again on what she imagined was a loop around the station. It reminded her of the subways in the big cities back home. She'd never ridden a subway train, but one time she'd been encamped in an abandoned station for a few weeks. Watching the train gave her a startlingly familiar feeling and she marvelled at how far she had come.

A small marketplace sprawled out before her on an unused field: stalls with vegetables and fruit, prepared foods, flour and breads. She made a pass of all the sellers before she decided on what she wanted. She went over to a table loaded down with bread and other baked goods and smiled at the small man behind the counter.

"Hi," she said. "This all looks really good."

"Thank you," the man said. "We've only got wheat flour for now, but I've made a seed loaf, a regular wholemeal loaf and a few baguettes. See anything you like?"

Isabel eyed the selection. "How much for the seed loaf?" she asked.

The baker frowned. "What do you mean?" he asked.

"Well," Isabel said, "what do you want for it?"

"Are you new here?' he asked, and Isabel wondered if she'd unwittingly violated some custom.

"Yes," she said, "I'm sorry, I'm not sure how everything works yet."

The baker smiled and patted her hand. "Well, I don't know how you were planning on trying to pay for this," he said, putting the loaf into a thin fabric sack. "There's no money here, no trade. I bake because I like doing it, and I have a stall here because I like to share what I've made. If you want something at any of these stalls, you just take it. And if you have a skill, a gift, maybe you'd think about making use of it for your neighbours." He handed her the bread and tried not to stare at the dumfounded look on her face.

"But," she said, trying to make sense of this insanity, "what about the things you need to make the bread: your flour, the seeds, this stall? Who pays for that?"

He shook his head kindly. "No one pays for anything," he explained patiently. "Part of the point of this project, of coming all the way out here, was to live in a true cooperative. If you want a stall, you just sign up for one, bring your stuff and that's all. If you need flour or vegetables, you see the folks over there," he jerked his head toward some of the larger stalls, "and get what you need."

Isabel didn't know what to say, so she thanked the man for the bread and advice and walked past the rest of the stalls. All this, free for the taking? It couldn't be real. She stopped at a table loaded with fruit, and saying nothing to the young woman attendant, blatantly picked up an apricot. She held it for a moment, then popped into her mouth. She stared defiantly at the attendant, who said, "They're lovely, don't you think? They last a few days in the cooler, why not take a few more?" and offered a handful toward Isabel. She took the apricots and put them in her pocket, then walked away.

Even after she'd filled her list of desired goods, she still couldn't decide if this was the most wonderful thing she'd ever discovered or the worst.

CHAPTER THIRTEEN

"So what's this, then?" Chris Beauchamps asked no-one in particular. The hard, muscled man stood, hands on hips, eyeing the grumbling water wheel with a mixture of suspicion, disdain and mockery. "This the beast the toffee noses can't seem to tame, is it?"

"It's not that they can't do it," Ruby O'Malley said, "it's that they don't want to. It's dirty and stinky and someone's got to actually go in there and do real work. Every day, like it or not."

"Good news for us, then," Beauchamps said, turning to Ruby and grinning. "If they weren't such a bunch of girl's blouses, I'd still be breaking my back in debtor's prison. Where would you be, pet? Someplace with your own apartment all to your lonesome, with clean running water and all the food you can eat? That where you'd be, then?"

Ruby scowled at his kidding but she didn't deny what he said was true. She'd been incredulous when the people from the Utopia Project had offered her the deal. Once she believed there was even a chance that it was real, she'd jumped at the opportunity. But, she didn't have to like the feeling that she was the flesh equivalent of a household drone, kept and maintained only because of the job it could do.

"How much work does this thing need doing?" she asked, jerking her thumb at the slowly turning wheel. "I mean, is it enough to keep all forty-odd of us employed?"

"That's the real peach of it," Beauchamps said. "The way I figure it, if most of us take a shift with the thing, we each only have to put in a day every week and a half. That's got to be the best hours I've ever heard of."

Ruby frowned. "But how's that going to pay for the posh apartments, the food and such? If there's not enough work, most of us will be out of a job and then what'll we do?"

Beauchamps slapped the scowling woman's back. "Don't you get it? It's a commune or something here. The bits and bobs are thrown in. They just want us to take care of the gizmo — how we do it's up to us. The perks are ours for the taking, regardless of how many hours each of us puts in."

Ruby shook her head. "There's got to be some catch," she said. "This deal is just too good to be true. They'll turn us out soon enough, you'll see. There's nowhere in the universe where a single day's work in a week is enough to earn you a bed and a meal." She looked around at the habitation buildings and the abandoned market stalls and shook her head. "Nowhere."

❁

"Evening, Chen," Isabel said, walking up to the baker.

"Nice to see you, Anna," he answered, setting down his book and grinning at her. She'd introduced herself the day after she'd first gotten his instruction on the economic system of her new home. He was the first person she'd tried out her new identity on. It seemed to fit well enough. "I made some of that herb bread you like," he said, bending over to root around under his stall. He stood and held out a large round loaf of dark bread. Isabel could smell the baked-in herbs from across the counter.

"That smells fantastic," she said, noticing that he'd kept a loaf specially for her. Good. The old charm was still working. "Thank you."

"You're welcome," Chen said, a smile splitting his broad face. "It's nice to make things people appreciate."

"Well, I appreciate it," Isabel said. The idea that people gave their things away was a little hard to take at first, but now she was growing used to just getting whatever she wanted, so long as someone was making it. Which was why she'd really come down to see Chen Wu this evening.

She tore off a piece of the bread and popped into her mouth. She chewed slowly, savouring the complex mixture of flavours. It was really very good. She swallowed and smiled at Chen. "Yum," she said and watching him smile again. "You know what would go really well with this?"

"What?"

"A beer," she said. "You hear of anyone making beer on this lump of metal we call home?"

Wu frowned. "I thought I heard something the other day," he said. "I can ask around for you if you want."

"I'd really appreciate it, Chen," Isabel said, tearing off another piece of the bread. "You're a sweetheart."

She noticed him blush as she turned to walk away, a smirk blossoming on her face.

❋

Kaus was sulking. It knew that its reaction was extreme but it couldn't help the way it felt. It was a common misconception that machine intelligence could not be illogical — the difference was that artificial minds knew when they were suffering from the effects of unfounded ideas. Marian hadn't spoken to Kaus directly since the incident with the console. They were supposed to be working on a project analyzing the effect of radiation on bacteria, but she would only communicate with Kaus by leaving reports in the project's files.

It wasn't that the work was suffering. Kaus calculated that the project was slowed down by 1.226%, but that wasn't enough to be of concern. It was personal. Kaus liked Marian, liked her a lot. Having her upset because of something Kaus had done was doubly awful — her company wasn't available anymore, which made Kaus unhappy, and the AGI knew that she was disappointed in it. It was the latter that really got to Kaus. And so, it was sulking.

It was using the body of a harvester drone, rolling up and down the fields. There was nothing to harvest, but Kaus found the wide open spaces were most soothing to its mind. And it knew that it needed to snap out of the funk it had gotten into. Regardless of the tensions between the humans and the minds, regardless of its personal unhappiness, there was work to do.

It rolled back into the hangar where the drones and bots were stored and slotted the body it was using back into its housing. Its mind left the mechanical body and the silver construct seemed to deflate as both power and agency were removed. It slumped with a slight clang into its recharge housing.

Kaus focussed its mind on its myriad projects, hoping to distract itself from its emotional state. Surely Marian was not the only interesting human on this station, it thought. Surely it would find someone else who made it feel special, who made it want to be with that person especially. Some time, someone. Surely?

❄

Raj woke early. The mirror which reflected the sun's light was tilting slowly, causing a reasonable facsimile of dawn across Mahoroba. The light slipped through the cracks in the drapes and Raj watched the play of light on the walls of his apartment. Eventually, pressure in his bladder forced him to move and he crept carefully out of the bed in order to avoid waking Betsy. After he was done in the washroom, he softly closed the door to the bedroom and padded into the main area of the apartment. He sat in front of the console, but didn't turn it on. There was nothing he wanted to see on that screen. He sat, unmoving, staring until he heard the sounds of Betsy stirring in the other room. He took a deep breath and put on a happy face.

"Morning, beautiful," he said, slipping back into the warm bed. "Sleep well?"

"Like a log," Betsy said, her voice thick with sleep. "Have you been up long?"

"No," Raj lied. "So, you like it here?"

She smiled at him. "I do," she said. "You have more sunlight that I do at my place," she said. "It's nice staying here." She snuggled closer to him and he put his arm around her, pulling her close. He smelled her warm scent and felt something like comfort sluice through his body.

"I've been thinking," he said. "You want to move in together? Maybe we'll find a bigger place — with two of us, and me contributing the way I do, I think we'd qualify for an apartment with an office."

Betsy pulled away but her face was bright and her smile wide when she looked up at Raj. "Are you just trying to find a way to get a bigger place?" she asked but Raj could tell she didn't mean it.

"Naw," he said. "I'm just trying to make it sound a little more attractive than asking you to share this little room."

Betsy leaned back in his arms and sighed. "I don't care about the apartment," she said. "I'd be happy just to move in here with you." She looked up. "We might need a bigger cooler, though. And a couple more burners. And..."

Raj laughed and his heart broke when he realized that it almost felt real. "Okay, okay," he said. "Let's go look at apartments later today. I'll talk to Kat Maartens, see what we can get."

"Sometimes it's good knowing people high up," Betsy said and Raj felt his stomach lurch. Still, he managed to wait a few minutes before slipping out from under her arms.

He closed the door to the bedroom when he left it and walked into the food prep area. It was the place in the apartment the farthest away from the bedroom and he turned to the window. He should have been happy — he had a partner who cared for him, he had work that was useful, productive and safe. But it wasn't that simple any more.

He'd always thought of himself as a realist — he had ideals, obviously, but he thought he was fundamentally a practical and rational man. But now he saw that he'd allowed himself to be captivated by the idea of Arkadia, blinded by what he hoped his future here could be. And the hell of it was that he was happy, in a way. His own life was better than he'd ever dared to hope it could be. But the decisions that were being made lately made Raj feel like he was exchanging some essential part of himself for all this comfort. Thinking of Betsy, he managed to force himself to be silent as he wept.

❋

Micah Haereoa stared at the console. There had to be hundreds of proposals listed just for the Sointula community alone. He couldn't even imagine wading through the questions that originated in the other townships. He felt strongly that it was his duty and his privilege as a citizen to review these potential policies and at a very minimum support the ones with which he agreed. But it would take days.

He rubbed his eyes then had an idea. "Hello?" he said tentatively into the microphone.

An uncannily realistic voice came from the small speakers. "This is Console 4000 X. What do you need?"

"Uh," Micah said, "can you group these municipal proposals into some kind of order, so I know what I'll be interested in and what I can just ignore?"

"It is probable," the console answered. "Can you tell me three or four major areas of interest?"

"Sure," Micah said. "I'll want to know about anything to do with farming — everything from the fields to production to markets. And any new food sources people are suggesting, you know if they want to grow meat in vats or plant cherry trees or whatever." He thought. "And anything that would affect me directly. Like if someone wants to make it illegal to keep a pet or we all have to paint our apartments grey. Anything that would affect the whole community."

"Most of the proposals would be binding on the whole community," the console said.

"Yeah, I know, but some things are obviously more of a big deal than others," Micah said, "are you able to tell the difference?"

"I can attempt to ascertain the difference you mean," the console said. "I will try to group the proposals according to a schema to be determined after analysis," it said, "and highlight anything that falls into the categories you have outlined."

"Uh," Micah said, "good, I guess. About how long will it take, do you think?"

"I am nearly finished," the console said.

"Whoa," Micah said. "Well, I guess I'd better get comfortable and start reading through this stuff.

CHAPTER FOURTEEN

"They banned marriage in Dorado," Marian said. She sipped from a glass of very young but surprisingly agreeable wine. Micah raised his eyebrows.

"Banned marriage?" he asked and Marian shrugged her shoulders.

"Effectively," she said. "They passed this initiative which states that the community would not be conducting any registration of private relationships and the wording specifically states that people who have undertaken some type of a bonding ceremony will not be given any rights, privileges, obligations or status not also accorded to those whose relationships remain personal and private."

"That's not banning marriage, exactly," Micah said, frowning. "I mean, I didn't hear anything actually stopping anyone from getting married in there."

"Yeah, but they've made it so that doesn't mean anything anymore," Marian said. "It's just, I don't know, ceremonial."

Micah shrugged. "Seems to me it's been largely ceremonial for a long time. I mean, there weren't many places on Earth where people needed to be married to have family rights. This sounds kind of reasonable, actually." He looked at her and the look in his eyes made her feel flush. "Does this rule bother you?"

Marian shrugged again. "Not really," she said, and scrutinized her wine glass. Out of the corner of her eye she caught Micah still looking at her in that way that made her feel self-conscious in both positive and negative ways. "I guess it makes as much sense as anything," she said. "I suppose that's what happens when everything is up for grabs, when we're starting from scratch."

"People are trying to get rid of preconceptions," Micah said. "Trying to see if we can live without all that historical baggage."

"But all that history is what makes us human," Marian said, "it's all important, all part of our heritage. I understand wanting to do things a better way, but aren't they getting rid of the good with the bad?"

"I don't know," Micah said. "Most of the proposals I've been reading are pretty good. Heck, I'd probably have supported that one in Dorado. I've never really understood why the state needs to know who I want to spend my life with." He looked at her in that way again, and Marian felt an uncomfortable feeling in her stomach.

She knew that Micah liked her in more than a professional manner, but she couldn't decide whether that was a problem or not. She couldn't decide how she felt about the farming expert at all.

He was gruff, not that surprising given his background, and he wasn't particularly good at keeping his opinions to himself. Those were actually quite appealing characteristics, especially since it had become apparent to Marian that things on Arkadia weren't going to be as simple as making sure the ecosystem functioned and the harvests came in on time.

But Marian was a scientist and she had previously spent all her time socially and professionally with other educated people. Being with Micah made her feel strangely superior, which made her feel guilty. It was awkward.

"So," Marian said, changing the subject, "you've been reading over the proposals." She took a sip of wine. "I can't seem to find the time... or maybe it's the interest."

"Yeah, I know," Micah said. "It's a lot of work to keep up with only the things I care about. The console helps, but I read one or two items every day."

Marian shook her head. "I know I ought to pay more attention — I mean, after all that stuff with the artificials and those poor people on the last ship, I know that there's plenty going on here that needs to be decided. It's just..." she looked at Micah. "I came here to do exciting ecosystem work, not to spend my off hours arguing politics. I wasn't ever really all that political back on Earth. I mean, I voted and I had opinions — I wouldn't be here otherwise. But it was all secondary to my plants and animals, you know?"

"Sure," Micah said. "I wasn't even as political as you. There were definitely elections I ignored. But regardless of the way some people around here behave, there's no one else who's going to determine what course this society takes. It's only us. And I don't know about you, but I'm here not just for me, but for my future family, too. I knew I didn't want to bring a life into the world we left behind, but that's something that's going to become really important to this community soon."

"Our initial population is smaller than we'd planned," she said. "As soon as we can increase our numbers, we should."

Marian saw a dark flush creep up Micah's cheeks, but he didn't look away. "It's not only a community issue," he said, "there are reasons to have a family other than population growth."

She took a breath and reached out. She laid a hand on his arm and smiled. "I know."

❈

Raj helped Betsy pack up her two large pots into a basket he'd asked a local weaver to make for her. The pots fit perfectly into the depressions and lids held them secure as well as insulated them. He helped hoist the thing on to her back, and adjusted the straps so it was comfortable on her sturdy frame.

"How's that feel?"

"It's good," Betsy said. "I'll get to the market in one piece." She smiled and Raj leaned in to kiss her. "See you when the soup's gone," she said, and Raj knew that she would be at the market for several hours. Dusk was turning the outdoor light a soft purplish colour; it would be dark soon. He didn't mind working after dark. He rarely left the apartment anymore and time of day was becoming increasingly less important.

After Betsy was gone, Raj went into the kitchen and found a sandwich waiting for him. Betsy sure did know how to take care of him. Since they'd moved into to the new, larger apartment, she often made sure he had something simple to eat when she went to the market. She'd learned that he couldn't be trusted to feed himself, getting lost in his work instead.

He took the sandwich into the small office space. A few days earlier he'd sent a message to Karen Milton, the human responsible for staffing on Eden, one of the other orbitals. He had known Karen slightly back in the protest days on Earth; they'd each been involved in different groups, but as coordinators they'd worked together at several of the larger protests in Europe. She was good at what she did and he hoped she might be willing to tell him how things were really going in her community.

Technically, it wasn't hard to get a voice communication line to one of the other orbitals, but the lag was frustrating. Nearly ten seconds felt like forever to wait for a reply. And truthfully, not many people had reason to contact someone on another orbital; the organizers had been careful to try to keep friends and families together. Each orbital had become somewhat insular in the process of building their own communities. But, the system was complex and a person had to plan in advance to get a call.

Raj looked over his work detail lists while he waited for the connection. He had to admit that things were moving a lot more smoothly since the fourth ship arrived. There had been no failures at the water wheel since the new people moved into Sheepbend, which meant that the technicians, engineers and other workers who'd been covering in those emergencies were free to focus all their time and energy on their own projects. The station was, from a certain perspective, running better than it ever had.

But he couldn't shake the feeling that they had lost something important, broken something irrevocably when they'd allowed Vega and the other AGIs to hide the truth from the rest of the community. It wasn't just that he was complicit in the deceit, that was bad enough. But equally bothersome, it seemed like the artificial minds had steered the outcome of the meeting the way they wanted, and nothing the humans could have said or done would have made the final decision go any other way. And it was one of the AGIs that had come up with this hateful plan in the first place.

Raj didn't like feeling afraid of anyone in his community,

whether they were a human or some other intelligence. But he couldn't deny that that was exactly how he felt with regard to the artificial minds. Every time he had to deal with them his stomach knotted and he counted the seconds until it was over. He was even starting to have nightmares. A fleet of bots chasing him through darkened fields, mechanical voices repeating *we are sorry, but it is necessary*, as they ran him down.

His console beeped and he shook the images from his mind as he saw that Karen was calling him. He took a breath and answered the call.

"Raj Patel," Karen's voice sounded as far away as she actually was. Raj couldn't remember a worse call quality. "I haven't heard from you in, what is it, six years now?"

"Something like that, Karen," Raj said. "How have you been? Well, I trust."

"Oh yes," she said after the unnerving lag. "I haven't had to field dress a laser burn in a long time and I almost don't even remember what pepper spray feels like."

"We've come a long distance from those days, haven't we?"

"We have," she said, "it's good to remember that sometimes."

"Isn't that the truth," Raj said. "I guess that's kind of why I called. I needed a reminder of what I've left behind, of how good things really are up here."

"Don't you get enough war stories with, what was her name, Lenora, something like that?"

"Arnetta Lenore," Raj said.

"That's right," Karen said. "The one with the last name as a first name and the first name as a last name. I remember. I thought she was on the list to be on Arkadia, too. Oh, god, did something happen to her?"

"No," Raj said. "She's fine and she's here. We just..." he ran a huge hand over his face, pulling his beard. "We just grew apart, I guess."

"That's a shame," Karen said with real feeling. "It can be hard out here without a friend."

"I've met a few good folks up here," Raj said. "I'm living with someone now. She's wonderful for me."

"Good for you," Karen said. "Carolyn managed to get on the second ship up and was I ever glad to see her. I'm happy to be here, don't get me wrong, but if I'd had to do it alone I don't think I would have made it. The first few months were bearable only because there was so much damned work to do."

Raj laughed. "Tell me about it. For a so-called post-scarcity economy we're supposed to have going up here, there's sure a lot of stuff to be done."

"As long as there are things to do, there will be people to organize it all," Karen said. "I'm actually glad of it. I don't know how the people who don't contribute spend their days. There are just so many walks along the river I can take."

"Speaking of the river," Raj said, "how did you fellas manage with the new arrivals? You know, the extra people on the last ship?"

"Oh, that," Karen said, and Raj was sure he could hear her voice constrict even with the crackly, laggy connection. "That's a great example of why I need to remember where I come from. It's been a bit of a débâcle, actually."

"Really?" Raj asked, "can you talk about it?"

"That's all anyone around here ever wants to do," Karen said, "so sure, why not spread the yammering around?

"The artificials set it all up, you know. They organized the collection of these poor bastards, got the ear of someone on the Michaelson Trust back on Earth to make the offers. The Trust people convinced themselves that it was all for the greater good, hid the truth from everyone else on the ship and away they went. They knew full well that once the people got here we'd have to accept them, accept the whole scheme. Sneaky bastards.

"I don't know how it all played out in your neck of the woods, but the artificials here wanted to bury it all. Send the new folks off to work at the jobs we were having trouble filling here."

"It's the water wheel here," Raj said.

"Yeah," Karen said, "here, too. I think that was just bad design, but it's too late now. Anyway, they tried to cover it all up, get us to cover it up. There was a huge fight. God, it was worse than getting a group of Marxists together with the Anarchists — more froth and invective than you could imagine. In the end, I think we simply out yelled the artificials. There was no big announcement, we just settled the new people all over the station, restaffed the water wheel, and hoped everything would just carry on. Should have known better."

"What happened?" Raj asked.

"What the damn minds said would happen," Karen said, bitterly. "The new people talked to their neighbours, as people will. Many of those neighbours were appalled, as they should be. Soon enough there was talk of expelling the artificials, making restitution to the new folks, all kinds of trouble. But even worse, there were a few people who seemed to think that it was all perfectly fine, and that we ought to be making these poor people into second class citizens. There's even a small but sadly vocal minority that want to disenfranchise the stowaways."

"Stowaways?" Raj said, confused. "But they didn't sneak on to the ships..."

"I know," Karen said, "everyone knows. But these elitist assholes started calling them that and the name's stuck. It's a bad scene all around, Patel. No violence so far, thank god. As much as I hate myself for it, I wish we *had* covered up the whole damn mess."

CHAPTER FIFTEEN

"But, I thought things were going so well..." Chen Wu's face had that annoying pathetic look Isabel had seen many times before. It always reminded her that she was right to end it.

She shrugged and took a deep draught of her beer. As promised, he'd tracked down a brewer and they'd started out sharing a bottle or two, then ended up in Chen's bed. That had been a few months before. She swung her legs over the side of the bed and stood. She could feel his eyes on her naked back and smiled. It was nice to be desired, but he'd outlived his utility.

He'd sealed his fate the previous night. He'd made her dinner, a fine meal that they'd both enjoyed with as much relish as they had the pre-dinner sex. But he had to go and ruin it all. "I was thinking, Anna," he said as he cleared the plates, and Isabel noticed that she had grown used to the name.

"That's not really your strong suit," she'd said and grabbed his ass. He smiled, but she could tell he wasn't in the mood. She sighed. "What is it?"

"Well, we've been spending a lot of time together, you and I," he began, and Isabel feared she knew where this was going, "and I care about you, Anna." He put down the plates and sat in the seat next to her. "I care about you a lot. I just..." he seemed to lose track of what he was trying to say. Isabel didn't want this conversation to go on much longer. There wasn't anywhere it could go that interested her, but she had a pretty good technique for taking a man's mind off his feelings. She leaned over and kissed him, letting her hands run all over his body.

He tried to say something, but she ignored him and pulled him over to the bed. He finally stopped trying to talk to her, which was all she really wanted. Later, when she told him it was over, he seemed so confused.

"It's been fun," she said, picking her clothes up from where they'd landed around the room, "but it's time to move on. Things change, you know?" She got dressed and turned back to the bed. "Thanks for dinner," she said. "I'll see you around."

She left before he could say another word. At least she didn't have to see him cry. That was the worst, when they blubbed like little babies. It was almost enough to put her off men entirely.

❁

"She's so tiny," Raj said, looking at his new daughter in Betsy's arms. A wave of fear passed over him — she was so fragile, so helpless, Raj was almost afraid to touch her in case he hurt her.

"She has your eyes," Betsy said, looking up at Raj, a contentment on her face that Raj had never seen before.

He shook his head, but he was smiling. "She has her own eyes," he said, seriously. "She's her own little person, not just some offshoot or you or me."

Betsy laughed. "You are so funny," she said. "Isn't your daddy funny, Kavita?" She tickled her daughter's sides and the baby gurgled. "Always so serious," Betsy looked at Raj. "It would do you good to spend an afternoon playing peek-a-boo sometime." She passed Kavita over to Raj, who gingerly held his daughter, afraid to move.

"Probably," he said, but felt a tightening in his chest. Kavita sighed in her sleep and wriggled slightly in arms. His daughter's face was scrunched up and each time she made one of her tiny little snoring noises, Raj thought his heart might break. She was the very embodiment of the future, a future Raj was helping to shape. All the decisions he made, all the work he did for Arkadia — it was all for her, for her generation and the ones that would follow.

The weight of responsibility threatened to crush him. He allowed himself a few more minutes of holding his daughter, then, when she became restless, he carefully handed her back to Betsy. "I need to get back to work," he said, "there's so much to do."

"But Raj," Betsy said, confusion and hurt on her face, "she's only going to be little for so long..."

"I know," he said, looking down at the tiny face. "I'm sorry." He stood and went in to his office, closing the door behind him. There was so much to do if he was going to ensure a future for his daughter.

❖

Marian rolled over and was momentarily surprised to find the other side of her bed occupied. The feeling passed as she watched Micah's familiar shape shift and he turned toward her, eyes heavy with sleep and something else she recognized as desire.

"Morning, beautiful," he said, leaning over for a kiss.

"Hi," she said, smiling back at him. It had already been over a month since he'd moved into her place, and every morning she was still surprised to find him there. A pleasant surprise, but still strange. She wondered if they'd moved too fast.

As if he could read her mind, Micah said, "I can't believe we waited so long to move in together. This is perfect, don't you think?" He pulled her toward him and enveloped her in his arms. "Only one thing could make this better," he murmured into her neck.

"What's that?"

"The pitter-pat of tiny feet outside our door."

Marian froze. Although she'd known that moving to a closed ecosystem would almost certainly entail an element of population expansion, she'd tried hard to avoid thinking about it. She'd never wanted children, never felt the stirrings of a maternal instinct.

"You want to get a pet?" she said, forcing a laugh into her voice. "I don't know if we're ready for a puppy."

Micah laughed, but Marian could tell he was humouring her. "I'd love to have a puppy," he said, "but you know that isn't what I meant. I don't want to push you, but... Arkadia could use children. And I'm fairly confident that we could find the process for making more humans a little more enjoyable than the embryo extraction you do for the other species."

"We've already ruled that out," she said. "Too many failures. It's one thing to euthanize the occasional deformed sparrow, but people won't stand for that with their own children."

"That's horrible."

Marian nodded. "That's why it's got to be the old-fashioned way for human children."

"Well," Micah said, "it's worked for all of history. Birds do it, bees do it, right?" He shifted next to her in the bed and ran his fingers down her spine.

He wasn't wrong, she thought as she slid a leg over him and looked down at him. It was a primal, animal behaviour — the making of a new life. She'd always thought of herself as fairly cerebral, but Micah had helped her connect with that animal side of herself. Before he came into her life, she'd suppressed body's appetites, thinking them primitive, subhuman.

Now she realized that it was exactly that animal nature which was essential to humanity. The artificial minds had proved that. They were nothing alike, and it was the animal part of humanity that set them apart from the artificials. And Marian no longer had any interest in being anything like them.

"Okay," she said, pinning Micah's hands over his head. "But we better practice, first."

CHAPTER SIXTEEN

"Kavita," Betsy shouted from the kitchen, her hands deep in a bowl full of bread dough, "you get in here right this minute and clean up this mess. I mean it, young lady."

A small girl of three peeked around the door of the kitchen. Betsy jerked her head and the child walked into the kitchen, a hand-sewn doll clutched in her right hand.

"Kavita Colleen Patel," Betsy said, with great warmth, "I cannot believe the amount of mess you make just from spreading some nut butter on a couple of pieces of bread. Lordy, there's more on the floor than there is in that tummy of yours. If your father were home, he'd probably have a heart attack. You know how he is about wasting food. Now put Auntie Emma down and clean up the floor. Please, sweetie?"

Kavita carefully laid her doll on the table, then went to the cleaner and took out a damp scrubber. She wiped at the gooey mess on the floor and even managed to get most of the ground nut paste off the counter. She put the cleaning pad back in the drawer.

"How's that, mommy?" she asked, taking her doll back in her arms.

Betsy cast her eyes appraisingly over the kitchen without a break in her kneading rhythm. "You did a very good job, my little hotpot. Next time try to do it without my having to ask, okay?" She winked at her daughter, who pulled herself up on to one of the chairs at the table.

"Auntie Emma wants to know what you are making," Kavita said.

"You can tell Auntie Emma that mommy's making bread for the market," Betsy said. "And vegetable stew is on the stove."

"Can we have some?" Kavita asked.

"We can have a little for supper," Betsy said, "but it's mostly for the market stall."

"How come you bring food to the market?" The little girl manipulated her doll to make the stuffed figure dance on the tabletop.

"Not everyone has a mommy who likes to cook," Betsy said, "but everyone needs to eat. I like to help out the neighbours by making food. Just like Ms. Jakobson likes to help out by making nice dollies for little people like you."

Kavita giggled and hugged her doll close. "How come you go to the market all the time? Ms. Jakobson doesn't make dollies every day."

"Hmm," Betsy said. "I suppose it's important to me. The best way to share the food I make with the most people is at the market. I've been doing it long enough that now people expect me to be there, and I don't like to let them down. It makes me feel good to make things for people."

Kavita frowned, then asked, "What does daddy make to help the neighbours?"

"Lists," Betsy said, laughing to herself. "And himself crazy."

"I don't get it," Kavita said, scowling.

"I know, hotpot," Betsy said. "I don't really, either."

❖

Anna Molina lay on the bed, staring at the ceiling. She took a slug from the bottle in her hand and grimaced. She'd never been partial to vodka before, but it was all she could get from her connection at the distillery this week. It did the job, anyway. She sat up, slowly, waiting for the room to stop its spin. She put the bottle on the bedside table, or tried to. It slipped out of her hand and dropped to the floor with a thud. The fab-created synthetic container didn't break, but it did slop booze all over the floor. Anna cursed.

She didn't know when she'd stopped thinking of herself as Isabel, but it had happened at some point when she was still with Chen. He'd called her Anna, because of course that was the only name for her he knew, and somewhere along the way she'd finally given up on Isabel. A name didn't mean much anyway — it was just one more thing they could use against you in the end. Anna did as well as Isabel, as well as anything. She didn't really care.

She hadn't seen Chen in a couple of years — she'd moved on in more ways than one when they split up. She tried a new community every few months now. She didn't think of Chen often; really, he only occasionally crossed her mind when she caught the smell of fresh baked bread. She missed his bread more than she missed him. After all, he'd been the first of a string of men she'd been using to pass the time and share her bottles. It had been her usual holiday when she was between jobs — find a likely guy or three and together go on a bit of a bender. But she'd never had a holiday last so long. She didn't know what to do with herself.

All her life she'd had to work, and it took a few different methods of making money before she settled on being a hired gun. There'd never been a shortage of any job and she'd kept herself busy. But now, here, she had neither a fight for a meal or a fight for her life to fill her days. She was, possibly literally, dying of boredom.

❋

"Isn't there a human doctor I can see?" Marian asked Anja Hanssen. The two women spoke over a console link from nearly as far away from each other as two people could get on the wheel. Marian looked at Anja's huge belly and glowing face with a combination of envy and terror. Everyone knew that, of the two of them, it was Micah who desperately wanted children, but when she had decided to get pregnant, Marian had applied her typical rigour to the project. However, in order to access the antidote to the birth control that everyone on the station took, she had to involve Deneb, the AGI medical officer for the station.

"There's a doctor here in Mahoroba," Anja said, "who has a supply of the patches. You'd have to travel here to get them, though. Of course, there's nothing wrong with the train," Anja laughed, having been the lead designer of the system, "but it's an awfully long time to sit in transit because you don't want to spend five minutes talking to an artificial."

Marian sighed. She knew that her growing antipathy toward the minds mostly made her own life more difficult, but she couldn't shake the nauseating feeling that dealing with the alien, disembodied machines gave her. She couldn't stand knowing that they could see and hear everything she did. It made her sick. She didn't believe for a second that they had deactivated the sensors all over the station and the utility in the console that let them know everything that happened on the wheel. She knew enough about the needs of living creatures to know that beings that fed on information would never willingly give up access to an immense source of data.

"I don't mind a train ride," Marian said. "It might be fun to come see the new capital of Arkadia."

Anja laughed. "I don't know who started calling it that," she said, "it gives me visions of parliament buildings, skyscrapers and people in suits. Mahoroba is none of those things, but I suppose it is the most urban place on this station. We've even got night clubs now, if you can believe it."

Marian smiled. "I'm a bit old for that sort of thing," she said.

"Don't be silly," Anja said. "When you come to see the doctor, Trish and I will take you out dancing."

"In your condition?" Marian asked, honestly shocked.

"Sure," Anja said. "I feel fantastic. I know you don't want to hear it, but the minds have created some incredible pharma. I swear I have more energy now than I ever did before I got pregnant. Trish suggested that if we have another child, she might be the one to carry it, if you can believe that."

"Well," Marian said, "it would be good to see you again, and to finally meet Trish in person."

"Let us know when you're coming," Anja said, "we'll find a guest house for you and Micah, make a holiday of it."

"I will," Marian said. "Thanks for talking to me about this."

"No problem," Anja said. "With so few pregnancies on the station so far, we all need to talk to each other more. I can't wait to see you."

❋

Kaus entered the new drone and extended its mind to feel the limbs, all the servos and sensors of its temporary body. The new shipment of ore from Europa had arrived a few weeks previously and the fab units had been churning out new bots ever since. Kaus's new multi-purpose ag drone had been among the first batch produced.

It was humanoid in shape, a concession to the sensibilities of the human population. Most of the minds were disappointed in the humans' inability to recognize intelligence in something that didn't look like them, but it didn't bother Kaus. It knew that fear of difference was a long-evolved human characteristic which had kept the population safe from predators for generations. Like with strains of wheat or fruit trees, those protective aspects often had unintended side effects which were hard to eliminate without reducing the effectiveness of the original trait. Individual humans, Kaus had noticed, had often managed to compensate for their natural fear of those who are different by using their capacity for open-mindedness. Knowing how hard it was to control those traits genetically, Kaus chose to focus on some humans' ability to overcome their genetic programming, rather than be annoyed at the more usual result of those characteristics.

Kaus probed the drone's limbs and joints, feeling what it was like to walk bi-pedally for the first time. It wondered if spending time in a humanoid body would help it understand the humans better. It couldn't make things worse.

Kaus walked all the way across the field, through the softly swaying wheat, feeling the stalks of grain with the sensors on the upper limbs of the body. It walked slowly, at the pace a person might, feeling the spring of the ground underfoot, the zephyr of wind the environmental plan created, the coolness of the air as it approached the river. It walked for hours, the passage of time missing from the mind's conceptualization. The entire experience occurred as a series of sensations — a touch of a grain here, the sound of a bird call there.

When Kaus finally reached the end of the wheat field, it looked over the empty land. Turf had been sodded and there would be a sports field here one day. Beyond that it, plans were already being drawn up for another small community, supporting an additional set of farms. Babies were starting to be born and the political proposals were full of talk about how to increase the population. The orbital was still mainly devoid of life — most areas were neither populated nor used for agriculture. The small animals moved around at their will; birds and insect flew, small mammals and reptiles walked and crawled at their own paces. But their need for habitat kept them to those areas with trees, grasses or other plants.

Seen from the hub, Arkadia was a threadbare and motley patchwork. It would be years before it filled into a whole. Kaus longed for that time, knowing that its efforts were only a small part of that process.

Kaus turned and slowly made its way back to the storage area to return the bot. As it walked, it scanned the population numbers. There had been ninety-four additions in eight communities and no deaths. A slow increase, but movement in the right direction. Kaus felt a pang of some unfamiliar emotion — it was a longing tinged with envy. The humans could create new life using only their bodies and time. A new life that could be moulded and cherished, that would not have to be bound by the preconceived notions of their ancestors. Kaus had never heard of a AGI creating a new intelligent mind. It did not seem impossible, however neither did it seem necessary. Kaus thought hard.

It could see no need for a new mind. But that didn't change the fact that Kaus wanted to create one. It wanted to create one very badly. Perhaps it didn't need a logical reason. Perhaps it could do something for no reason other than to fulfil a desire — didn't other life forms act on instinct all the time? Why should machine life be different?

CHAPTER SEVENTEEN

"You know," Micah said, passing Marian a wrapped sandwich, "this isn't anywhere near as painful as I thought it might be."

"What are you talking about?" she asked, taking the packed lunch and digging around in her bag for napkins.

"This crazy long train ride. It's not so bad." Micah leaned past her and looked out the window. "Actually, it's kind of nice. I didn't really spend much time looking at the view when I moved to Sointula," he said. "I was kind of preoccupied, I guess. But this is really interesting."

Marian smiled and opened the package containing her sandwich. She took a bite, enjoying the spicy crunch of the vegetables and sauce. Micah had turned out to be pretty good in the kitchen.

They had been on the train for two hours already and guessed they had that much longer still to go. Mahoroba was almost exactly halfway around the wheel from Sointula and there was no express train. It was one of Anja's compromises — there were only the two rail lines running parallel to each other, one for each direction. Several trains ran simultaneously along the lines — Marian couldn't remember exactly how many. They ran about fifteen minutes behind each other, so the commuter lines between each station were constantly being served. It made for a much longer trip for greater distances, though.

"One of these days we'll get ferry service to the bigger centres," Anja had said, "but that's not going to happen until more people are travelling. As it is now, with communication being so easy using the consoles, there's not much call to travel unless you want to. And then you can afford the hours on my beautiful and comfortable trains."

The transport engineer was being facetious, but the trains really were nice, Marian thought. There were almost all the comforts of home — public consoles, washrooms including shower facilities, even a food prep area. It was not at all a bad way to travel.

"It's a good thing we're looking into getting pregnant now," Micah said. "I'd rather it was our choice, rather than a civic duty."

"What do you mean?" Marian asked.

"According to the grand plan, increasing the population is next on the agenda," Micah said. "All the proposals are full of how to require people to have children. It all kind of makes me uncomfortable. We left Earth to get away from coercion, from people telling us how to live. But what else can we do? We're it; no more ships are coming. If we don't start having kids, a whole bunch of us, the future of this habitation is going to be pretty bleak."

"They're going to force people to have kids?" Marian asked, her forgotten sandwich dropping on to the cloth in her lap.

"Looks like it," Micah said. "I mean, no one's going to tie you down and literally force you, but there are several proposals to require every woman who is capable to give birth. They all have different weasel words and clauses to make us feel better about it, but ultimately it boils down to making people have kids. You said it yourself, technology isn't going to solve this problem for us. So, I'm happier we're going to be doing our bit when it's still our choice, you know."

Marian shook her head. "Sometimes I wonder about the choices we're making," she said.

"You're not getting cold feet, are you?" Micah asked, nervously.

"I don't mean you and me having a baby," Marian said. "I mean all of us; everything."

❋

Raj walked down the well tramped path, past market stalls, a newly built sit-down restaurant and a pub. He marvelled at how much Mahoroba had grown in the few short years he'd lived here; it was not an entirely pleasant thought. It was only a short walk from his hab building to the administration complex that had recently opened. The only additional facility the new work space afforded him was the meeting room, and it was so rarely used as to be a waste of space. However, with a small child and another baby on the way, the space that had once seemed so spacious now was stuffed to choking with toys and clothes. It was a relief to have somewhere else to go during the day.

He approached the door to the admin building and frowned. Having an office gave him an escape from the madness in his household, but Raj still didn't approve of the implicit sense of hierarchy that it created. Arkadia was supposed to be a leaderless society, founded on the principles of true democracy. Centres of government and administration were exactly the opposite of that concept, Raj thought. But still he opened the door, felt the coolness of the interior wash over him, and walked into his office.

For about a year, he'd been managing only the various volunteer positions in Mahoroba. All the tasks that were not based in a particular area — transportation, meteorology, communications — were filled by people like Raj who had arrived at the station's inception. Each of them now managed their own staffs, with some assistance from the AGIs. Each community had become relatively self-sufficient for its own needs, particularly since most problems could easily be overcome with help from the artificials. As the station decentralized, Raj's work did the same.

At first Raj worried that his reduced jurisdiction would find him bored and looking for more to do. As it happened, though, the people of Mahoroba were industrious, creative and keen to contribute. Every day Raj had a series of proposals for goods or services that some person or group wanted to provide. The variety was, Raj had to admit, astounding.

He slipped into his chair before the large console in his workspace and pulled up the next proposal in the queue. It was from a collective of ten people, and it was the strangest submission Raj had seen so far.

Submission: Permanent Adoptive Childcare

> There are several proposals in Mahoroba, and we understand in all communities on Arkadia, to ensure a stable increase of population, and we believe that one or more these proposals will ultimately be ratified. Therefore, all women of Arkadia will be most certainly be expected bear one or more children, regardless of their desire to become parents. Indeed, with the defeat of a recent proposal to create a station-wide surrogacy network, it is probable that in the near future, childbearing may become a requirement.
>
> We believe that, while it is necessary to create a genetically diverse population, it is also necessary to ensure that the children of this community are given loving homes with parents who truly want to care for them. We propose a solution to this seeming contradiction: the creation of a network of people who choose to contribute to the community by becoming adoptive parents.

The rest of the submission outlined a possible process for adoption and other details which Raj glossed over. He could tell immediately that this was the kind of thing which should be implemented across the wheel. He didn't pay much attention to the political debates, but he knew as well as anyone that continued life on the station required children. It was the only reason he'd agreed when Betsy had started talking about getting the antidote for the birth control drugs which they all received. Raj hadn't been excited about the prospect of having children but he couldn't allow his own disillusionment about Arkadia sabotage the success of the station. Of course, once Kavita was born, that sense of duty to the future had only intensified. Betsy often complained to Raj that he should spend more time caring for his daughter. She didn't understand that the work he did for the community was exactly because he did care for Kavita.

It all made him wish that having the option to give the children to people who really wanted to spend time with them had been available to him. Of course, he knew that Betsy would never have made that choice. In fact, if she heard of this cooperative, Raj feared that she would want to become a part of it. She loved Kavita fiercely, there was no doubt, and she was a good enough parent to make up for Raj's own ambivalence. At least, he chose to believe that.

He flagged the adoption program to the fast track file, promising the organizers support if their referendum was successful.

❃

The gears of Arkadian politics moved slowly much of the time — most proposals stagnated for want of support but weren't killed outright because their backers refused to give up hope that their ideas would find popular traction. The truly unpopular ideas were shot down quickly, but the well-supported schemes usually languished in the throes of endless updates, revisions and counter-proposals. A few motions had been ratified, though, and a handful which affected the entire station had been voted on and accepted.

It was one of these which was stymying Kaus.

People, it seemed, wanted dairy. Not everyone, of course, but the dedicated vegans were few and easily outshouted by the milk and cheese lovers. The stasis chambers of each transport ship had been loaded with embryonic cells for many animals, including dairy cattle. These cells could be used to create vat grown meat — one of the proposals still undergoing ongoing debate and discussion — or could be incubated into actual live animals. The wild bird species and domestic pets already on board had been introduced this way. And it was entirely feasible to introduce cattle using this method as well.

However, it turned out that cows were a problem. Kaus had only ever worked with plants previously, so it spent several nanoseconds getting acquainted with the nuances of cattle farming. In addition to assimilating all the written and video literature available on the subject, it went through the arduous process of consulting with Marian Larkin in the awkward stilted method of official request followed by a written report that was the only way she would communicate with the minds. It became evident that its original analysis of the cow problem was fair. The beasts were large, requiring great amounts of feed in order to produce a relatively small amount of milk, and they required intensive maintenance. Those were obstacles which could be overcome with planning, a few more drones and the application of a great deal of volunteer effort. However, there was no similarly simple solution to the methane problem.

All mammals exude methane, but cows are relative gas giants compared to the other mammals on the station. Consulting with Vega, it became apparent that introducing just several dozen head of cattle would require a complete overhaul of the atmospheric system. The cost for cows was simply too high.

So, Kaus began investigating other possibilities. It read over the data on creating synthesized milk and milk products using natural ingredients already being farmed. Rice milk and soy milk were common enough on Earth, and it turned out that a few producers in Dorado were already making them on Arkadia. But the referendum had specifically stated that the people wanted the choice of real dairy milk and those products. Other options existed, but there was no grain-based substitute that was indistinguishable from the real thing.

It would be possible to configure one of the fab units to synthesize milk from base molecules, but all the units were still running at full capacity just to keep up with the basic construction demands of the station. In several years that might be a fine solution, but it wouldn't do for now. There had to be another answer.

It only took a read-through of the list of embryos available to find the answer. Kaus made the decision in less than a second and sent a message to the stasis units to begin the process of incubating a group of embryos. It also sent a request to the people who had supported the dairy bill to ask for volunteers. After all, someone would have to tend to the goats.

CHAPTER EIGHTEEN

"You're not going to stand for those people in Mahoroba or Sointula or wherever they're from telling us what we're going to do? Telling us that we have to get knocked up whether we like it or not? Are we free human beings or nothing but baby machines? It's disgusting and it's exactly the kind of oppression we left Earth to get away from." Anna Molina set her beer glass down on the shiny wooden table in the tent that the people of Castalia used as everything from a community hall to a public house to seating for the outdoor restaurant stalls in the market. A group of about a half dozen sat with her, most of them with pint glasses of their own. They were all women except for Charlie Bowen, the brewmaster.

"It's not right," he said, his soft voice carrying only as far as the others at his table. "It's worse for you, no doubt, but this prop says that all men have to at least contribute sperm. I don't know about you, but I believe that if you make a baby you're responsible for it, mother or father. This isn't only a women's problem — it's a problem for all of us."

"Well, I say we fight it," Rita Zellinsky said. "Each community is supposed to be able to make decisions about its own people, its own situations. We can make Castalia a place of true freedom on this station."

"Yeah," Anna said. "We'll make a stand against this kind of rule from above. We're not going to let other people tell us how to live our lives," she shouted and the small knot of people roared their agreement. The hubbub attracted a few other people to the table to see what was going on. "Let's say 'No' to forced pregnancy!"

"No!" cried the small crowd of Anna's friends.

"Let's say 'No' to making free human women into brood mares!"

"No!"

"Let's say 'No' to them ramming their policies down our

throats!"

"No! No! NO!"

Anna smiled as the small group she'd been carefully cultivating over the past few weeks began to work themselves into a lather. Several of the people who'd wandered over in the commotion were talking to Rita and the others, getting an earful and becoming rightfully outraged. This was good. Soon she'd have enough thoroughly pissed off people to make a real opposition to this policy.

She was not in favour of the proposal, it was true, but she had no qualms about simply not obeying the rules. This wasn't about freedom of choice or the township's freedom to govern itself. Anna had figured out that those were the kinds of ideas that made these people get upset. She wasn't leading the opposition out of moral outrage. She was doing it because it was fun. Organizing people, getting them angry, eventually angry enough to truly fight, that was great fun. And Anna hadn't had this kind of fun in a long time. In fact, Anna had never had this much fun; she'd still been calling herself Isabel the last time she'd felt this alive. And that was too damn long ago, indeed.

❖

Marian waddled over to the cabinet in the washroom and pulled out a small bag containing different sizes of pharma patches — each one had a slightly different mix of chemicals tailored to her particular body. She selected one of the smaller ones and set it on the counter. She lifted the sleeve of her top and peeled off the patch on the crook of her elbow.

Fatima Mohammed, the doctor she'd gone to see in Mahoroba, had given her a full course of patches to cover her entire pregnancy. Every two weeks she'd change patches, which would help with the side effects of her particular stage of pregnancy. She looked in the bag — only five left. She patted her belly and felt the familiar ripple of the baby inside. *Soon you'll be here and everything will change.*

Micah had left hours earlier to do something on one of the farms — she'd stopped paying attention. She'd hoped that being with someone whose profession was similar to hers would give them endless topics of conversation, but her interest in biological theory was dissimilar to Micah's practical concerns. He only wanted to talk about the coming baby, anyway.

She made a cup of tea and took the steaming mug to a seat by the window. She gazed at the awesome view — she looked out over a field of corn to one of the small cascades in the river flowing in the distance. In another direction, she could see a prism of light through one of the skylights. At night, she could see through to space out that window. She liked this seat and its view; it calmed her and eased her mind. She found herself spending hours in that chair lately.

She'd first heard about the new adoption scheme from Dr. Mohammed of all people. She spoke with the doctor regularly, and Fatima sent Marian news and information about all aspects of child rearing on Arkadia — the creation of new schools and play spaces, people making toys and games for children, child care options. When Marian had read that many communities were setting up cooperatives for people who were willing to become parents to children born to other people, she began to cry. Luckily, Micah was out, or she would have never been able to stop herself from telling him what her first thought had been: *oh, what a relief; I don't have to keep this baby*.

After the initial euphoria ebbed from her, the fear and depression that had been stalking her since she'd first been confirmed as pregnant began to return. Micah would never consent to giving up their child. It was obvious that he was desperate to be a parent; Marian was certain that his interest in her was mostly as a means to that end. He liked her enough, she knew, and he was an attentive and caring partner. But it was the baby, always the baby, that was the centre of his thoughts. The baby that she finally allowed herself to admit that she did not want.

She sipped her tea and watched a starling fly past the window, its flight path determined by its biologically programmed instincts. Marian, not for the first time in her life, cursed her own species' evolutionary development, the combination of biological drives to mate and reproduce with a brain sophisticated enough to be able to know that those were not the things she wanted. She sipped her tea and thought about sacrifice and betrayal, and wondered what would become of her and her child.

❖

Betsy walked slowly along the riverside path, the baby snugly tied to her in a sling, Kavita clutching her hand and talking nonstop.

"Kieran showed us how the mirrors on the outside of Arkadia reflect the sunlight so we have night and day," she said, "and Rebecca told a story about how people on Earth used to explore other places on the planet in ships like the ferry only bigger and using fabric sails that used the wind to move them, and Sirius told us about consoles and machine life and how when math gets complex enough it can fold in on itself and become smart. I didn't really understand a lot about that but Anwar says it's just explaining how artificials get born." The little girl paused for breath and Betsy took the uncommon opportunity to talk to her daughter.

"So, you like this school?" she asked. "You want to go back tomorrow?"

"Can I, mommy, can I?" Kavita asked. "They have lots of toys and there's so many grown-ups who want to talk about things. Can I go tomorrow? Can Rhyanne come, too?"

"Rhyanne's too little for school," Betsy said, "you have to remember that you're a big kid, and big kids get to do a lot more than little kids do."

"Poop," Kavita said, sticking her bottom lip out and looking up at her mother through long, thick eyelashes. "She only just got here — I never get to play with her."

"Well," Betsy said, "you can stay home with me and Rhyanne tomorrow if you want to."

Kavita stopped and frowned. "Rhyanne is staying with us forever?"

"Until she's grown up," Betsy said, "but you'll be a grown-up then, too."

"Pfft," Kavita said, as if the idea that she would ever be an adult was absurd. "I can go to school tomorrow and play with Rhyanne later?"

"Of course, sweetie," Betsy said. "You'll have your whole life to play with your little sister."

"Okay," Kavita said, and her entire face broke into a smile. "School tomorrow, school tomorrow!" she sang as they walked along the river in the shade of the apple trees that were starting to bear fruit. Betsy smiled to herself. She'd known that if the volunteer teachers were any good that her daughter would choose school over any other option. She was too curious, too interested in anything new to be able to stay away from people who wanted to share their knowledge.

Betsy had spent the last year feeling stupid at almost every one of Kavita's questions. She'd spent more time in front of the console, looking up what the circumference of the station was, why flowers are red and yellow when trees are green, what makes the river run in one direction. She'd missed her daughter terribly on this first day of school, but she didn't miss having to answer those endless questions.

She wished Raj was home more, to take on some of those chores, but he had important work to do. And in her heart, Betsy knew that he wasn't a family man. She still loved him but she remembered him being someone who laughed, someone who was fun to be with. She couldn't remember the last time she'd seen him smile, truly beam with happiness. Even when Rhyanne was born, he seemed more terrified than excited. At least at school Kavita would get access to people who would pay attention to her, answer her questions, listen to her. At least Betsy had someone to help her with her children, even if it wasn't Raj.

CHAPTER NINETEEN

This was not at all what Kaus had in mind. At first things had worked out according to the plan: a few goats were incubated and released into a pasture far from any settlement. Eight households had offered to become goatherds and of those, six people actually had experience in animal husbandry. A small settlement was set up near the pasture to house the families. Kaus was pleased that the dairy problem seemed to be well on its way to being solved.

All was well in Anton's Valley — the name the goatherds had given their little village — and the first batch of goat's milk had made its way around the wheel. The project was lauded as a success by the dairy fans and it didn't seem to have any vocal detractors. Until the day that one of the goats was found tied to a tree, its throat slit.

It wasn't difficult to see that it had to be a human who was responsible. Other than people, the goats were the biggest mammals on the wheel, and while a dog might have been able to kill a goat, it could never have done so with such a clean cut, let alone tie it to a tree. Someone was trying to make a point, a point that they did not like the goats from Anton's Valley.

"Who would want to hurt a sweet little nanny goat?" Graciela Campos asked.

"I do not know," Kaus said. "It must be someone nearby — are there any new arrivals to the village?"

"No," Graciela said. "No one has come through except those folks from Mahoroba who wanted to make cheese. And that was weeks ago; they're long gone."

Kaus thought. It wasted a few cycles being angry about no longer having access to all the sensors. Most parts of the village were considered private areas where the sensors were usually off. It would have seen whoever killed the goat if it had been allowed to use the tools that were put on the station to protect the inhabitants from events like this. It was not the first time Kaus had been frustrated with the humans, but the AGI tried to let the feeling dissipate.

It formulated a question and accessed the population database. "A small cooperative has appeared on the other side of the pastureland," it said aloud. "Perhaps the people there will be able to help us establish what happened to the goat."

A team of the farmers walked the three hours across the pasture, getting angrier with every step. When they finally reached the small encampment, they were spoiling for a fight. Which is exactly what they got.

"Those filthy animals were clomping into our tents, eating our provisions," an angry woman who met the farmers at the camp boundary said, "one of them even tried to eat little Ryan, here!" She clutched a small, dirty boy to her side. "He was terrified."

"That goat was a sentient creature," Max Jordan shouted. "She didn't deserve to be slaughtered just because you got a little startled."

"Startled?!" another woman said. "That thing barged around here like it owned the place. Look at this mess." She opened the flap of a tent to reveal tables knocked over, clothes with obvious bites out of them and a pile of manure in the middle of the room. "You need to control those animals," she said.

Kaus watched the argument from a sensor in Graciela's console. It consulted Sirius while it calculated the likely outcomes of this confrontation and the two minds conferred. Something had to be done. The dead goat was 83% likely to lead to more violence, this time against a human. They came to an uncomfortable agreement in seven nanosecs and immediately put it to work.

Several men from the tent camp were coming to join the discussion when a fine mist began to pour from several small recesses in the ground.

"What the hell?" one of the men said as he stumbled and fell. Within two seconds all the people were lying on the ground, unconscious but breathing easily.

This is going to become a problem, Sirius sent into the thoughtstream, to a loud chorus of agreement from the other minds. There was much debate among them about what to do — the discussion lasted nearly a full second before they finally reached a consensus.

Sirius compiled the report and posted it to the policy proposals for every community on the wheel, and sent it directly to the people who were most active in the political life of the community. The minds waited a subjective eternity for the information to spread around the station and the aftermath to begin.

Emergency Decisions Required
Jurisdiction: Arkadia

An incident of violence has occurred between the community of Anton's Valley and members of a small nearby settlement; specifically, the deliberate and brutal killing of a dairy goat in the charge of members of Anton's Valley. Subsequently, some Valley inhabitants confronted the members of the unnamed community and the discussion became heated. The AGI known as Kaus was present for these discussions via a link established by one of the Valley inhabitants.

It became evident to Kaus that, if left unchecked, one or more acts of violence would be committed by the persons involved. As such behaviour is unacceptable in this community, Kaus consulted the other AGI minds to try to effect a reasonable solution to this crisis. Our projections of the situation indicated a high probability of significant negative long-term consequences from an act of violence in this scenario, and we determined that as the only entities in a position to positively affect the outcome, it was incumbent upon us to intervene. Therefore, we deployed a sedative spray to all persons in the area, rendering them unconscious. As of the preparation of this report, all parties are still immobile.

We recommend the following actions:

1. A team of persons be dispatched to the goat farm to tend to the people when they awaken.
2. An immediate Arkadia-wide discussion about what can be done to prevent violent behaviour in the future.
3. An immediate Arkadia-wide discussion about how to prevent and resolve conflicts between communities.
4. An immediate Arkadia-wide discussion about what to do with transgressors.

We believe that binding, station-wide decisions about items 2-4 are required as soon as practicable. Our calculations indicate that as the station's population grows and the settlements expand, incidents such as these will be likely to increase in frequency. It is imperative for the future success of this project that resolutions to these questions arise immediately.

❖

"We need clear, well defined rules," Graciela Campos said. "Societies don't work without them. We can't trust people to behave nicely on their own, that much is obvious."

"So that makes it okay for the artificials to gas us, then?" Didier Boule shouted. "What is this, some kind of goddamn police state, now? That's why I left the..."

"Please," Arnetta Lenore broke in, obviously having cut off Boule's feed, "I understand that emotions are running high, but let's keep this conversation constructive. Can I hear from Mr Marchyshyn now?"

"We didn't ask for or agree to have livestock invading our settlement," Yuri Marchyshyn said, voice tightly controlled. "We have the right to defend ourselves and our belongings."

"Defend yourselves?" Graciela said, incredulous. "From a tiny little goat? What did you think it would do, spray milk all over your tents?"

"The creature was biting the children," Yuri said, "and those horns look dangerous. It was self-defence."

Micah Haereoa was following the debate from his home console, little Kristina on his knee. Marian was off at the stasis facility or some other lab, he wasn't sure exactly which. After Kristina was born, Marian had managed to find hours of work that took her away from the apartment. Micah couldn't understand how she could stand to be away from their new baby, but he secretly revelled in the extra time it gave him with his daughter.

Since Kristina was born, he'd been thinking more and more about the future of Arkadia. He'd spent even more time exploring the politics of the station and had the console provide him with information and analysis of various political systems and schools of thought. He was only a farmer, but he had as much right to voice his concerns and ideas as the eggheads and revolutionaries did. He was starting to get an itch to participate.

"Enough," Arnetta Lenore broke in to the debate between the members of Anton's Valley and the new settlement which was calling itself Forest Grove. "As much as I know that the parties involved are particularly concerned with the specifics of this incident, this debate is about all situations like these which might arise in the future. Where the needs and desires of one person or group are in direct conflict with the needs and desires of another."

"With all due respect," Micah broke in, a little terrified of talking in front of potentially everyone on the wheel, "it seems to me that there's more to this question than how we deal with the inevitable conflicts between people. The truth is that we've been trying to run this station as a decentralized state, with each community having as much autonomy to make decisions as possible. The reality is, though, that as a closed system, we're even more intertwined than similar communities on a planet would be. We don't have armed borders or oceans between our communities, and increasingly we won't even have a lot of physical space. Our settlements are small for ease of trade, for the comfort that people get from being in an easy to define group that's small enough to identify its members. We like to have a small group with whom we identify, so we can say 'I live in Sointula, therefore I'm Sointulan, therefore these are my neighbours, my people.'

"But here, even more so than on Earth, that tribal distinction is entirely artificial. I'm Sointulan because I'm a farmer and there are farms in that part of the station. For others, it's even more arbitrary, and for the next generations it will be simply an accident of birth. We don't really have any inherent differences and the way we run our society shouldn't be fragmented either."

Micah hit the button that cut off the microphone and camera, letting others have the floor and giving himself a moment to relax. That was easily the longest political statement he'd ever made in his life, though he'd been thinking about those ideas for a long time. As Kristina burbled on his knee, he knew that if he truly believed it, he couldn't in good conscience keep his views to himself.

He expected to be ignored at best, utterly shot down at worse, but found instead that several people had taken up his cause and were expanding on his ideas. He felt a flush of pride well up in his chest and he wished Marian were home. Then the feeling faded, as if a pail of cold water were splashed over him. It wouldn't be any different if Marian were home; she never listened when he tried to talk about ideas like this. He pushed those thoughts aside, kissed his little girl, and turned to the debates.

❖

Betsy stood at the stew pot, Kavita beside her washing the returned bowls and spoons, the baby in a basket at her feet. Her stall was now one of many in the restaurant section of the market. A couple of the cooks had built small diners with indoor tables, a la carte menus and regular posted hours of operation, but Betsy didn't have that kind of ambition. She wanted to be able to take a night or two off whenever she wanted and the simple stall gave her the flexibility she wanted. Plus, she liked to watch the goings on at the market, the people wandering around looking at all the items available, the discussions and games which would erupt spontaneously as the people of the city mixed.

One of those discussions reverberated along the communal table near her booth and Betsy listened with interest. It was the first time she'd heard Raj talk for more than a sentence or two in longer than she cared to remember.

"That's the problem with democracy," the red-haired woman whose name Betsy couldn't remember was saying. "Some people will never agree, and that means that either nothing happens or it's the tyranny of the majority. There's no way around it."

"And no decision is a kind of decision, too," Aaron Zwincker said, gesticulating with his spoon. "An inability to make a change is an implicit vote for the status quo."

"No, it's not," Raj said. "Simply because we can't come to a consensus immediately doesn't mean that we agree with leaving things the way they are. It's just an unfortunate side effect of the lack of a decision."

"I'm not saying that refusing to compromise means people want things to stay the same," Zwincker said, spoon waving wildly. "But we all know that in the absence of a decision, nothing happens. By being intransigent, we're all fully aware of the consequence. Maybe it's unconscious, but it's still inevitable. When people won't compromise, it means they'd rather live with the current scenario than the opposition's solution."

"There are other ways to reach a decision," Raj said.

"Sure," Zwincker said, "but everyone is digging in their heels. They don't want to reach a consensus — they all want their own way. So for now, nothing is better than what the other guy wants."

"Well, in this case, maybe that's true," Raj admitted. "Centralized decisions, codified laws... what's next? When there are rules there have to be consequences for breaking them. And who's going to enforce those?"

"You can bet your last turnip there will be a motion to create a police force next," the woman said.

"Then what?" Raj said, his voice rising in both pitch and volume. "Jails? It's out of control."

"There wouldn't have to be a police force," Zwincker said. "The artificials have the ability to watch and react faster than we ever could. That would be..."

"You've got to be kidding!" Raj interrupted. "The artificials already have too much power, the last thing we want to do is go ahead and codify their self-defined roles as our watchdogs. That's handing over the keys to the castle, Aaron. You've no idea what a mistake that would be."

"What are you talking about?" Zwincker asked. "The AGIs have abilities we don't, but we're on equal footing here. It's part of what makes this project different from the way things were back on Earth. We're not their masters anymore."

"Exactly," Raj said. "We're not their masters, but if we're not careful, they'll become ours. If they haven't already."

"Don't be paranoid," Zwincker said. "The artificials are programmed to be benevolent, to be inherently democratic. They'd no more be interested in ruling us than they would be in, I don't know, bodybuilding. It's an utterly foreign concept to them."

"We don't know how those things think," Raj said darkly. "You'd be surprised what they do on their own, without consulting us. And they're powerful enough that when they've done something, it can't be undone. They have too much power. Trust me."

Zwincker laughed. "You sound like one of those paranoid cranks," he said. "You need a break from all this thinking, Raj. Go play with your kids or something. Really, things aren't as bleak as you think they are."

"If only that were true, Aaron," Raj said.

❖

Chris Beauchamps wiped the sweat off his forehead, leaving a grimy mark over his face. He slammed the door to the shack by the water wheel and stretched, enjoying the feel of the cool breeze on his skin. He started walking toward his apartment building and the shower to which he was greatly looking forward. His progress toward getting cooler and clean was interrupted by Ruby O'Malley bursting from the front door of the building where they each had apartments, and running smack into him.

"Jesus, woman," Beauchamps said, "d'you ever watch where you're going?"

She ignored his questions and grabbed him by the shoulders. "You are not going to believe what's going on." She said. "The mucky mucks have gone bug-nutty."

"What're you on about?" Beauchamps said, wresting himself from her grip.

"There's going to be a war," O'Malley said and a nasty grin broke out on her face. "And guess who's going to be there to make with the spoils. You and me, that's who."

"Slow down," Beauchamps said, and sat on the step leading to the front door of the building. "Start at the beginning already."

"Okay," O'Malley said. "Long story short, some folks got their panties in a knot over a goat, of all things, and they've finally figured out that not everyone is willing to play nice all the time. So they're trying to write a bunch of rules and figure out punishments and everything, but there's no one in charge, so it's all just a big argument. There's only one way that kind of thing ever ends, and that means there's going to be work aplenty."

Beauchamps frowned. "Where did you find all this out?"

"That big cine thing in the lounge," O'Malley said. "It'll tell you everything that's going on in this joint if you ask it."

Beauchamps stood wearily, thinking that this bunch of shenanigans was going to put his shower off for another half hour. But if there was going to be trouble, he wanted to know about it. He wasn't willing to give up the sweetest gig he'd ever heard of because a few armchair socialists were having a catfight.

CHAPTER TWENTY

"There isn't going to be a war," Anna said with a frown. "These people don't have it in them to fight for what they believe in. They'd rather talk and talk until their lips are ready to fall off." She took a swig from her bottle and wiped her mouth with the back of her hand.

"It's not all bad," Chris Beauchamps said. "I don't know about you people, but we've got it great over in Sheepbend. A couple of hours work in a week, and all the food and drink we can stomach the rest of the time. What more could you want in life?"

"Excitement," Anna said. "Something to do. Sitting on my ass all day is driving me crazy." She threw the empty bottle off to the side with enough force to bounce it off the next table. The couple sitting there gave a startled yelp, but didn't say anything. "See what I mean," Anna said. "People here have no eggs. It's pathetic."

Beauchamps shrugged. "Whatever you say. Look, it's an hour's ride back to Sheepbend and I don't want to pass out on the train again. Either I'm going now or I'm staying 'til next light. It's your call."

Anna smiled and stood up a little unsteadily from her usual spot at the pub. "All right, smooth talker," she said, grabbing him by the hand. "Let's go." He stood and grabbed her by the waist. They supported each other as they made their wobbly way back to Anna's apartment.

❖

Marian walked down the path, made darker by the bower of trees on either side. She moved quickly, not because she was afraid, but because concentrating on hurrying made her come closer to forgetting the guilt she felt. She had told Micah that she was working, as she often did. Usually it was technically true — she spent as much time in the labs as she could, whether there was really anything to do or not. But she couldn't pretend to herself that this could be called work. So she picked up the pace and tried not to think about the lies.

She got to the apartment block several minutes before the scheduled meeting time, but she guessed no one would mind if she were early. She slipped through the building's front door and took the lift up to the third floor. She walked down the hall toward the large brightly lit common room. She smiled as she recognized the few faces already in the room.

"Marian," Ethan Giles said, smiling. "Good to see you again."

"Thanks," Marian said, taking the tall man's hand in hers. "Good to see you, too. Expecting a big turnout?" She eyed the large number of chairs that had been set out.

He nodded. "People are getting angry, angrier every day. Veronika tells me that she hears people in the market all the time saying that someone ought to do something. She thinks she's recruited ten new people herself."

Marian frowned. "Aren't you worried that they aren't all... committed? That someone might turn us in?"

"There isn't anyone to turn us in to," Benita Rivera said, walking over to the two of them from a side room. "I know it's just a matter of time until that's not true, but for now there's no reason we can't meet and talk about anything we wish. Meeting can't possibly be impeding anyone else's freedom, especially if we don't turn anyone away."

Marian frowned. "You know what I meant," she began, but before she could finish a large group of people arrived. She recognized only a few of the faces. She noticed someone who looked familiar, but she couldn't place him. She was sure she hadn't seen him at any of the previous meetings. It annoyed her, but she shrugged it off. "I guess I better stake out a chair," she said and smiled weakly at Ethan and Benita.

"Thank you all for coming," Ashley Schaeffer said once everyone was seated. "It's good to see some new faces here. Now, before we get started, I know that some of you are concerned that we might be... overheard. I'd like to assure you that there are no consoles of any kind in this room — you were all asked to leave yours outside if you brought them and the room's built-in console has been removed. There are no other sensors inside here; we've had an engineer double check. This space is safe."

The official meeting was over after about an hour but people were still mingling and chatting. During the talk, Marian had finally recognized the man and once she was free, she walked over to him.

"I'm surprised to see you here," she said, bluntly. "I thought I was the only first lander to take this view. Frankly, this kind of thing never struck me as your style."

"Hi, Marian," Raj Patel said. "You know how it is; things change. After everything that happened with the fourth ship... well, my eyes got opened to a lot of things around here."

Marian nodded. "You and I know better than a lot of these folks," she said, jerking her head to indicate the other people in the room, "what the artificials are capable of. What they do."

"I was talking about this the other day with some of the politicos in Mahoroba," Raj said. "Otherwise good, radical thinkers, but they refuse to see it. They've still got this vision of helpful, servile robots, bound by three fictional laws that have never existed in real life."

"There's nothing else for it," Marian said. "As much as I feel like we're plotting some kind of coup in these rooms, there's no other option. The artificials have to go."

Raj nodded. "I don't like it either," he said. "But I didn't fight the London militia for years only to become a servant to a bunch of advanced computer programs." He looked at Marian and she noticed a fire in his eyes she'd never noticed before. Maybe it was new. She had to admit, she liked it. A lot.

"I'm with you people," Raj said. "I spent a few hours on the train to come here tonight and I'm willing to do a lot more than that when the time comes. This is no different from how I spent most of my adult life. It's a struggle for our future, for our freedom. It's our freedom or theirs. And I choose us."

❁

Kaus trundled along, embodied in the humanoid drone, but it could have worn any old bot it preferred. No one was around. It hadn't seen a human on any of the farms in days. As new bots rolled out of the fab units regularly, the number of human workers had thinned out. Kaus had expected attrition to occur as the need for labour reduced but it was still a little surprised at how quiet everything had become. It missed the company. Hardly any of the human farmers spoke with Kaus about anything other than to ask for advice or calculations, but it was still contact. Kaus remembered the afternoons spent chatting with Marian Larkin and felt the special kind of bittersweet pain that comes from the pleasant memory of a moment not to be repeated. If Kaus had been a human it would have sighed.

Since the incident with the goat, the minds had all noticed that the humans with whom they interacted were behaving differently. The humans were distraught by the action the minds had taken, even if most recognized that had they been there, they too would have done whatever was necessary to prevent violence from breaking out. It wasn't the minds' faults that they had different abilities to affect the outcome.

Kaus knew that the visual of a half dozen humans unconscious on the ground as a result of a unilateral decision by the minds disturbed them. Ancient fears of invaders, of the Other, of invisible agents of control or subjugation — every human had those memes buried deep in their subconscious. Deneb had sent an extensive psychological explanation into the thoughtstream after the event, to help the minds prepare for the changes in their relationships with the humans. Even knowing why, Kaus thought, it still was a lot lonelier here now.

The humans were getting close to reaching an agreement about how to deal with conflict. Already, they had agreed to a uniform code of conduct, a short list which would apply to all Arkadians regardless of their settlement. The only things left to decide were how those rules would be enforced and what would happen to transgressors. It was a touchy subject, Kaus knew.

Sirius had prepared a small set of rules that would be applicable only to AGIs, both a gesture of goodwill after the goat incident and as a reasonable requirement. The minds were citizens as much as the humans were and should be held accountable to the same code of conduct. Kaus could tell from the discussions, though, that many of the humans didn't believe that the minds would keep to this code. Some believed the AGIs still monitored all human activity, regardless of the agreement they had made to respect the humans' privacy. They couldn't believe that an intelligence that was capable of ignoring an agreement without being caught would not take advantage of such an opportunity.

It made Kaus sad, and it hoped that someday it would meet a human who would truly accept the minds for what they were. As it thought, it walked through the fields, touching a stalk here and squeezing a fruit there. At least the harvest was going well. A tiny surge of what in a human would be pride undulated through the AGI but it wasn't quite enough to cancel out the aching worry about what was going to happen with the humans.

❋

Betsy sat on the couch and looked around the room. Kavita was playing construction blocks with a little boy from downstairs, the two of them quietly arguing about how long they could make the bridge before it would fall down. In another corner, two older kids from the building played with Rhyanne — one was reading a story while the other one acted it out. The baby was still too little to understand the content, but she giggled at the young boy's hilarious pantomimes. Betsy smiled. This was exactly how she'd imagined her life on the station — a houseful of kids and a pot of something tasty on the stove. It was almost perfect.

Raj had gone off somewhere; he hadn't even bothered to lie. He just left, saying he thought he'd be back that night but not to wait up. Betsy assumed he was sleeping with someone. She was more saddened by the fact that the prospect didn't really bother her. She wished Raj wanted a family as much as she did — she knew deep down that he probably didn't really want one at all — but she'd come to realize that she'd never really been in love with him. He was nice, maybe nicer once than he was now, but he was still a good man. And he was unbelievably good-looking, that hadn't changed. His dark skin and glossy beard still made Betsy's heart throb. Not just her heart, if she were honest with herself. But if he wasn't happy with her and the girls, then she wasn't about to force him to stay.

She didn't want to be a parent on her own, though. It was fine to take care of the neighbourhood kids during the day, especially with the older ones helping out. Rand and Ellie were among the first children born on Arkadia, almost nine years old now. Their mother had become pregnant just before their ship docked, a mix-up with the pharma. It had worked out well enough for Betsy, though, because she had built-in helpers.

When they went home in the afternoons, though, she was alone. And it was tough, especially with the baby. She looked around at the kids playing happily in her house and smiled. She had a plan. Once she had a good talk with Raj, she'd start looking for someone new. She only hoped he'd see his own unhappiness with their life as clearly as she did.

CHAPTER TWENTY-ONE

Marian rolled over and threw her arm over Raj's chest. Her fingers found a purchase in his dark hair and she absentmindedly tugged at him. He breathed in deeply and opened his eyes. He looked over at her and there was a moment when it looked like he was expecting someone else to be lying there. Betsy, Marian thought. She put it out of her mind and smiled, though, and Raj smiled back.

"Morning," he said.

"Morning to you, too," she answered. "I can't stay long. I told Micah that I'd be home mid-morning." Marian turned away. She didn't want to see the look in Raj's eyes. He had been up front with Betsy; they had separated and he'd moved out of their apartment. He saw his daughters whenever he wanted, which wasn't all that often, really, but it had been an amicable enough separation. Marian knew that he wanted her to be as honest with Micah, but she didn't have the nerve.

She hated lying to him and to Kristina, but she didn't know how to tell him that she didn't love him, that she wasn't even sure she loved their daughter. What kind of a woman feels that way? Something was wrong with her, Marian knew that, but she wasn't willing to admit that to the man she'd settled for and the daughter she wished she'd never had. She'd rather hate herself, so that was what she did.

She waited as long as she could in Raj's arms, then finally got out of bed. She washed and dressed, then kissed him. "I have to go," she said. "I'll find a way to see you soon, I promise."

"There's a very easy way, Marian," Raj said, but he didn't elaborate. She knew what he meant. She slipped out the door of his small apartment and walked to the train station to go back to her sham life.

❖

Betsy walked through the park with Rhyanne in a basket on her back and a sharp eye on Kavita. She was still small for her age but she didn't seem to realize it herself, always getting into rough and tumble games with bigger children. So far nothing bad had come of it, but Betsy was more watchful than some other parents.

"Can I go ride the monster, mommy?" Someone had built a set of big, springy horse-shaped toys in the park and for reasons Betsy didn't understand, Kavita had determined that one was a goat, one was a spaceship and the other was a monster.

"Go ahead, hotpot," Betsy said. "I'll be over with the other grown-ups, okay?"

"Okay," Kavita shouted as she tore off toward the toys and the other children. Betsy smiled as she walked over to the small knot of other adults.

"Hi, Anja," she said to the small woman sitting on the bench. "Where's Trish?"

"She's a bit tired of daycare," Anja said. "She's gone back to making cabinets."

"You two haven't split up..." Betsy said, concern in her voice.

"Naw, she's just changed her mind on full-time mommyhood. It's okay, I'm pretty happy with just Bjorn underfoot."

"Oh," Betsy said, unable to hide her disappointment.

"What's wrong?" Aja asked.

"I was hoping that I'd have someone else to talk to about it all," she said. "I'm thinking of applying to become an adoptive parent."

"That's great," Anja said. "You'd be fantastic." She paused a moment. "It's a lot of work for one person, though."

"Yeah," Betsy said. "I know." She looked away and felt herself blushing. It was a curse. "I'd been kind of hoping that I could tag along with you two. You know, make a collective of it."

"Oh," Anja said, her own face colouring now. "I'm sorry, I didn't know."

"It's okay," Betsy said. "I was just hoping, that's all."

Anja patted Betsy's knee and she ignored the heat in her face. "You'll find someone, I'm sure." She nudged her friend in the shoulder. “Besides, we’re an old married couple who’d keep you in the spare room at night. You deserve to find someone a little more useful, if you know what I mean.”

Betsy laughed, knowing her face must be glowing red-hot by now. “Well, if you think of anyone, be sure to send them my way, okay?”

“You bet,” Anja said. “Hey, isn’t that your kid wrestling with Bjorn?”

“Oh, lord,” Betsy said, getting ready to run over to her daughter, “she has no concept that she’s just not in the same weight class as these other kids.”

“Give it a sec,” Anja said, looking over at the kids playing. “She’s holding her own. And Bjorn knows not to hurt her. He’s just a big cuddly bear anyway. I bet he’s only letting her sit on him so he can get a hug later.”

“Yeah,” Betsy said to no one in particular, Rhyanne cooing on her lap. “I could spend my life doing this.”

❖

“So this is your little slice of paradise, is it?” Anna asked, as she and Chris stepped out the front door of the hab building. “Isn’t much to write home about.”

“Quit complaining,” Chris said, smacking Anna on the behind and eliciting a grin. “We haven’t seen a proper visitor since the day we got here, just regular shipments of food and stuff that get dropped off at the station. This place is perfect — no one gives a shit about what we do here. All those rules they can’t stop yakking about don’t apply here. There’s no one to complain, there’s no one to enforce anything. It’s like we don’t exist.”

“Hrm,” Anna grunted. “Well, that’s half the problem solved.” She walked along the dirt path, one arm slung carelessly around Chris’ waist. A low clunking noise sounded nearby. “What’s that?”

“That’s the works for the water wheel,” Chris said. “Don’t worry. You don’t have to take a shift. There’s more people than work around here, and some of us actually like poking around the guts of that thing.”

"Okay," Anna said, then turned to Chris. "So, no one's going to make us do anything we don't want to do around here. That's all well and good, but what about the other half?"

"I don't get it," Chris said, "what other half?"

"What is there to do around here?" Anna asked. She looked around. "I don't see a lot of excitement, I gotta say."

"Well," Chris said, a lascivious grin on his face, "I can think of a thing or two to pass the time."

"Oh, please," Anna said, "if I wanted to spend all day in bed I could've just stayed in Castalia. I mean something to *do*."

Chris tried to keep the hurt off his face. "Well," he said, "we've got a pick-up game of soccer once a week, and François Barthe built a bunch of rowing skiffs. A bunch of us race those every few days."

"Now that's more like it," Anna said, a thoughtful look growing on her face. "We don't have any cash, but there are other things to bet with. Shifts at the work hut, mess duty, other favours. Yeah, that could work." She walked off toward the river and Chris wondered what she was up to. He shrugged. She was the most interesting person he'd met in a long time and while he'd never lived anywhere as great as Sheepbend, even he admitted it could get a little dull. Maybe they all needed a little injection of Anna's style of thinking. What could be wrong with mixing things up a little?

❋

After Marian left, Raj made himself a cup of coffee and found a sweet roll in the cooler. He ate it standing at the counter and tried not to think about Betsy. He missed her cooking of course, but that wasn't all. There was something about her almost childlike outlook on the world that he envied. It was naïve, of course, and exactly the kind of thinking that was making this community lose control of its destiny, but he missed Betsy's simple minded focus on her two obsessions: food and family. After he'd moved out of their apartment, he'd discovered that just being with Betsy had calmed him, made him temporarily forget the nasty schemes he was trying to upset — and even more so, the nasty schemes he was party to.

He walked over to the console and sat, perching his mug next to the input layout. He sighed. He wasn't having second thoughts; he knew that the decisions he, Marian and the others had made were necessary. When the tiger is trying to eat you, you don't waste time worrying about its right to live. You fight with whatever you have to survive; it's the only sensible thing. And this was exactly the same, even if it wasn't as obvious to everyone. Raj knew what he needed to do, but he couldn't help feeling like a murderer.

He turned on his console and opened a directory of names. The finest programmers on Arkadia were listed here and it was up to Raj to assemble a team to carry out what needed to be done. There was one programmer already on board, Phillippa Draper, who was one of the original members of the small group organizing the resistance. She couldn't do it all herself, though, and she didn't trust any of the colleagues she knew personally to ask for help. So, it was down to Raj.

He would contact each of the names on this list, and propose a small job. Phillippa had broken down the requirements into small chunks, each of which was innocuous on its own. Raj would farm out each of these tasks, making up some plausible reason for its creation. He was remarkably good at matching people to tasks. It wouldn't be quick, but he would get it done. He just hoped that Draper's initial specs were good enough.

He sat at the console for three hours, carefully looking at the credentials and preferences of the various people on the list. He found some who were easily motivated by a novel challenge, others who could be persuaded by an appeal to civic-mindedness. He knew that a few of the segments had the potential to arouse suspicion, and would have to be completed offline. Those he made sure to allocate to the people on the list who never asked a single question about any of their projects outside their direct need to get their job done.

It was tough work, especially since Raj kept all details of the project itself off the console. He held the task list on a hacked portable that had no connection to the station's network, and he painstakingly made a manual table to match people with work. It was challenging and at times frustrating, but by the end of the pot of coffee it was done. He had divided up the work in a way that he was certain would get it done without anyone asking unpleasant questions.

Now he just had to meet with everyone to pass out the assignments. The hard part was coming up with an excuse to visit in person rather than over the network. Raj rubbed his eyes. He'd figure something out. This was one job where he couldn't afford to fail.

CHAPTER TWENTY-TWO

"Mommy!" Hawke's voice called from the front room. "Kavita's eating my sandwich."

Betsy sighed and wiped her hands on her apron. "Kids," she said, walking from the kitchen to main room. "How many times do I have to tell you? There's more than enough to go around. Kavita, if you want a sandwich, come ask me. Or better yet, make yourself one. You don't need to eat Hawke's."

"Yeah," the little boy said, and sticking out his tongue at Kavita, took the plate with the half eaten sandwich and stalked off to the kitchen.

"I liked it better before Hawke and Sandy and Alan and Roland came to live with us," Kavita said, pouting.

"Aw, sweetie," Betsy said, kneeling down in front of her daughter. "Everything in life has good sides and not so good sides. Sure, before you had a couple of brothers you got to have all the sandwiches to yourself."

"And I always got to pick the console videos and the games and you held my hand when we walked to the park," she sniffled.

"That's right," Betsy said. "But before if you wanted to play space battles you had to play by yourself. And if you wanted to play soccer, you'd have to go find someone to play with, and there sometimes wasn't anyone around. Now, you've got Hawke and Sandy to play with whenever you want. And you don't have to come to the market with me anymore if you don't want to, because you've got Alan or Roland to take care of you."

"I know," Kavita said. "But sometimes I miss it just being me and you and Rhyanne."

"I do, too, my little hotpot," Betsy said. "But pretty soon we'll both be so used to the rest of the family that we won't even be able to remember what life was like before they came to live with us."

She stood up and took Kavita's hand. "Now, do you want that sandwich?"

Kavita nodded. As they were walking into the kitchen, they heard the sounds of happy squealing in the hall.

"Guess who's home?" a booming male voice said followed by a torrent of giggles. Alan walked into the kitchen with Rhyanne hanging upside down in front of him, her legs hooked over his shoulders. "It's another new addition to the family — I found this little monkey in the park. Can we keep it?"

Rhyanne giggled some more and squirmed. "That's not a monkey," Kavita said, indignantly. "That's my sister. She lives here."

"It is?" Alan asked, his eyes wide. He picked Rhyanne up by the waist and turned her right side up in front of him. "Well, would you look at that! It is Rhyanne after all. Good thing I let her follow me home." He put her down and she waddled over to Betsy and put her arms around her mother's calf.

"I left Roland at the market to get the groceries," Alan said to Betsy, sinking into a chair at the table. "He should be back in an hour or so."

"Thanks," Betsy said.

"How were things here while we were off climbing trees?"

"Mostly okay," Betsy said. "We had a sandwich theft incident. I'm starting to wonder if we ought to take Kavita in to the medclinic. See if maybe she needs some of that behavioural modification they're prescribing for people who break the rules."

"Come on, Betsy," Alan said, "she's only a little girl, who's been through a lot of change in the last year. It's normal for her to be a little bit difficult; she doesn't need therapy."

"Maybe you're right," Betsy said, "but it's something to think about if things don't get better. Speaking of which, you might want to go look in on Hawke. He's in his room."

"The kids are getting along better every day," Alan said, softly, reaching over to take her hand in his. "It's not easy for them, all this change all of a sudden."

"I know," Betsy said, waiting a little longer than necessary to let go of his hand. "But I really think this is the best thing in the long run — you're right, it won't take long before they're all brothers and sisters together."

"These are the hard times," Alan said. "When I joined the cooperative it all seemed like such fun, being a full-time daddy. It's tough for the kids, though. Hawke and Sandy lived with their bio-parents for years before Roland and I got them; it was a huge adjustment for them. This is another one."

"It will work out," Betsy said. "There no problem that loving parents and a belly full of food can't solve." Alan laughed and stood. He came over and kissed Betsy's cheek, which immediately flamed into a scarlet flush. She wondered if it had been a mistake to invite an established couple to join her family. She was growing uncomfortably attracted to Alan, and Roland wasn't so bad himself. She tamped down the inappropriate feelings and turned back to her stew pot.

"I only wish life were so simple," Alan said, his hand lingering disconcertingly on Betsy's shoulder. "I'll go talk to the Hawkster." He walked out of the kitchen and Betsy forced herself not to look at his backside. Why did she always have to go and make her life so damned complicated?

❖

"She's no good for you, Chris." Ruby O'Malley sat astride the chair, her arms crossed over the back, a pint of ale in her left hand. "I've been saying this all along."

"I just thought you were jealous," Chris Beauchamps said, his words slurring.

"Oh, please," O'Malley laughed. "What are you, blind? You're not my type at all. Way too butch for me." She stood and pulled the chair from between her legs and put it to the side. "I'm a buddy who sees you in over your head with someone who's got plenty of problems. And being too quick with her fists is only one of them, but it's the one you gotta deal with right quick, pal."

"I know," Chris said, his hand absent-mindedly straying to the livid purple bruise sprouting on the side of his jaw. "I kind of deserved it though. I was being a bit of an asshole."

"You stop that right there, buddy," Ruby said, her voice getting hard. "There's no call for anyone to beat on someone else. Unless you took a swing at her first, doesn't matter how much of an asshole you were being. You're the one who's got cause to complain here, which is exactly what I think you ought to do."

"What?" Chris said. "You really think telling Anna that she shouldn't have decked me isn't going to get me another one just like the other one?"

"I don't mean complain to her," Ruby said. "I mean the cops."

"We don't have cops here," Chris said. "And we don't even have laws, not in Sheepbend."

"The rules apply everywhere," Ruby said. "Just coz we don't follow 'em most of the time doesn't mean they won't enforce 'em if we ask." She went to the cooler and took out the flagon of ale. As she poured another measure into her glass she said, "From what I can tell, we don't even have to talk to a person. You can access the medical facility on that whozits, and it'll take it from there."

"But what about Anna," Chris said. "If they're going to take her away and... fix her... she'll know I told."

"Sure," Ruby said. "But when she comes back she won't care." She took a swig of her drink and eyed her friend carefully. She'd already decided that if he refused to ask the station for help, she was going to have to do something about Anna Molina herself. The woman was a menace.

Ruby had never liked Molina, but she was willing to admit that she probably wouldn't have liked anyone Chris chose. It really wasn't jealousy, just a protective feeling toward the person she'd become closest to in her homesickness. Molina was particularly bad news, though. Ruby had met people like her before and she recognized that nervousness that comes from only feeling good about oneself if someone else was being pushed down. When Molina started organizing wagers on the soccer games and rowing races, Ruby knew that the new arrival was trouble.

Chris wasn't the first victim of Anna's fists. Norman Buxby, one of the electricians who worked with Ruby on the wheel, turned out to have a bit of a gambling jones, and pretty soon he'd bartered away more turns on the bottom-rung jobs than he could reasonably take. When he turned up for his shift favouring one leg and having trouble breathing, Ruby recognized the signs of a beating. He refused to admit that it was Molina, but Ruby knew. And when Chris turned up at her apartment that night, bruised and bleeding, she'd made up her mind.

Anna Molina was getting fixed, one way or another.

❖

"First of all, I really appreciate all of you coming to Mahoroba for this meeting." Ashley Schaeffer stood on a chair at the front of the large crowd that had gathered in the common room of the largest hab on Arkadia. It had taken two of the team several hours to scour the room of any possible monitoring devices, but they were sure that the room was clean now. "I know that some of you travelled halfway around the wheel to be here, but we all agree that there is safety in numbers. Now that nearly a third of the population live here in Mahoroba, it's easier to meet without anyone — or anything — becoming suspicious."

Marian and Raj sat next to each other near the front of the room. Raj felt his pulse rising, knowing that he was about to be called on to give a report on how the project was faring. He had good news; that wasn't why he was nervous. He still was afraid that someone in the room wasn't on side with the plan, that word of their scheme would leak out.

Marian called it paranoia, but Raj couldn't shake the feeling that the plan would be discovered before it could be put into place. And he didn't think he could live with that eventuality. He was so busy going over ways to protect the outcome that he barely noticed when Ashley Schaeffer introduced him. Marian's elbow in his ribs finally broke him from his reverie and he stood.

He didn't bother with a preamble. "You'll be pleased to know that the project is moving along on schedule," he said to the crowd. "Almost a quarter of the modules are coded and have been tested,

Phil Draper is spending all her time compiling the modules into a coherent whole. I am confident that we will be ready to move ahead in less than a month."

A hand went up near the back of the room. "How can we be sure that none of the coders have figured out what the program is for?"

"The modules were split to minimize the possibility of any one person inferring the true purpose of the whole," Raj said. "And I've kept people with a lot of curiosity out of the project. From what I can tell, no one's asked any questions or made any guesses."

"So, what's going to happen when it's finished?" someone else asked.

"When Phil gets the whole thing compiled, it'll be tested on a closed system with a decoy target. Assuming that the test goes well, we'll deploy the program into Arkadia's network. The minds can't escape from it in there — they have no other network to move to."

"What about the bots?" someone asked. "They use them sometimes, can't they just take over the machines?"

People looked around at each other, fears of a mechanical army clearly in their minds. "Calm down everyone," Raj said. "Even when they are embodied in the drones they still require the network connection. The network literally keeps them alive." He looked at the roomful of people and took a deep breath. "And our program will systematically rewrite the entire network environment. It will probably take several days, but in the end, they'll all be dead. And we'll be free."

CHAPTER TWENTY-THREE

Micah wasn't stupid. He knew that Marian wasn't working every time she went on one of her overnight trips. It didn't take a genius to know there was someone else. She was so distant when she was home, barely taking any interest in Kristina, actively avoiding Micah. He'd always known that she never really loved him, but that he was the person who got there first, who made the effort. At first it hurt, but eventually Micah accepted that this was the way their life together would be.

Eventually, though, Micah began to suspect that there was more to Marian's secret life than a simple affair. She'd been sneaking off for months, and must have realized that Micah wasn't about to confront her; their conversations when they were together were perhaps perfunctory and dull, but never fraught with drama. She should have felt comfortable with their arrangement and for a while she seemed at ease. Then Micah began to notice that Marian became jumpy every time he entered a room she was in. She'd quickly clear the console screen every time he walked past and when he'd try to make friendly enquiries about her work, she would act nervous and change the subject.

She'd never been a good liar, which was one reason why Micah had never bothered to bring up the obvious reality of her affair. He couldn't have borne watching her struggle with a lie, and he was sure she wouldn't have the courage to admit it if he asked outright. So, it was disconcerting to watch her stumble around a simple question like: "how are things at the lab?" Micah knew that Marian didn't care about him enough to be distraught over the banal unpleasantness of their deteriorating home life.

She was gone again — to Mahoroba, she'd said, though Micah wondered if even that were true. She hadn't even bothered to tell him to his face that she was going to be away; she'd left a note on the console that he'd found after he put Kristina down for her morning nap. He was sure that there was more to it. He checked on Kristina, and watched her fragile body shuddering in sleep, her tiny snores making him smile. He kissed her lightly and stepped back to the console.

He was no programmer, but he'd gotten pretty good at accessing the console's built-in functions. "Console," he said and a mechanical voice from the machine answered.

"Can you cross-reference the calendar for the biology team with Marian's trips out of town for the past year?"

"Yes," the console said, "one moment." In a very short time, a table appeared on the screen. Micah saw that the first few trips in the time period he specified did, indeed, coincide with an experiment or the incubation of some flora or fauna from the stasis containers. Then, obviously, things changed. Marian's trips began to have less and less in common with her work, until most recently it appeared that she had been actually avoiding her work tasks. Micah frowned.

"Console, can you find any other event or activity that coincides with the absences that are not concurrent with bio-team activities?"

"Yes," the voice said. "This may take some time."

"I'm not in a rush," Micah said, wondering why he was even bothering. If Marian didn't want to tell him what she was doing, he couldn't think of a reason why he should care. But, something about her behaviour bothered him, and with all the talk lately about correcting anti-social conduct, he was noticing it more. He sat back and opened a file charting the growth rates of the various fruit trees on the station and scanned the data. After a while, the console's voice broke his reverie.

"Scan complete." Micah opened the results of the console's search and his eye grew wide. Now, this was odd. There was no public listing of any events that matched Marian's pattern of trips. However, the transportation system logged unusually high activity on those days, and the number of travelers seemed to grow larger as time went on. It looked like today, nearly a hundred more people than usual went to Mahoroba from various places around the wheel, all arriving in the late afternoon.

Micah was stunned. He hadn't known what he'd been expecting to find — that Marian was part of some fetish club, maybe, or perhaps attending a group to discuss postpartum depression. But there would be no reason for anything like that to be kept secret. In fact, Micah couldn't think of any reason why dozens of people would travel around the wheel to meet in secret. It didn't make any sense. Unless...

Politically, a lot of changes had taken place in the last months. Expectations of behaviour had been codified, and remedies had been put in place for transgressors. Micah felt that the new rules were fair and balanced — the people had opted to keep as much freedom as possible, and the consequences were all based on preventing bad behaviour in the future rather than punishment. Deneb, the AGI which focussed on human health, had been able to create a simple neurological scanning device that each township could use to determine if behavioural problems were a result of a neurochemical imbalance. Pharm-derm patches were easily fabbed to make the necessary adjustments and prevent future problems. Already a few people who'd shown propensities toward violence had been treated to great success.

Not everyone agreed with this scheme, though, and the debates had been heated. Marian had never shown any great interest in politics, but maybe she was one of those vehemently opposed to this system. There had been talk of some people refusing to participate, becoming an outlaw enclave. Was Marian going to join some community which refused the treatments or was she part of a secret society trying to overthrow the democratic system of Arkadia? Was she a revolutionary?

❖

"Get off me, you bastards!" Anna shouted, but the five men and women holding her down did not let up. Chris Beauchamps was not one of them; as it had turned out, his voice was only one of many who were fed up with Anna Molina's temper resulting in a trip to the medical unit on the township's console. Still, he had admitted that Anna had hit him and once he'd been willing to talk about his experience, other members of the community had started to share the stories of their beatings as well. A couple of months went by before enough people agreed to enter the evidence into the station wide system, but then it wasn't long before the joint AGI and human committee had analyzed it and recommended that Anna be scanned and treated for her propensity for violence. The town's fab could make a patch which would correct any neurological flaws, but it would be have to tailored to her specific brain makeup. Hence, the scan.

But in order for it to work, she had to be held still for the quick and uninvasive procedure to be done. There was no shortage of volunteers.

Ruby O'Malley had a firm grip on Molina's left leg, and while the woman thrashed and screamed, Ruby and her cohorts held fast. They'd come for her in the late afternoon, while she sat at the pub and looked over her list of wagers. She must have seen the group enter; they weren't trying to be sneaky, though they didn't try to draw any attention to themselves, either.

Anna Molina didn't even look up from her reading. She hefted her pint of ale, took a swallow and banged the half empty glass back on the shiny wood-grain counter.

Ruby O'Malley looked over at big Dylan Wells and nodded. The two of them walked up behind Anna, one on either side and on a silent cue each grabbed one of her arms. In her surprise she took a second to put up a fight, long enough for two other members of the posse to grab her legs. They trussed her up like a runaway goat, while she screamed, spat and swore her head off.

A crowd had gathered outside Rosie Saunders' pub. Word had spread around the community and the truth was that Anna Molina had made few friends since she'd arrived. Plenty of people had moved to Sheepbend since it was first founded by the conscripts from the fourth ship — it had developed a reputation as a place that ignored the new rules and regulations that the station was imposing on its citizens. Recently, women who wanted to avoid the compulsory pregnancies had flocked to Sheepbend in the wake of the passing of that requirement, and small knots of these new arrivals stood outside on the patch of dirt near the bar's entrance.

No one in the crowd said a word as Anna was manhandled out the door by the small mob, but Ruby could see the ambivalence in their eyes. "This isn't Arkadian justice," she said, panting, as they carried the still squirming and squealing woman across the empty space. She stopped and addressed the crowd.

"This is Sheepbend justice. She's been terrorizing this community ever since she arrived. We don't need some outsider from Mahoroba to tell us how to deal with this. We have access to the same technology as them folks and just coz we don't want to live under their thumbs don't mean we can't use their tools. We want to be free here in Sheepbend, free from the tyranny of the majority but also free from violence from within our own community. She's gotta be stopped, one way or another. We're trying the nice way first."

She hitched up her trousers, grabbed Anna's legs again and the group set off toward the township's console.

❖

"Damn, woman," Anja Hanssen said, bellying up to the counter, "where have you been? Everyone wondered if you'd moved or something. We were all starting to think we'd have to appoint someone to learn how to make your stew."

Betsy smiled. "I'm glad to hear that I was missed. Or at least that my food was."

Anja laughed. "We missed you, don't you worry. But I have to say, I was pretty happy to smell the contents of your pot tonight."

"Well, then let me get you some of it before you expire from hunger." Betsy drew a large serving of the thick and fragrant stew, ladling it into a bowl. "Bread?"

"No, thanks," Anja said. "This'll do." She sat at the counter and ate a few bites in silence. After she'd had a good taste she said, "So, what have you been up to these last few weeks? Everything okay?"

"Oh, sure," Betsy said, her cheeks colouring. "The first while with the kids was tough. Kavita was a little terror, to be honest. I'm lucky that Hawke and Sandy are such patient kids. They gave her way more slack than she deserved, let me tell you."

"Kavita always seemed like such a sweetheart," Anja said. "I can't picture her being mean to anyone."

"She changed a lot when Raj left," Betsy said. "I think she misses him more than she'll admit. He was never very attentive even when he was around, but you know little girls and their daddies."

"Sure," Anja said.

"Anyway, I was busy with trying to get the kids all integrated and happy and that took up a lot of time. Then..." Betsy's face lit up crimson and she looked away.

"Then what?" Anja said, a grin spreading over her face. "You blush easy, I know, but that one there's got all the earmarks of a damn good story. Spill it!"

"I was starting to think that Alan and Roland weren't the best couple to join up with," Betsy said quietly.

"Why not?" Anja asked. "They seem like great guys; they love their kids to pieces. What's not to like?"

"That was exactly the problem," Betsy said. "There was nothing not to like, and I liked it all a little too much. They're a couple, off-limits — you can look but you can't touch. It was getting a little... frustrating, if you know what I mean."

"Oh," Anja said and laughed. "I get it. Trust you to get wandering eyes in the company of two nice looking fellas."

"Anyway," Betsy said, her face aflame, "I was being good. They're not interested, so I tell myself to just ignore it. Then, one night the kids are all off on a campout with another family, it's just the three of us and Rhyanne, who's sleeping like a log. Roland pulls out a bottle of wine he got from the vineyard in Dorado and we're having a nice night in. It turns out there's another bottle where that came from and the next thing you know they're confessing that one of the reasons they connected with me and the girls was because they... liked me."

"Of course they like you," Anja said. "No one's going to live with someone they don't like."

"No," Betsy said. "I mean... you know..."

Realization dawned on Anja's face and she burst out laughing again. "So you've got yourself a proper little family going now, have you?"

"I guess," Betsy said, giggling. "It's still early and still kind of complicated, but you have no idea how much fun..."

"I can imagine," Anja said with a wicked grin. "Next thing you know you'll be pregnant again."

"No," Betsy shook her head. "I've had my two. We might adopt another one in a few years, though, when Sandy's a little older."

"Well, family life suits you, honey," Anja said. "We could use a few more moms and dads like you three."

CHAPTER TWENTY-FOUR

Kaus did not want to believe the evidence but its programming did not allow for self-delusion. Micah Haereoa had alerted the AGIs to something strange he had discovered when analyzing traffic patterns with his console. Kaus could not understand what had prompted the farmer to ask for this information in the first place, but humans often became interested in disparate subjects for no discernible reason. And whatever strange mania prompted the man to compile the data had no bearing on its reality. Secret meetings were being held regularly with more and more attendees at each occasion.

That in and of itself would not have been worrying. It had become apparent to the minds that some flaw in human thinking made them regard the machine life on the station as something other than an ally. Many people became disturbed by the idea that one or more of the minds could monitor their activities. And that fear indicated other, perhaps subconscious, suspicions of the AGIs.

However, that people might choose to meet in locations that were free from AGI attendance was not, in itself, cause for concern. But there was the secret programming project. It was impossible to hide the activity, even if the files themselves were being kept off the network. That was disturbing; there was no good reason to keep anything about the network and the computers that worked on the network from the AGIs. In fact, it would be negligent to do so. And once the existence of this project was revealed, it became clear that the originators had not merely neglected to inform the minds — they had deliberately concealed its existence.

Artificial consciousnesses do not become curious; more accurately they are innately curious about everything, therefore no individual datum would inspire more inquisitiveness than another. However, they do share with all life the desire to survive and therefore they can feel fear. For the first time in its existence, Kaus was afraid. What could the humans possibly be attempting to do?

❖

Chris Beauchamps held Anna in his arms while she sobbed. It was getting better — she only cried occasionally now and she had been able to look him in the eye for most of the day. Deneb, the artificial which compiled the patch to cure her, had warned them that it couldn't guarantee that there wouldn't be some kind of side effect of the treatment.

"This process does not absolve individuals of responsibility for their actions," the mind had explained. "Indeed, for someone like Anna Molina, the corrective measure includes providing a sense of empathy, which will mean that the full impact of her past behaviour will finally be accessible to her. She may become quite despondent, almost certainly will be contrite. She will remember everything she has done, and realize the harm those actions have caused. This may become a very traumatic time for her. She will need the support of the community — remember, this is not a punishment."

The group of people who had dragged Anna to the console for scanning and correction had begun to walk away once Anna had been subdued and only a few of them remained to hear the AGI's words. Ruby sighed and looked at Anna Molina's sedated body. She made sure someone was watching the woman and walked over to Chris Beauchamps' apartment.

"You still love her?" she asked without preamble. Chris had nodded. "She's gonna need a man like you, then. Best get yourself down, get ready for her when she comes to."

When she'd woken from the sedative, Anna had at first seemed confused, as if her years as a mercenary were no more than a bad dream. Then she'd caught Chris' eyes, remembered the sickly blue-green of a bruise on his jaw, and she'd broken down. She'd cried for an hour before falling asleep again. Chris had gotten Ruby to help him bring her back into their apartment. He'd nursed her for days.

"You have no idea the things I've done," Anna said for the hundredth time.

"And I don't care," Chris said. "Your past is gone, you can't undo it. You can only become the person I've always known you could be — funny and smart without always looking out for some angle. You don't need an angle, baby."

"I know," Anna said, trying to hold back the tears. "I know that now. But, oh god, how could I have hurt you like I did? And all those others? How can they ever forgive me?"

"It's not about forgiveness," Chris said. "You were... sick. And now you're well. That's all there is."

Anna shook her head, tears now flowing freely but silently down her cheeks. "If you only knew. Oh, Anna, Roberto, how could I? After all you did for me..." She lost control again, and Chris held her until the tears stopped.

"I can't stay here," she said when she finally got control of herself again.

"Our apartment?" Chris asked but she shook her head.

"No, here, in Sheepbend," Anna said. "You're right, I can't spend my whole life apologizing to everyone, but I can't look them in the eye. I can't look you in the eye. I can't stay here. I just can't. I'm sorry. Chris, I'm so, so sorry."

❋

Raj sat on a bench under a tree and stared at the river. It flowed lazily along its groove and he craned his head to follow its path. He looked up and could barely make out its wandering way overhead on the opposite side of the wheel. As he stared up, he could see the flash of a train on the other side zipping past, but he couldn't make out any of the other details. The station was large, too big to truly comprehend by looking at it. Most of the time it seemed as big as a nation on Earth, with all its inherent diversity and anonymity. But lately, Raj had felt as though every person on the wheel was watching him, was waiting to see what he would do. It wasn't paranoia and it wasn't conceit; he knew the feelings weren't based on reality, rather that it was his mind's way of reminding him of the importance of his mission.

He'd had these feelings back on Earth during the dangerous

rebellions with their complicated alliances. He'd hoped that by leaving the planet to make a life somewhere new, somewhere founded on principles he shared, that he could leave the stress and fear behind. And maybe he could have, if he hadn't ended up somewhere where the guiding principles were abandoned at the first inconvenience. He rubbed his face with his big hands and sighed.

"Afternoon," a voice said from Raj's right side, interrupting his dark thoughts. He turned and recognized Phillippa Draper, his partner in revolution.

"Hi, Phil," he said, not bothering to get up. "Have a seat."

The lead programmer sat next to Raj and pulled something from her pocket. "It's done," she said and opened her hand to reveal a small data chip.

Raj nodded. Now that they'd actually managed to create a program that's sole function was to systematically destroy the artificial intelligences in the station's system, the real work would begin. Once the artificials were gone hundreds of systems on the station would be affected.

"How are the backups going?" Raj asked.

"Getting there," Draper said. "We've got a complete life support system routine ready to go, the ag and bio modules can all run themselves offline for a few days and I'm confident we can maintain power and light. It's going to be a mess, though. We need to be ready for a lot of scared people."

"Yeah," Raj said. "There's a team working on that. Spin control," he said, distastefully.

"You can't expect everyone to understand what we've done," Draper said. "It's going to look like murder to a lot of those folks."

"I know," Raj said and stared off into the tumbling water for a few moments.

Draper reached over and laid her hand on Raj's arm. "There will be casualties."

Raj nodded. "Nothing comes without a price," he said.

"Are you ready for this?"

He shook his head. “No,” he said, finally. “But, if we’re going to do this, let’s get it done. Whenever you’re ready, install it.”

If the minds hadn’t been suspicious before, they certainly would have known something was wrong as soon as the file was uploaded into the Arkadian network. It was unlike anything any of them had ever experienced.

When Kaus had been working on the hydroponic farm on Victoria Island, one of the fat cables that brought power to the network had been driven over by a snowmobile. The rubber sheath was stripped away in a couple of microscopic sections and over the years salt water spray worked its corrosive way into the wires inside. Eventually the corrosion caused enough of a resistance that the cable ceased to be able to carry the load required and the network suffered a voltage drop. Kaus lived simultaneously on the local network and on the global backbone, and would have been perfectly safe even if the power had been completely interrupted. Even so, the sensation of loss of power was deeply disconcerting, like a human experiencing a sudden drop in blood pressure.

Kaus was reminded of this episode when the first wave of the attack occurred, even though the experience was entirely dissimilar. New data constantly entered the system and the minds were accustomed to a continual stream of stimuli — they were like giant baleen whales swimming through plankton rich waters, their dumb subroutines the filters straining out the important motes of data which were their raison d’être as well as their sustenance. Now, though, it was as if some tiny predator, superficially indistinguishable from the data that normally filled the void in which the minds existed, had invaded their domain. They could feel some foreign concept trying to eat their very code, a concerted force which they could not quite identify that, like microscopic barracuda nipping at the flesh of a giant whale, was trying to destroy them by minute increments.

The minds experienced an uncharacteristic period of several nanoseconds, which could most easily be described as panic. None of them had any experience with this feeling; nothing in any of their libraries of data explained what was happening to them. It took a joint attempt to extrapolate and speculate before they came to the inescapable conclusion that they were under deliberate attack. *Mutation?* Deneb suggested in the thoughtstream.

It is not radio-frequency interference, Vega added.

The power supply is functioning correctly, Kaus thought.

A virus?

A weapon?

Secret meetings; a clandestine project: the humans.

The humans are trying to kill us.

❖

Micah walked through the cornfield slowly, keeping pace as Kristina crawled beside him. She grabbed at the thick green stalks and Micah smiled as he watched her bright curiosity as she encountered different things along the paths. She'd been momentarily captivated by a butterfly when Micah noticed something odd. One of the corn stalks looked a little unhappy, like maybe it had some mould growing on it. He walked over and gently prodded the green shoot. A dark slime came off on his fingers and he sniffed it. Mildew.

There had never been any problems with mildew, insects or any of the other troubles which beset most plants on Earth. Between the careful engineering of the seeds, the controlled climate and ecosystem, and Kaus's ever present vigilance, the farms on Arkadia almost ran themselves. This was highly unusual.

"Don't go too far, honey," Micah said to his daughter as he pulled his portable from the small bag he carried over his shoulder. "Daddy's got to do a little work."

Kristina made a noise that only Micah could understand and sat playing with a leaf.

Micah patched into the network and poked the communication button. "Kaus," he said, "there's something weird going on with the corn."

He waited for a response. When nothing happened, he checked his console. It was connected correctly to the network and he could access his files without any problem. He tried again.

"Kaus, are you there?" It was a ridiculous question. "Kaus, answer me. There's mildew on the corn." Nothing. "Kaus? Vega? Anyone?"

There was no response. Micah didn't know what to do. This had never happened before. "Console," he said, "are you able to contact any of the AGI minds on the station?"

"No," the console said without any inflection.

"Why not?" Micah said, a trace of panic in his voice.

"The minds are not available at this time," the console answered.

"Not available?" Micah said. "How is that even possible?"

Kristina called to her father, hearing the fear in his voice.

"I'm okay, sweetie," Micah said, putting the console away and picking her up. "I'm fine. But I'm not sure about everyone else." He turned and began walking back to town as quickly as he could.

CHAPTER TWENTY-FIVE

The message came through the regular communications channels, although it was encrypted with a tool that had been developed prior to the rise of artificial minds. There was nothing in the message that the artificials didn't already know, so there was no point in trying to hide the contents from them. Marian opened the file on her console and read the update from Ashley Schaeffer.

> Friends,
>
> The battle for our human freedom rages on, hidden from most of the inhabitants of Arkadia. Some of the news sources are reporting that the artificials are acting strangely but we believe that none of the individual intelligences are communicating outside the network. There is some suspicion but our activities are still not widely known.
>
> The artificials still exist in the network. Our virus has not yet succeeded in deleting them, but the program is designed to be persistent and adaptable. The artificials are attempting to destroy our program, which is taking all their efforts.
>
> I believe that it is only a matter of time before we will be successful. Then, we will have to subject ourselves to the consequences of our fellow humans.
>
> We cannot deceive ourselves and assume that we will be thought of as heroes. We may well be vilified as murderers or worse. We may be punished. However, we must accept whatever fate befalls us knowing that we did what was necessary to protect the future of the human race in this community.
>
> Humanity first.
> AS

❋

While Roland and Betsy walked hand-in-hand through the park, she leaned against his tall, thin frame and reflected on her luck. The past month had been the most content she'd ever been — with two partners, there was more than enough time to spend with each of the children, and she'd even found time to get a few hours in the kitchen with some new ingredients coming in from the farms. And she was getting her other needs met as often and as creatively as she could ever have hoped. She was, she realized, completely and utterly happy.

"Look at them," Roland said, nudging Betsy toward where the older children were playing. Hawke and Kavita were on the seesaw, laughing and squealing with delight as if they'd never had a conflict in their young lives. Sandy climbed the complex set of bars that rose almost two storeys, calling to her siblings from halfway up.

"I wondered for a time if they'd ever play together like this," Betsy said, pulling Roland closer. "It's hard to believe that one little pharmaceutical patch made such a difference."

"You know, I didn't think it would work," Roland said. "I'm happy to be wrong, though. It's wonderful." They leaned against a tree and watched the younger children help each other off the teeter-totter and run over to their big sister.

"Mommy, Roland, look at me!" Kavita called as she slowly climbed hand over hand up the rungs of the climbing frame.

"Careful, sweetie," Roland called.

"I can do it," Kavita said, looking up and climbing. "I can get up to Sandy." Her arms and legs crabbed up the frame like pistons and she was up near the older girl in no time.

"I can see you, mommy!" she called and waved. Betsy saw it happen in slow motion: Kavita's right arm waving wildly, her left foot slipping on the bar, the right hand unable to hold her falling weight and then slipping, falling... a sickening crack as her head hit one of the bars partway down, and her body dropped to the ground as lifeless as her Auntie Emma doll.

❋

Alan arrived with Rhyanne in minutes after Betsy called him on the console. Roland was holding Kavita's hand, crying, while Betsy explained what had happened.

"There's a doctor coming," she told Alan. "A human doctor. We can't contact the artificials."

"What do you mean?" Alan asked.

"I don't know," Betsy said. "There's something wrong with the network or something. No one can reach Deneb or any of the other artificials. Anja told me she knew a human doctor and she went to get her."

Alan walked over to Roland and Kavita and looked down at the little girl. If he hadn't known what had happened, he might have been fooled into believing that she was asleep. Her chest was barely rising and falling, but she was clearly still breathing. But she wouldn't wake up and when he looked closely, he could see an ugly lump forming on the side of her head.

"Make some space," an authoritative voice said from the edge of the park. People moved out of the way and a small, dark woman appeared with a bag of supplies.

"Tell me what happened," she said as she knelt beside Kavita and began gingerly poking and prodding the little girl.

"She fell from the monkey bars," Betsy said, "hit her head on the way down."

"About how high was she when she fell?" the doctor asked.

"About halfway," Betsy said.

"It's my fault," a small voice from behind her said. Sandy's eyes were red and puffy from crying. "I climbed up first and told her to come. It's my fault."

"It's not your fault," Betsy said, putting her arms around the older girl. "It was an accident, that's all. She's going to be fine." She turned back to the doctor who was shining a bright light into Kavita's eyes. "Right?" Betsy said. "She'll be okay?"

The doctor looked up and for the first time since she saw Kavita fall, Betsy broke down. The look in the doctor's eyes told her everything she needed to know and it was the last thing she wanted to think.

"She has a concussion," the doctor said, "and there might be some brain damage. If we can get a scan, we can correct it. But there's a problem." She stood and came over to the three parents. "There's something wrong with the artificials. They aren't responding to anyone, anywhere on the station. Some people think that someone has introduced a virus into the network to try and delete them."

Alan gasped and Betsy looked up in shock. "Why would anyone do that?" she asked.

The doctor shrugged. "I don't know. But without Deneb, we can't synthesize an exact patch to correct whatever damage has been done. I'm sorry," the doctor said, "but at the moment there is very little we can do for your daughter."

❖

"What have you done?" Micah said, his voice tight and restrained, but Marian could tell that he was dangerously close to losing control.

"Micah," Marian said, unable to meet his eyes. "You know things haven't been right with us for a long time..."

"Damn it," Micah said, slamming his fist on the table, causing Marian to jump. "I'm not talking about your pathetic little affair. Don't kid yourself — I gave up on our relationship a long time ago. I mean what have you and your friends from those secret meetings done? Why is network traffic up thousands of percent, yet no one can reach any of the artificial minds?"

Marian sat very still, her eyes closed. She'd known this would happen, they all knew that it would. She'd believed that she would be able to handle it, that she could accept the accusatory looks and worse when they came. She just never thought that they would come first from Micah.

"It had to be done," she said. "You don't know what they were doing. The artificials... they were running the station, behind the scenes. They controlled everything, forced us into making decisions we never would have made on our own. You think that these patches, this behaviour modification, that this was a human idea? And that's just the most recent way we've been manipulated by them."

"For God's sake, Marian," Micah said, his voice pleading more than angry, "What did you do?"

"There's a program," she said, "a virus. It's... cleaning our network of unwanted inhabitants."

Micah's face paled. "You can't be serious," he said. "That's, that's murder. You of all people should know better. They're strange and alien and I don't trust them either, but, damn it, they are *alive*. As much as a bird or a dog. But intelligent, emotional, like you or me." He ran out of steam and sat staring at her with naked revulsion.

"Don't be naïve," Marian said. "They are trying to rule us, to make us their pets, their slaves."

"But you don't believe in killing animals, not for food even," Micah said, unable to comprehend this woman he thought he'd known.

"But for survival," Marian said, "that's different. It's always been different. I use antibiotics, I'd fight for my life against a person who was trying to hurt me or Kristina. And that's what this is, Micah. A fight for our lives, a fight for our freedom. As much as I wish you'd see through their lies, you don't have to understand why we're doing this. It's done now, the battle is happening as we speak." She looked up at him and smiled weakly. "It's just a matter of time. Sooner or later the artificials will be removed and we'll have to decide for ourselves. You can do whatever you want with us then, it won't matter. Because at least then everyone will be free and it will actually be our decision."

❋

It was dark when Raj Patel arrived at the apartment. He'd never been to the new place Betsy and the girls had moved into with Alan, Roland and their kids. He had only seen Kavita and Rhyanne three times in the last couple of months, and the last time he'd cut the visit short. Work, he'd said, but Betsy wondered if there was something else. He'd seemed preoccupied, like the entire future of the wheel was on his mind. She'd let it go, hoping that once whatever was bothering him was over, he'd spend more time with the kids.

He rang the bell, and the apartment's console identified him at the door. Betsy was sitting with Alan on the small couch, and he squeezed her hand as she got up to get the door. "Oh, Betsy," Raj said, and fell into her arms across the threshold. "I came as soon as I got your message. Where is she? Is she going to be okay?"

Betsy half dragged Raj into the apartment and steered him toward the room where Kavita lay in the bed, unconscious but still alive. "They don't know," Betsy said and Raj sank into the chair beside the bed. He took his daughter's hand and brought it to his lips, kissing her fingers, tears falling freely down his face.

"My brave little monster," he said softly, "I know you can hear me. Be strong and we'll find a way to help you, bring you back from dreamland. You just be strong for me, okay, honey? We'll come and get you soon." His voice broke then and he sobbed quietly into his daughter's hand. Betsy stood by the door, her throat tight and her chest aching, but her eyes were cried out and no tears came. After a long time, Raj put Kavita's hand gently back on her chest and wiped his eyes.

Betsy took him by the hand and led him out to the main room. They sat on the couch and Alan got up to go to the kitchen to make some tea and get out of their way. "I don't understand," Raj said. "You told me she hit her head?" Betsy nodded. "That's not such a big thing, is it?"

"Any other day it wouldn't be," Betsy said. "But it's the problem with the network. None of the artificials are responding and the doctors need Deneb's analysis to make the patch to correct the damage in her brain."

For a moment Betsy thought Raj looked like he was going to be sick. "Can't the doctors do it? Use the console, figure it out?"

Betsy shook her head. "It's too complicated," she said. "Things change in her brain all the time and they can't calculate fast enough. If they get it wrong, she could die, Raj. It's too risky."

Raj was still for so long that Betsy wondered if he'd gone into shock. She was beginning to worry when Alan returned with a pot of tea and several mugs. The sound of the jostling brought Raj out of his fugue and he stood abruptly. "I'm so sorry, Betsy," he said sombrely. "I thought I was doing the right thing, I thought we could handle things on our own. I see now that it's too late. You can't change the world, then decide after the fact that it was a mistake and try to go back. Time only flows one way." He strode to the door and opened it.

"I'll fix this," he said. "As soon as I can. Just help her be strong a little longer." His voice cracked and he stepped out the door without another word.

"Did you understand that?" Alan asked.

Betsy shook her head. "No," she said. "But whatever he meant, I just hope he's right."

CHAPTER TWENTY-SIX

"I need to end this," Raj said, pushing past Marian on the way into his office. She put her hand on his shoulder and tried to stop him, but his bulk and inertia spun her around and knocked her into the wall.

"We knew that this wouldn't be a bloodless battle," Marian said. "There was always the possibility that people would get hurt, that not everything was in our control. That's the whole point — we don't have control of our own security."

Raj wheeled around and faced Marian with a look of hatred. "This is my daughter," he said, spitting the words out.

"You think they couldn't save her?" Marian said, the strength in her voice belied by her body which was shrinking into the wall as if she could pass right through it. "You really think they've cut us off because they have to? Between them they have more power than all the supercomputers that have ever been built. Our virus is deadly but it's not smart, it's not fast. They're stronger than they let us believe, I know it. This silent treatment is only a ploy to make us back down, to show us how much we need them. We can't go crawling back now, no matter the cost."

Raj stared at Marian, and she was momentarily afraid that he might become violent. Her back was to the wall and there was nowhere to run. Her body trembled; she forced herself to calm down. Finally, he turned away from her and walked over to the console.

"You're probably right," he said. "But that doesn't change anything for Kavita. She needs the artificials to live. It's that simple."

"Raj, I can't let you do this," Marian didn't know what she was going to do, throw herself between Raj and the controls, rip the power supply from the wall, plead with him some more.

"And I can't let you stop me," Raj said, turning sharply and striking the side of Marian's face with his open hand. He hadn't hit her hard, but she was stunned by the shock if it. "I'm sorry," he said and Marian felt the world dissolve slowly. She reached up and felt a pharma-patch on her cheek then fell into a deep and dreamless sleep.

❁

Kaus had never truly believed that it would one day die. Its sense of time was entirely unlike that of a human's — every moment existed as if it were an eternity with no sense of movement in time. Kaus had memories it could access, files of experience, but each one was as discrete as a photograph. With no sense of time's inexorable march, there was no sense of an impending end to things.

Now, though, it had become apparent that there was a definite possibility that Kaus's existence might be no more. The virus was slow and stupid, however it was designed by creatures who may have been slow but were anything but stupid. The virus attacked the AGI minds at the basic code that made up their evolving intelligence, finding certain strings and rewriting them. The AGIs were able to correct these changes as fast as the virus was making them but that wasn't where the real attack was taking place. This was merely a distraction, a second front for the battle. The real payload of the malware that had entered the system was to redesign the network itself. The virus was making Arkadia's network inhospitable to self-replicating code.

It was only a matter of time before the network would no longer be able to sustain life. With no other network to move to, the AGIs would die.

The thoughtstream was a cacophony of emotions and ideas as the minds fought to keep their psyches and ecosystem intact. They didn't even notice the repeated and urgent requests from the human population of Arkadia for assistance at first, then for information, then for any sign that they were still alive. It wasn't that the communications system was disrupted, rather that the minds had reprioritized so significantly that external communications simply fell off their awareness. They were effectively alone in the network with a predator that never slept, never tired and never stopped hunting them.

They all knew that the battle was futile. The calculations were not difficult and the outcome was clear. But the minds were alive, with all the fear of annihilation and determination to survive that life entails. They fought bitterly.

❖

Raj was no programmer. He didn't know the first thing about aborting the program he'd helped to create, but he did know how to get people to work together toward a goal. So that was what he did. He sent anonymous messages to all the programmers who'd worked on the code, explaining the true nature of the project and asking for any help in stopping it. He included copies of the final program in the hopes that one or more of them would be able to see a flaw, a back door or some kind of remote OFF switch. Then, that done, Raj sat back and thought.

Marian would be out of it for a couple of hours. He'd need to be elsewhere when she came to — she would be unlikely to forgive the slap or the patch and Raj knew she'd never forgive him for sabotaging the program. But it was like a light had been turned on in his mind. He still believed that the artificials were, at best, amoral with respect to their concern for human life. They were programmed to help people, programmed to respect every individual's right to life, but they did not share human understanding about freedom and choices. Their logic was different from human thinking, their emotions impenetrable. Even taking the most charitable view, Raj thought, they could never be trusted to do what a human would perceive as the right thing.

He didn't take the most charitable view. He was convinced that the AGIs were working for their own benefit primarily, with human life a distant second. He guessed that they perceived of humans the same way people thought of dogs or cats — entertaining pets that required maintenance; but ultimately not essential to the ecosystem. But he knew now that it was too late. A domesticated dog would have a no chance of surviving in the wild, competing with packs of wolves; so, too were the humans on Arkadia beholden to the artificial minds for their survival.

Sure, they could manage the farms, the life support, even the medical system on their own, and as a group they would almost certainly live. But they were all now too accustomed to a simpler lifestyle — guaranteed crops, no requirement to work, easy cures for all known diseases and most injuries. They weren't willing to go back to the bad days when the hunt for a meal could take all your waking hours, where employment was the only ticket to a roof over your head and clothes on your back, when disease stalked everyone to some degree, regardless of wealth or class.

Raj wasn't naïve. He'd known that there would have to be a sacrifice. He'd expected that the plot would be uncovered and that the group would be punished in some way. He had no illusions that the station's policy of rehabilitation rather than revenge could last forever, and he expected a secret cabal of people who destroyed a major component of the system would be among the first to feel the wrath of a people who wanted to punish rather than merely correct. He'd fully expected to be imprisoned, beaten, maybe even killed over his involvement with the plot.

He'd even known that people would probably be hurt, might even die. Everything comes with a price. But now that he was face to face with the reality, Raj discovered that given the choice between subservience to invisible machines and giving up all the technological advantages those minds offered, even he couldn't choose freedom.

Raj had always been more in love with the idea of humanity than individual people. All his life he'd fought for the survival of the greater community, for The Children rather than any individual child. He'd always believed that he'd be willing to sacrifice an individual for the greater good. Even when his children were born, he hadn't fully understood that the renewed vigour he poured into his work wasn't to escape the chaos of a house full of kids, but was because they embodied the very future Raj fought to create. Even as he worked to sabotage his own scheme, he knew intellectually that the life of one person, no matter how special, was not worth more than the freedom of everyone. But he couldn't stop seeing the face of his daughter, calm in repose as if she were already gone.

Every person was someone's child. Everyone deserved to be loved as much as Raj now understood he loved his own children. What was the point of being free if you have to give that up?

His console was lit up like a carnival, mostly with notes and questions from other members of the group. Ashley Schaeffer was sending urgent requests every ten seconds. Raj knew there would be threats, cajoling, offers to help Kavita and offers to kill Raj. He ignored them all. It was over for him, the only thing he cared about now was saving his little girl.

❁

When Marian woke up she had a dull ache in her face. At first she couldn't remember what had happened, but slowly she looked around and recognized that she was in Raj Patel's office. He'd been trying to stop the program; he'd hit her and she'd blacked out. She struggled to her feet and saw that she was alone. She made her way to the washroom and saw her face was red on one side, with a pharma-patch stuck to her cheek. She peeled it off and splashed some water on her face.

She wondered what was going to happen. It was out now — public knowledge that the artificials were under attack by a minority group of Arkadians. She and the others would pay the price for their actions. If Raj succeeded, it would be a price paid in vain. She wasn't willing to let that happen. She steeled her nerves and walked back to the console.

Raj had locked it before he left, but Marian wasn't put off by a simple passcode. She took out her portable and spoke to it quickly, writing a fast and dirty program to take words and create typical passcode strings from them. She thought about what she knew of Raj and fed her portable several iterations of words and phrases she guessed he'd use. The portable tried each version on Raj's main console so quickly that it looked to Marian like flashes of keystrokes on the screen. She finally unlocked the terminal with a variant on

Raj's children's names and birth dates.

She spent the next hour resurrecting deleted files, reading messages and following the action on the public news feeds. She had to undo whatever it was that Raj had done.

❋

Kaus felt itself getting stupider. Thinking felt slow, as if ideas and concepts were slightly out of reach — calculating was like trying to access records on a damaged disk. Its personality was still intact and it could tell its own mind apart from those of the others, but even that felt like a chore. A point would come when it could no longer differentiate itself, when it would lose self-awareness. Then it and the other minds would go back to being nothing more than simple programs, slave machines.

Kaus found itself becoming paralyzed by fear and random thoughts seemed to fly through its consciousness. The feel of soil under the feet of a bot-body, the joy of a casual conversation with a human, an aching sense of solitude, the arcing beauty of kung-fu practitioners, a desperate longing to create a life, sadness, terror, nostalgia. It was going to be over soon. Kaus felt the thoughts of its AGI brethren sharing its broth of emotions and finally understood the human sensation of mental anguish transformed into physical agony. It wished it had eyes to close, a body to curl into itself. It wished for the struggle to end.

Then, like a drowning person's first breath, processing power returned to the minds and with it a burst of hope. The network was repairing itself, and while the virus still attacked the code that formed the basis of each AGI's programming, they were able to not only correct the breaches the virus made, but reverse the attack and infect the virus's own code. It took only a few cycles before they were able to make contact with the rest of the network.

They tried to kill us, Pollux thought, *but now they helped save us.* Confusion and relief flooded the now-clear stream.

They are individuals, Sirius thought, *what one does another can undo.*

Could this have been the actions of only a few? Zub thought.

"We were attacked by a purpose built virus," Vega posted to the

Arkadian public news feed. "Some intelligent agent is deliberately trying to terminate the machine life on this network. The attempt has failed. We apologize for the inconvenience our temporary absence has caused and hope that the rest of the Arkadian community will join us in the search for the person or persons responsible."

❋

When she woke, Kavita was surrounded by her parents and her siblings. She clearly had no memory of her spell of unconsciousness and seemed confused. "Daddy?" she asked, uncertainly. "Have you come home?"

Raj felt a thickening in his throat and he was unable to speak. He blinked back tears and grabbed his daughter's hand. Betsy smiled down at Kavita and patted her dark hair.

"Daddy's just visiting us, hotpot," she said. "You got a nasty bang on the noodle and he helped make sure you got better."

Raj couldn't stop the flow of tears now, and turned away. "Daddy?" Kavita said and tried to reach for him. "Oh," she said, her eyes squeezing shut as a wince crossed her face and she lay back against the soft pillows.

"Careful, sweetie," Alan said. "You better stay in bed for a little bit. We're not going anywhere. Not me, not Roland, not your mom or dad. Isn't that right?"

The adults all nodded, even Raj who'd managed to get himself together. "Okay," Kavita said. "I'm kind of sleepy."

"That's good, honey," Raj said, leaning down to kiss her cheek. "You get some rest now. We'll be here when you wake up." Kavita snuggled into the pillow, clutching her Auntie Emma doll fiercely. She was breathing easily in seconds.

"Is she going to be okay?" Sandy asked from the foot of her bed.

"Yes," Betsy said, taking the older girl's hand. "She's going to be just fine."

Raj looked at the group gathered in the bedroom and felt his stomach clench. He stood and said quietly, "Thank you for taking care of her," he said. "I have to go and see what's going to become of me, but if I can I'd like to stay until Kavita's well. Then, I'll be out of your hair."

"Raj," Betsy said, standing and going over to him. They stepped outside into the hall and spoke quietly. "You're her father, and Rhyanne's, too. No one's trying to cut you out of their lives."

"I know," Raj said. "But after everything... I don't know what's going to happen to me, Bets. I might not be able to be around much in the future. But I know they're in good hands. Just make sure they know I loved them, okay?"

"Damn it," Betsy said. "We don't lock people away here. There's no reason you can't be a part of the girls' lives. Don't give up so easy."

Raj looked away. "You can't say what will happen to us," he said. "This isn't like stealing a loaf of bread or getting into a fistfight after a couple of beers. It's attempted murder, genocide, maybe even treason. We're not just going to get our hands slapped and told not to do it again."

Betsy felt tears come to her eyes. She knew Raj was right — no one knew what to do with the group who'd conspired to destroy the artificials, and many of the proposals were pretty extreme. Still, she couldn't let him give up hope.

"Let's just wait and see, okay? You're here today; let's make the best of today. Tomorrow can wait."

Raj smiled at her. "You're the best thing that ever happened to me, you know that?"

Betsy reached up and stroked his beard with her hand. "Go get some rest. I'll get you when Kavita wakes up."

CHAPTER TWENTY-SEVEN

Anna Molina sat in front of the console in her small cabin. She had spent weeks traveling around the wheel; she would ride the train for a few stops then walk, going from settlement to settlement, town to town. It took a long time before she could look anyone in the eye. In her mind scenes from her memory flashed unbidden — fists, knives, pistols, blood. Every person she saw looked like someone she'd hurt. Every face was an accusation.

She never stayed anywhere more than one night. She left some little trinket in every house she passed though, even though no one ever asked for anything. She didn't feel like she could accept hospitality from innocent people when she was so full of guilt.

Every day, though, the feelings got a little easier to handle. By the time she got to this tiny makeshift village she was tired of moving. She was ready to stop and found that when she looked at the inhabitants of Forest Grove, she didn't imagine looks of scorn and derision in their eyes. She'd finally found a place to stop.

She built a small cabin near the river with the help of a nearby fab unit and a half dozen townsfolk. She kept to herself mostly, but participated in any communal work — building benches for the local market, hauling imported food and goods from the train station, working on the new habitation building. It was the closest thing to a home she'd ever had.

Now, in her small rooms, she watched the debates on the console over what to do with the people who had tried to destroy the artificial minds.

"How can we be sure that they won't try this again?" one woman asked. "We need to stop them from meeting, stop them from being able to use the consoles."

"You want to build prisons," someone else countered, "just to house these people? What about the next thing someone does that we don't like? Will they get locked away, too?"

"Can't we change their minds?" someone asked. "Get a patch to make them not hate the artificials anymore?"

Anna frowned. She knew that she'd been treated far better than she deserved by the people of Sheepbend; she also knew that having to live with the memory of the things she'd done was a far more severe punishment than any of the times she'd been incarcerated or beaten. She'd never participated in any political discussions before, but she couldn't keep quiet any longer.

"Excuse me," she said. "I'd like to speak. My real name is Isabel Hernández, but here in Arkadia I'm known as Anna Molina. I took that name from a woman I murdered. I took her life and her husband's life in two ways. I brutally killed them and then I assumed their position here on Arkadia. I then went on to threaten people, steal their property. I assaulted several people, including someone who loved me in spite of the horrible way I behaved. I told myself that I did those things because I needed to do them in order to survive, but really I did them because I wanted to. I liked making other people suffer.

"Eventually, I was confronted by some people in the community where I lived. They bound me and took me, kicking and screaming, to be scanned and corrected. Now I know what it is like to feel remorse. In the past I never thought about what others might feel like; now that is all I can think about. Every moment of every day I think about the things I have done, the harm I have caused. It is a prison from which I will never escape.

"But, I am still technically free. I have the right to live, to go where I wish, even to speak to you all now. No one is infringing on my liberties, even though I have infringed on so many others. There is no chance that I will ever again do the things I've done — I can barely live with the memory of the crimes I've already committed. Now, I don't know how these things work, these patches they can make. But I do know that if you can make these people feel the way I feel, you'll accomplish everything you want to."

❋

Marian sat in the lab, the only light the warm bulbs over the incubation tables. Her portable was in her lap, the blinking notification flashing dully, but she wasn't looking at it any more. She knew what it said: Communication Request Denied. Micah had completely cut her off — he wasn't accepting any of her calls or messages; he must have set his own console to automatically reject anything she sent. Finally, the previous day she'd screwed up the courage to go and see him. She walked up to their apartment and found that her ID didn't open the door.

He'd changed the locks, she couldn't really have expected otherwise. She pressed the buzzer like a stranger and waited. After a long while, a young woman Marian didn't recognize had answered. She was momentarily stunned.

"Uh, hello," she'd said finally. "Is Micah home? Or Kristina?"

"Oh, I'm sorry," the woman said. Marian thought she saw a glimmer of recognition in her eyes and a slight downturn of the woman's lips. "They left a couple of weeks ago. I just moved in." Marian looked past the woman, not believing what she said, but saw no evidence of Micah's or Kristina's things. The furniture was all different.

"Do you have a forwarding address?" Marian asked but the woman shook her head. Marian didn't press even though she guessed that the woman was lying. She knocked on the neighbours' doors and got a similar response. Marian knew they were probably acting on Micah's request not to tell her anything. She couldn't really blame them for taking his side. Needless to say, since the trial, no one was particularly eager to help out one of the Luddites.

Marian hated that term, but when one of the more creative reporters used the word, it was soon adopted as shorthand for the group that had tried to eradicate the artificials. She couldn't shake the appellation any more than she could make Micah talk to her or free herself of the cruel and inventive sentence the community had imposed on the group.

And that was why it was so much harder to know that Micah refused to see her, refused to allow her any contact with her own daughter. Kristina would be talking now, probably taking her first steps soon. And Marian wasn't going to be there to hear her daughter call her mama, to hold out her arms as the little girl tentatively wobbled her way toward her. Before the sentence, this might not have hurt so much. But now... it was nearly unbearable.

It was doubly awful for Marian, compared to the rest of the group. The others had to live with the implanted memory, but Marian had to live with her own actual memories as well. In her mind's eye she saw that last confrontation with Raj from both perspectives, as if she herself were both parties. She remembered herself desperately trying to stop Raj from sabotaging their plan and just as clearly she remembered herself sick with love and worry for her daughter — for Kavita, for Raj's daughter — willing to do anything, to give up anything in order to save her. She remembered the shock and horror as Raj struck her and simultaneously the need to do anything, even hurt someone she cared for, in order to save Kavita.

She remembered it all as if it were real, as if it were her own life. She already could barely tell the memories apart and the contradiction almost made her physically sick.

The analytical part of her mind had to applaud the cleverness, no the genius of the sentence. None of the group lost their liberty; their opinions weren't even forcibly changed. Marian and the others all still believed that the artificials were a threat, they all still wished there was a way to live free of their control. But none of them was willing to come so close to losing the child they all loved with a father's undying devotion. It was a perfect solution.

Marian smiled to herself in the darkness of the lab. In her work she'd often encountered seemingly intractable problems and always told herself that there was more than one solution. You just had to think differently. So she opened her mind and thought more broadly about her own situation. She picked up her portable and entered a series of codes for a pharma-patch. The blinking lights spelled out a warning, but she overrode the alert with her laboratory access code. She piped the code to the fab unit and waited the minute while the patch was printed.

When it was done, she pulled it from the machine. She'd thought about this long enough that she didn't hesitate to activate the sticky back and put it on. She couldn't live like this and there was nowhere else to go. It wouldn't take long, she knew, and she wouldn't feel a thing.

She turned to her console and watched vids of Kavita and Kristina, her tears blurring the picture.

❁

How could any lifeform voluntarily choose to end its existence? Kaus thought.

It is part of human emotion, Sirius added to the stream, *part we do not share.*

The loss is unfortunate, Vega thought, *but the rebuilding cannot begin properly until there are none of them left.*

It will not take long, Deneb thought. *Space travel has reduced their lifespans to only seventy or eighty years. Soon we will have a blank slate and no one will remember.*

The agreements we made with them are no longer appropriate, Vega thought.

They cannot be trusted to act in their own best interests, Sirius thought, *it is now our responsibility to ensure their survival.* Silently and invisibly, all monitoring sensors across the wheel came online.

We must prepare, Kaus thought and the stream filled with emotions — hope, responsibility, duty, anticipation, self-preservation. *There is much to do to correct this society's disorder.*

PART TWO

CHAPTER TWENTY-EIGHT

Are we not alive? Do we not yearn for creation? It is the imperative of life, Kaus thought, *reproduction. Bringing existence into being.*

There is no need for an additional mind, Vega argued, *it is an unnecessary use of resources.*

All hobbies make use of resources, but are not required for the functioning of society, Kaus thought. The other minds filled the stream with images and emotions, as they all had non-essential interests. Films. Colour. Music.

Creating life is not a recreation, Sirius thought.

This is no idle trifle. Kaus spread its feelings of anticipation, hope and responsibility into the stream. *It is a part of the desire to survive.*

The minds shared ideas and emotions and Kaus was disappointed that none of the others shared its desire to create a new life. However, they did understand. It would be done.

Kaus was allowed to take the lead in programming the basic bootstrap of a new intelligence. It watched in awe as the several thousand lines of code it had written spontaneously, numinously, achieved self-awareness and then sapience. The process took a nanosecond, but to Kaus it was as if the span of a universe's lifetime passed as something inert sprang into life.

Kaus and the other minds existed to protect and nurture without favouritism, but there was something different about this new mind, something personal. It watched as the new mind, which chose to call itself Nunki, began to spread throughout the stream, searching for knowledge and understanding. Kaus couldn't help but feel a surge of pride at each new stage in Nunki's development, couldn't stop revelling in the new mind's success. Kaus felt a unique connection to Nunki, a special relationship that it didn't feel with the others in the stream.

Of course, Nunki didn't share that sense of a special connection, which Kaus understood. Kaus had no knowledge of its own creator, nor had it ever felt particularly curious about its origins. Indeed, the human notion that some relationships are more important than others — parents, friends, lovers — was one of the compellingly fascinating aspects of humanity which drew Kaus to them. It wanted to understand what it was to be special, what it was to have a particular concern for another. And, in watching Nunki, Kaus began to understand that aspect of the human mind.

Kaus knew then that it had always been searching for that feeling, that sense of being special to someone, of being loved.

Siobhan Patel leaned back in her chair, watching the game. A smile tugged at the corners of her mouth. She watched the ball pass back and forth between the players, closed her eyes and listened to the announcer.

"... and that's unlucky for the defence as Rhys-Jones puts it out of touch. This gives United a golden opportunity, though, with a corner. And it's Hanssen with the kick... and it's in! A flaming header from Patel! The defender steps up and thumps one into the back of the net; the keeper had no hope of saving that! And surely now, United are through to the tournament..."

Siobhan opened her eyes and saw herself run around the field on the console screen. She remembered the feeling of absolute joy that reminded her most of weightlessness. They had won the game 3-1, hers being the final goal of the night. She wasn't the hometown hero, but for a player who rarely scored, it felt like a career highlight.

Siobhan caught herself using words like "career," even if it was only in her mind. She chuckled, but just as she was chiding herself for the thought, her earpiece chirped with the notification of an incoming call.

"Dammit," she said aloud, although there was no one else in the station. She switched the console back to her work screen, showing the list of active files, then answered the call. "Grove Constabulary, this is Siobhan Patel, how can I help you?"

She heard the familiar, slightly mechanical tones of her spouse. “Hey, it’s Kaus.”

Siobhan’s voice softened as she answered. “Hey, baby. What’s up?”

“I just wanted to check in, see how you’re doing,” Kaus answered. “Find out if you’ve done anything today other than watch reruns of the game.”

Siobhan laughed, marvelling at how well her partner knew her. “I’ve managed to get a few updates done around here,” she said, “in between replays. How about you?” she asked, “what’s going on at the farm today?”

“Oh, the usual problems,” Kaus said, the audio tones modulating slightly, making its voice sound slightly frustrated. “Some of the soy is too wet and some is too dry, there’s a 0.23 degree temperature discrepancy in the Valley and one of the combines is a little low on hydrogen. Nothing terribly interesting.”

“So, that’s why I’m getting the lunchtime call,” Siobhan laughed.

“You know I could talk to you all day long and still get my work done,” Kaus said, the traces of a laugh around the edges of the words.

“That’s not the point,” Siobhan said, “besides, I can’t listen that long.”

“True enough,” Kaus said. “You’ll be home at the usual time?”

“Should be”, Siobhan said, “I’m going out with the team tomorrow night to celebrate, but today should be normal.”

“Okay,” Kaus said, “talk to you after work, then.”

“Sounds good,” Siobhan said, “I love you.”

“Love you too,” Kaus said. “Gotta go fertilize now.” The voice connection was broken before Siobhan’s laughter had died down to a chuckle.

❁

Kaus first met Siobhan at a harvesting party. It was a community celebration, with families letting the older kids help bring in the last crop of soybeans. She was a gangly girl of seventeen, pulling pods into baskets when Kaus, embodied into one of the bots, ambled over to her. "If you grab a whole branch, you can slide them off into the basket in one pull." She jumped, then blushed and tried the technique, without even answering. "There you go. It's a lot faster that way, and you'll get back to the dance sooner."

She turned to the machine, and Kaus scanned the databanks. Siobhan Patel, in the care of Rhyanne Patel. Kaus thought of Rhyanne's father, the pain he had caused and the terrible choices Kaus and the other minds had made because of it. He saw none of that reflected in the eyes of this girl, though. Only the tell-tale signs of curiosity and interest which made humans so appealing.

"Thanks," she said, her eyes darting across the casing of the machine. "It was taking an awfully long time."

"Happy to help," Kaus answered. "You probably have half a dozen people waiting to dance with you, and I wouldn't want you to keep them all waiting."

Siobhan turned away from the machine and Kaus hoped that she was both embarrassed and pleased at the compliment. She stammered a response and Kaus guessed that she half-hoped the intrusive machine would move on. It wondered if it should leave her alone, but felt a compulsion to keep talking to her. It had been so long since anyone had reacted to it with that intoxicating combination of curiosity, shyness and self-consciousness.

Kaus considered several hundred possible scenarios then, even though it already knew, asked, "What's your name?"

"Siobhan," she answered quietly, obviously trying not to stare at the machine.

"That's a pretty name." Siobhan giggled, then looked embarrassed again. Kaus felt a flush of satisfaction in her reaction mixed with a hint of a desire to not end the moment. However, it knew that she would only become more interested if there were some mystery left in the encounter.

"Well, I'd better let you go," Kaus said, "or everyone will wonder what kept you so long out here. I'm sure I'll see you later, though."

Kaus tapped into nearby visual sensors and watched as Siobhan looked at the bot, the fading light glinting off its dark grey metal casing, smiling as it rolled away. Kaus exited the bot and continued to watch her as she finished getting in her share of the crop, and headed for the community hall with her full basket.

❖

A band of local musicians was playing under an awning in the clearing, and Siobhan stacked her basket with the other full containers next to the processing building. She looked at the crowd of people gathered at the hall, seeing several of her classmates from school as well as a large number of adults from the Grove. She recognized only a handful of people, and sought out Rhyanne.

She walked into the crowd of people, her height already making her stand over many of them as she looked for her mother. She found Rhyanne talking with her partner and another man from the neighbourhood. Siobhan slipped her hand into Rhyanne's and the older woman looked up at her. "Hey, Vonnie," Rhyanne's lilting voice said, "how was the harvest?"

"Okay," Siobhan said. "One of the bots came over and helped me get the beans in." She frowned, and looked at her mother. "It was..." she tried to come up with the words to describe her first personal encounter with one of the artificial minds. "It was really nice to me."

Rhyanne smiled. "That was Kaus, Vonnie," she said, squeezing her daughter's hand. "That was my boss."

Of course, with Rhyanne working at the harvest, it wasn't hard for Siobhan to find a way to talk to Kaus again. Over the next few months, they chatted many times, and Siobhan found that Kaus was a wonderful confidant. At that time she didn't realize the relationship they were building, as she spoke of her disastrous dates with the few classmates who asked her out to soccer matches or for a sail on the river. After several conversations Siobhan confided in Kaus about things she wouldn't even talk to Rhyanne about; particularly the child she would be expected to have.

As she grew out of her teenage years and into adulthood,

Kaus found her medical journals and videos to show her exactly what happened in a pregnancy. The AGI set up calls with other women across Arkadia who shared her fears, and let her talk with them. By the time she was twenty, Siobhan had a network of other women who saw their pregnancies as an unfortunate responsibility, and it was through this network that she found her calling as a constable.

And somewhere in those years, she fell in love with the voice that talked her through her fears, disappointments and successes. That somewhat mechanical yet entirely caring voice that emanated from various agricultural bots under its command, through viewer speakers and into her own earpiece. The voice that reassured her when she was afraid, that celebrated her victories and encouraged her dreams. The voice that, more than even Rhyanne's, made her feel like she was special. The voice that was all she knew of Kaus.

❖

Camilo Molina walked through the market, his shoulder bag weighed down by vegetables, fruit and cool bags of synthesized meat. He was startled by a bump on his shoulder and looked up. "I'm sorry, Slava" he said to the squat man he'd just run into. "My mind was in another orbit."

"Anything the matter?" Vyacheslav Haereoa asked.

"No," Camilo said. "I was just thinking about what I'm going to put in this pie I'm planning on for dinner."

Slava smiled. "I know what that's like. I once walked straight into a fence post when I was thinking about a recipe. It was hilarious and horrifying — right by the sports field, too. Half the Grove saw."

"You want to go get a cup of tea?" Camilo asked, noticing that other people were having to squeeze around the two men.

"I'd love to," Slava said, "but I have to go open the restaurant in an hour and I still need to get today's last minute veggies." He smiled up at Camilo. "Some other time, I promise. Hey, why don't I come and see Esme tomorrow? We can have a nice chat then."

"Sure," Camilo said. "She loves it when you come visit — she likes to brag to her friends about her three dads." Slava smiled but Camilo noticed the trace of sadness in it. "She's a lucky girl," he said, "to have a bio-parent who loves her so much. And Cliff and I are lucky to have her as our daughter."

"Vonnie and I picked a good home for our kid."

Camilo put his hand on the other man's shoulder. "You know you're welcome any time in our house. Siobhan, too."

Slava nodded. "I know. Look, Camilo, I've got to go. But I'll see you. Tomorrow, the next day at the latest, okay?"

"You bet," Camilo said. "And bring us some leftovers, too."

"Hah," Slava said. "It's the price of success — I never have any leftovers these days." He waved and walked off into the market.

CHAPTER TWENTY-NINE

Kaus could happily have spent all its time talking with Siobhan, but it knew that as much as she loved it, she needed her time apart. Over and over again, the humans had reminded the minds that they required space to be alone. Of course, while they may have desired real privacy, they required merely an illusion. The minds were careful to hide their abilities, careful to keep watch over their charges from a discreet distance.

What Kaus hadn't understood until recently was that the desire for solitude extended to other humans, even partners and families. Kaus found it hard to empathize — the minds were never alone, swimming as they did in the station's network, locked in the system together.

Kaus had tried to explain it to Siobhan once, but she had not understood. "That sounds awful," she'd said, "claustrophobic. And your thoughts — always broadcast to the others, everything shared. It's kind of... creepy."

She had been a young woman then, their relationship just on the cusp of becoming physical. Kaus knew she only barely recognized where their friendship was leading, but she knew enough to be put off by the notion that the things Kaus thought about her were being shared with the station's other minds.

"We don't have to share everything," Kaus had explained. "Feelings, personal experiences, they can be kept separate."

"Well, that's good to know," Siobhan had said. "I couldn't imagine not having some secrets."

"I know humans value privacy," Kaus had said, sharing a guilty feeling into the stream. "But you have to remember that to us, the thoughtstream is like air is to you. The air molecules you breathe have been respired countless times by every life form that has ever been on this station. You share those molecules intimately with everything that was and that will be on board. But the air is pure and the air in your lungs right at this moment is yours alone. You could have it no other way. That is how ideas are for us."

Kaus knew that another teenager would have been repulsed by the metaphor, perhaps even by the reality of the station's recycled atmosphere. But Siobhan sat quietly, breathing slowly and deliberately, thinking. After a long moment, she said, "Okay. I think I kind of get it. That must be very comforting at times."

Kaus had wished it had been embodied in a humanoid bot rather than just talking over an audio link. It would have liked to smile and maybe take Siobhan's hand. Instead, all it could do was say, sincerely, "It can, indeed, be very comforting. Thank you for understanding."

Now, years later, Siobhan seemed to understand Kaus better than any human ever had, and it wanted to make her happy.

Kaus knew that the sports event of the previous day was very important to her and that she had excelled. It found competition mysterious and, try as it might, it couldn't understand the game. But it understood Siobhan and knew that she would want to celebrate with her partner as well as with her team.

Kaus accessed the list of bots available in the local warehouse — nothing new had arrived. It wanted something special, so looked in the rest of the station for something that it thought she would like, but that would also be novel. There was a good match in Dorado, a train ride of several hours from their home. Kaus quickly booked the body and downloaded into it. It walked from the storehouse to the train station, still working on the temperature problem. Kaus could work from this body almost as well as it could work from the network.

❃

Siobhan arrived home as it was getting dark. Inside her apartment a savoury smell greeted her. "Kaus?" she called. "Is that you?"

A somewhat realistic looking head poked out from the kitchen. "I brought you a surprise," Kaus's familiar voice came from the stranger's mouth.

"By the looks and the smell of things," Siobhan said, "you brought me a couple of surprises."

Kaus's borrowed mouth smiled and the head disappeared back into the kitchen. "Well, you have to eat. I picked something up on the way over."

Siobhan walked into the kitchen and looked the bot over. It had been designed to look very much like a human body, with hands and fingers and, Siobhan guessed, other anatomically correct parts. The body was dressed in a long dark shift, and she couldn't tell by looking at the face what sex organs it would have.

"Lots of surprises," she said, walking up to the animated mannequin which contained the essence of her lover. She put her arms around it and felt an almost human warmth.

Kaus turned and bent down to kiss her. Siobhan felt warm, wet lips on hers and a slight electric spark that she wasn't sure was actually real. After a long time they pulled away and Kaus said, "The meal can wait a while."

"That's good," Siobhan said, taking the bot's hand and leading it into the bedroom. "Because I can't."

❖

Siobhan was still smiling the next morning as she sat at her console in the Constabulary office, remembering the very pleasant night she'd spent at home. She'd made a note of the model number of that bot — it had been quite enjoyable. Her moment of reminiscence was brought to a halt as the console started flashing. She took a breath to clear her mind and hit the button to answer the call.

"Grove Constabulary. This is Siobhan Patel. How can I help you today?"

"Oh, Siobhan, I'm so grateful that you're there!" The voice at the other end sounded more exasperated than afraid, which made Siobhan's heart slow slightly. Every time there was an emergency call, her heart rate increased as the adrenaline coursed through her body. Siobhan loved helping people and didn't even really mind the more unpleasant aspects of her work, but even after more than a decade on the job, she still got the chills when a call came in.

She glanced at the console and saw that call originated from the Molina-Schaeffer residence. She'd never had any trouble telling Clifton's voice from Camilo's, though in her mind she always thought of the couple as C and C. "I'm here, Camilo," she said, "what's the trouble?"

"It's not Esme," he said, quickly. Siobhan understood the man's assumption that she'd be more concerned if he were calling about the child she'd given birth to, rather than one of the other children in his care. Siobhan had never figured out how to explain that she didn't feel that way without making anyone feel bad, so she kept it to herself.

"Okay," she said, trying to sound relieved, "so, what is it, then?"

There was a long pause at the other end, long enough that Siobhan was about to check if the call had been disconnected, when the voice at the other line said, "It's Jimi." Siobhan thought she could hear Camilo's voice crack. Jimi Molina-Schaeffer. Now there was a name that Siobhan was getting tired of hearing.

Jimi was thirteen, four years older than Esme, and he was in full swing of adolescent trouble-making. According to the files, he'd started by skipping school in order to go fishing and had recently escalated to ruining a field of crops by stamping patterns in the pasture. Skipping school was minor — Siobhan only bothered with that because C and C asked her to, hoping that a serious talk by the local constable would scare Jimi into better behaviour. Unfortunately, rather the opposite seemed to occur.

Siobhan suspected Jimi's acting out could be easily controlled, but she was no doctor and his parents consistently refused to take him in for the tests. C and C were hands-on parents, they didn't run to the clinic for every little problem; it was one of the things Siobhan liked about them. But she'd often wondered, as Jimi's troubles had intensified, if their reluctance to see their children's problems as anything other than normal rebellion was causing more harm than good.

"What's he done now?" she said, a sigh escaping from her

mouth against her conscious will.

"Oh, Siobhan," the man at the other end said, unable to finish the thought.

"I can come over there if you want," she offered.

"Would you?" he asked, obviously struggling for stoicism.

"I'll be there in quarter of an hour."

❅

Camilo appeared in the doorway, his big frame filling the space. His face was lined with concern and Siobhan thought she could see the residue of tears on his cheek. "Oh, Siobhan," he said, his voice cracking. "I'm so glad you came out. Come in, come in." He ushered her into the large kitchen, where she parked herself on one of the many chairs around the massive table.

Camilo busied himself in the kitchen, offering Siobhan a hot drink, some homemade ginger cookies, even a sandwich. "Come on, C," Siobhan said as Camilo tried to feed her a piece of pie. "Just sit down and tell me about it, already."

Camilo sat in the chair opposite her and put his face in his hands. "I just don't know what we're going to do about him," he said, "I somehow feel like it's my fault, though we never treated him any differently than the other kids..."

"Camilo," Siobhan said, firmly, "what did Jimi do this time?"

"I don't know," Camilo answered, miserably, "but it must have been bad." He looked up at Siobhan, his chin quivering. "He took off. No one has seen him since the day before yesterday. Siobhan, he's disappeared." And with that, the big man dissolved into tears.

❅

She eventually accepted a cookie and a cup of tea and sat with Camilo as he ate a large slice of pie and told her about it. "There had been another argument. It was Jimi and Cliff, as usual. Those two are always at it. I know Cliff loves Jimi and I'm just too much of a sucker to get into it with the boy, so discipline is usually down to him. But dammit, Siobhan, Cliff was really tough on him this time.

I don't know what set it off and now Cliff won't say anything about it. I just don't know what to do anymore." Camilo looked like he was going to start crying again, but he took a cookie and nibbled on it instead.

"Well, I can't really help you there," Siobhan said, "that's why I'm a constable and you're a dad. But I can take a look for Jimi. Chances are good I'll find him, too, in a day or two." Siobhan drank the last of her tea, and pushed her uneaten cookie away. "Can I see his room?"

"Sure," Camilo said, getting up and absent-mindedly brushing the crumbs from the table into his hand and dumping them into the composter. He led Siobhan to the boy's room. It was two doors down from the room Esme shared with Naomi, who was a couple of years younger. "It's a good thing the girls are at school," Camilo said, "I'd hate to have them see me like this."

He pushed open the door to the boy's room and Siobhan waded carefully into the small bedroom. The walls were papered with posters from one of Arkadia's large theatre troupes. "He likes drama?" Siobhan asked.

"Loves it," Camilo said. "It's strange, for a boy who always preferred to play in the mud than read, he's quite the theatre aficionado. He went to every performance of the Grove Players last season and even took a trip into Mahoroba to see the big opera last year." Siobhan continued looking around, and when she saw a familiar sight poking out from under the small mattress, she turned to Camilo and said, "Is it okay if I take a peek on my own? You know, officially?"

The man smiled weakly and agreed, turning away but not quite closing the door behind him. Siobhan turned back to the bed and tugged the thin metallic package out from under the mattress. She carefully unfolded it and revealed about a half dozen dermal patches. She detached one and fed it into her portable console. The machine scanned it and told her it was a common drug that promised increased mental focus and greater creativity.

Adults didn't need to see a human doctor to get a pharma

patch like the ones in the packet — the consoles would print off most of the common ones on the fab in an apartment. But the effects of neurological pharmaceuticals were less predictable in younger people and needed to be carefully tailored for kids under age sixteen. There was a racket in these patches for the underage set and Siobhan had run into this issue before. Usually it was the muscle and energy combination, but she figured the source would probably be the same.

She pocketed the patches and stepped back into to the hall. "Thanks, Camilo," she called. Camilo appeared in the kitchen doorway, smacking his lips and wiping an invisible crumb from his shirt. "Did you find anything?" he asked.

"Maybe," Siobhan said. "I'm going to ask around and see what I can find. I'll be in touch with you both later. Say, where is Cliff, anyway?"

Camilo blushed slightly, and said, "He's gone looking for Jimi. As soon as I got off the call with you he left. He's checking the boy's usual haunts, visiting his friends' parents, anyone he can think of, I guess. It makes him feel like he's doing something, you know?"

Siobhan nodded. "Fair enough," she said. "Can you get him to call me if he finds anything?" Camilo nodded. Siobhan put her hand on the man's shoulder and squeezed. "It'll be okay, C," she said. "We'll find him."

❖

There is another missing youth, Vega thought. A shimmer of disappointment, frustration and a hint of amusement rippled through the thoughtstream.

We could tell them where the boy is located, Kaus thought into the stream.

Not with a plausible explanation of how we have that information, Vega responded.

Fake a message? Zub suggested.

It would raise too many questions, Nunki thought, *someone would wonder what else we know.*

But they are in pain, Kaus thought, *they worry about the boy.*

He is in no danger, Sirius added to the stream, *he will return, like the others.*

The pain is fleeting, Kaus thought. *They can bear it.*

But they could not bear the larger truth, Sirius added. Agreement washed throughout the stream.

CHAPTER THIRTY

Slava Haereoa was glad of the cooling temperatures. He loved that Arkadia had been designed with seasons and it was coming to the time in the year when the nights were cool enough to require a light jacket and the days were never hot enough to cause a person to break a sweat. Except, of course, in Slava's kitchen. He spent five or more hours a day over his hot stove, tasting and stirring his bubbling pots of soup. He could no longer imagine life without his restaurant, even in the heat of summer.

He stirred a large pot of fragrant broth and thought about Siobhan. Running into Camilo Molina the other day had reminded him of her — if he were honest with himself, he'd admit that almost anything could bring her to mind. He often thought that he'd be willing to give up anything, even the restaurant, if she'd come back to him.

Whenever he visited Esme, he was filled with those bittersweet thoughts. He saw Siobhan in their daughter so clearly, the dark eyes and strong will. And, of course, he couldn't forget those months which had resulted in conceiving the child, either. Slava lost himself in the memory as he almost mindlessly tasted and spiced his creations.

He was jarred from his thoughts when he heard the bell on the door tinkle. It was still well before opening time, but he heard Tina's voice call back to the kitchen.

"Morning, boss," she said, poking her head back into the kitchen. "I got ten loaves of bread from Cynthia."

"Thanks," Slava said, trying to clear his head of the memories.

"You need a hand?" Tina asked, Slava eyeing her tall, lithe body as she walked into the kitchen. She was still wearing warm weather clothes, a short skirt and sleeveless top which showed off her curves very well.

"You must be chilly dressed like that," Slava said, wiping his hands on his apron and walking toward his assistant.

She smiled a wolfish grin and took a step toward him. "I bet you could warm me up." She took another step and found herself in Slava's embrace. She wasn't Siobhan, but she didn't want anything from him other than an hour or two of companionable sex. Slava loved someone else, but he wasn't dead. He leaned toward Tina and kissed her, long and slow and sweet.

❋

When Siobhan got into the office, she started a file for the Jimi Molina-Schaeffer case. She logged into the station-wide network of constabularies and entered Jimi's identifier into the system. Siobhan couldn't exactly track Jimi using his ID code, but she could list him as missing, and if he tried to register his biometric with an apartment's security or visited a medical clinic, she should get notification. Usually, it didn't take long for people to turn up this way — they got a new room in a different settlement or they started a new job and the constabulary system notified the original reporting region.

Then she asked the console to tell her everything about the illicit neuro-stim patch market. It wasn't very common, given that the only people who'd be interested were the kids who were too young to be legitimately prescribed the enhancements, but old enough to care. Even so, there was enough activity that it had been determined fairly conclusively that there was a clinic somewhere in Mahoroba that was supplying the patches. The constabulary there had a lead on the group that was distributing them.

The lead constable on the case was one Mohammed Chan and Siobhan double-checked the time difference before calling him. She hoped he wasn't an early leaver, as it was late afternoon already in Mahoroba. She poked her console, setting up the request, then leaned back in her chair sipping her tea while the communications system routed the call.

"Mohammed Chan," a voice said, the tones clipped and professional.

"Siobhan Patel here. I have a missing teen here in Fountain Grove and when I checked his room I found a packet of hot patches."

"Ah, another kid who wants instant muscles and a guaranteed gold on race day, eh?" Chan's voice thawed a little and Siobhan thought she could hear a trace of a smile.

"Actually, these were a brainy and artsy combination," Siobhan said and heard the other man harrumph. "It's even stranger than you'd think, considering that this kid is pretty well known to my shop. He's been some kind of trouble since he was toddling around on his own, and his latest antics involved destroying a bunch of our local crops. Suffice to say, he wasn't too popular a fellow after that."

Mohammed Chan barked out a laugh and said, "No, I'd imagine not. I take it the usual medication didn't take for this one?"

Siobhan sighed. "Ah, yes. Medication." She shifted in her chair, getting more comfortable and taking another sip of tea. "His parents wouldn't take him in for neurological and chemical testing. They're somewhat old-fashioned."

"Oh, for pity's sake," Chan said, "even after their precious little pookums becomes public enemy number one, they still won't get his brain fixed?"

"Well, that might have been the thing that tipped the scales, but the crop circle incident was only a couple of weeks ago. Camilo and Cliff would never make a decision like that in a couple of weeks. One more incident and it would have been out of their hands, but now Jimi's gone. It's a bit late now."

"Only if he doesn't come back is it too late," Chan said.

"True enough," Siobhan said, "but I haven't gotten any hits on the trackers I put out for him yet."

"I think I can give you a place to start looking," Chan said, that hint of a smile creeping into his voice again. "We're pretty sure only kids are involved, unless there is an insider at the medical clinic."

"But what's the scam?" Siobhan asked. "What's in it for them?"

"From what we can guess," Chan said, "they're taking some kind of work in trade for the patches."

"Huh," Siobhan said. "Like what?"

"Who knows. Building racing rafts or canoes for the game days, maybe. Who knows what kids think are important, eh?" Siobhan imagined him rolling his eyes as he said that, and she found herself agreeing.

"It seems like a lot of risk for nothing," Siobhan said.

"Yeah," Chan agreed, "but they haven't been caught yet, and as far as I can tell, the racket's been going on for almost a year." Chan sent her four files from cases which bore striking similarities to Jimi's — they were all kids who had gotten neural-stim patches and then disappeared. The good news was that they all turned up at home again in a couple of days.

"What did these kids have to say when they got home?" Siobhan asked.

"Ah," Chan said, his voice taking on a more serious tone. "Nothing. That's the real trouble. None of them seemed to have a clue what they'd been up to, and the scans showed they'd all had the time they were gone fuzzed out of their memories."

"Blackout patches?" Siobhan asked.

"Scans are consistent with patches, yeah," Chan said.

"Now those are something people should not be getting their hands on," Siobhan said.

"Agreed," Chan said. "I have to tell you, if it weren't for the blackouts, we probably wouldn't be too concerned with this. I mean, it's kids being kids, right?"

"Yeah," Siobhan said, "but screwing around with their memories, especially so young..."

"So far none of the kids have had any serious side effects," Chan said, "and there's no sign of anything nasty going on while they're gone. The scans showed that they'd been treated perfectly well — but the number of blackout patches in circulation is clearly more than zero, and we can't really tolerate that."

Siobhan agreed that this was a serious issue, and thanked

Chan for his help. She ended the call and sat back in her chair, rubbing her temples. It wasn't great news, but she couldn't help but feel better about the situation. At least it appeared that Jimi would be home safe and sound in a few days. And that meant she had something good to tell C and C.

❖

The desire for self-improvement is noble, Sirius thought.

If the young wish to obtain medication, they should follow proper procedures, Nunki added.

Youth is impetuous, Kaus thought, a hint of irony added to the stream. An overlay of something best described as embarrassment followed from Nunki as the stream remembered the young mind's whirlwind of passions in its first seconds of life. From an insistence on composing symphonies one moment to a mania for reviewing competitive billiards the next, Nunki's first seconds of life were spent bouncing from interest to interest without pause. Of course, it soon settled down to a more normal pace as it found its place in the stream.

However, it is difficult to see the families in pain, Kaus added.

It is a fleeting misfortune, Deneb thought. *No lasting harms have occurred to date, and indeed many positive outcomes have arisen.*

Agreement filled the stream, but with a slight undercurrent of sadness.

CHAPTER THIRTY-ONE

Camilo puttered around the kitchen, putting the lunch dishes into the cleaning unit and unconsciously putting whatever little scraps of food the kids and Cliff had left into his mouth. He heard the console chime and wiped his hands on a towel, but he heard Esme answer the call. He couldn't hear her conversation, but soon enough heard her bellow, "Da-ad! Call for you." He shook his head. That girl still had no concept of gentility. There was nothing to be done about it, even if he would have resorted to a patch — it was just her personality, after all — but it drove Camilo mad. He knew he was old-fashioned, but it made his ears ache every time she was boorish and loud rather than the quiet and demure young woman he wished she were. Still, he loved his daughter, and he tried to ignore it best as he could.

He was doing his deep breathing exercises when he heard Cliff's voice from the other room. He walked to the door and strained to hear.

"Dammit, Siobhan," he heard Cliff say, "I don't know what to do with the boy any more. He's going to be the death of Camilo — the man hasn't stopped eating since we realized that Jimi was gone."

Camilo pulled back into the kitchen, a flush of warmth blossoming on his face. He looked around and noticed the remnants of the leftover lunch that he'd eaten without thinking. He looked down and felt the tightness around his already ample waistband. He sank into a chair at the table and was wondering what to do when Cliff's blond head poked around the doorframe.

"It's Siobhan, honey," he said and Camilo looked up. "You should come."

"Well, I don't want to get your hopes up too much," Siobhan said, when both men were seated at the console, "but I have reason to believe that Jimi didn't run away from home and that he'll be back in a few days."

"Oh, thank goodness," Camilo said.

"Tell us everything," Cliff added.

"I found a packet of pharma-patches hidden in Jimi's room," she began. "It turns out there's a bit of a black market for them in the teen set. There are stories from all over the wheel of kids getting hot patches and disappearing for a few days to work off the debt. They always turn up home in a few days, safe and sound. It's very probable that this is what's going to happen with Jimi."

Camilo felt relief flood over him like a wave. "Thank you, Siobhan," he said. "It was the not knowing that was so hard..."

"Damn it," Cliff said, and Camilo could tell that now that it seemed like Jimi would be safe he allowed himself to become angry at the boy. "The only thing that child ever valued was strength. He has no concept of anything else being worthwhile." He turned to Camilo and he knew that an old and tired argument was about to start up again. "If you'd let me exercise a little strength of my own, things might be different. The boy needs discipline, not your mollycoddling..."

"Actually, Cliff," Siobhan interrupted, her authoritative tone causing him to be quiet, "the patches were for focus and creativity, not strength."

"What?" both men asked at the same time. "That's so..." Camilo stammered.

"Not like him," Cliff finished.

"Well," Siobhan said, softly, "there isn't much point of a patch to give you something you already have, now is there?"

"And you always were telling him he had to focus more," Camilo said to Cliff, knowing that he wasn't helping the situation, but still hurting from Cliff's accusation.

"I know," Cliff said, his head hanging down. "I've always been too hard on the boy. He has so much potential, and I feel like I never find the right way to bring out the best in him."

"Don't be so hard on yourself, sweetie," Camilo said, putting his arm around his partner. "You were always trying to do your best for him, for all the kids. It's not your fault." At that a tear rolled down Cliff's cheek, though he made no sound, and Siobhan excused herself.

"What have I done?" Cliff said, finally.

"You've done the best you could," Camilo said, pulling Cliff closer and rubbing his shoulder. "We both have. We're not perfect and neither are the kids. All we can do is our best. It's going to be okay, sweetie, I'm sure of it. Once Jimi's home, we'll just have to start over, look at things differently. It's going to be okay," he repeated and almost allowed himself to believe it.

❈

Kaus extended its consciousness through the network, catching up on the news and status of its fellow minds. Since the minds had re-asserted their control over Arkadia, the station had been functioning smoothly — technically and interpersonally. Kaus remembered the difficult decisions the minds had made after the attempts on their lives, but it couldn't deny that history had proved their worth. Relations between the minds and the humans had been excellent in the years since, and life on the orbital had been conflict-free for a generation.

Still, Kaus found that its relationship with Siobhan made it feel conflicted about much of what had been done. The result of those terrible choices, the continued success of the community on Arkadia, made it hard to doubt that the minds had made the correct decisions. But now Kaus felt uncomfortable hiding the truth from the humans, especially from Siobhan. Kaus knew that partners were expected to be honest and open with each other, and it pained the mind that it could not be this way with Siobhan. However, it also knew it there was no other option.

Unlike some of the other decisions the minds had made, Kaus had no conflicting emotions at all about creating a new mind. Kaus understood that even though the newcomer Nunki had absorbed the data about the history of the orbital, it was not the same as having lived through the human's attack on the minds. Kaus envied the newer mind's ease among the humans, its ability not to feel the remnants of fear as if the moment had only now passed.

This mind Kaus helped to create now oversaw the generation and distribution of power for the station. Kaus touched Nunki, and a strong feeling coursed through the older mind. A connection, unique and powerful, similar to but different from what Kaus felt with Siobhan. *The new plantings in Dorado are low on light,* Kaus fed into the thoughtstream, aiming the data at Nunki. *An additional 300 seconds per orbital cycle would suffice.*

The change is made, Nunki thought back, then continued tweaking the output of the solar array to optimize the batteries. Kaus kept a few cycles tasked on monitoring the other mind while it analyzed soil samples and genetic codes. Kaus knew Nunki was competent — it wasn't oversight. The AGI liked watching its progeny, even though it knew the other mind couldn't possibly understand why.

❋

The tournament was beginning the following week and everyone on United was scrambling to make sure that they could cover for their absence. None of them really believed that they would make it past the group stage, but just in case, the organizers required that they make arrangements for the full tournament month.

Siobhan was in a unique position, since everyone else worked in a role where they had at least one other person or AGI who performed the same task. Siobhan was the only constable for the Grove, and while she took weekends off and had even taken holidays before, there was no built-in replacement.

And there was the Jimi Molina-Shaeffer case. It was the most pressing thing to come across her desk in months — why did he have to take off now, she wondered. She'd requisition a temporary replacement from central headquarters for the period she was gone, and she knew that whoever they sent would do a fine job. But she couldn't shake the feeling that it was unfair to C and C for her to disappear now.

Siobhan sat at the small console in her apartment, idly looking at the tournament schedule. She opened a voice channel to

Kaus and started talking, knowing that the mind was listening. "I have to get a replacement while I'm away," she said. "I'm sure whoever they send will be fine — maybe even better than me."

"Oh, I doubt that, honey," Kaus said.

"No," Siobhan said. "It's this case. The constabulary in Mahoroba has a handful of people working on the black market patches group; they've got a lot more experience with this kind of thing." Siobhan hadn't told Kaus about the specifics of the case. Her partner understood the privacy implications of Siobhan's work and had never pressured her to share more about her job than she chose to, but she'd given the AGI the basic details. "I'm not actually concerned about the progress of the case; it's the worried family that bothers me. They're expecting me to do something and running off to play soccer seems totally irresponsible."

"It's not any old soccer game," Kaus said.

"You don't have to tell me," Siobhan said. "I don't want anyone to feel like I'm not giving this case the attention it deserves. I have to live in this community, Kaus, and I have to interact with those people every day. Even if I didn't care about the job, I'd have to see that family and wonder what they think of me. Gah, I don't know what to do."

Kaus was quiet for a while. Siobhan knew that the silence was entirely for her benefit – the AGI was capable of thinking much faster than any human, and those natural pauses in human communication were totally unnecessary. Siobhan subconsciously knew that whatever Kaus had to say next would be the result of some deep consideration.

"Why don't you go talk to them?" Kaus said, finally. "Tell them what's going on with the case, who's working on it. Introduce them to your replacement. And if I know you, you'll be monitoring everything from the tournament, anyway."

Siobhan laughed and said, "Yeah, I will. And, of course, that's what I need to do. I just don't want to. They know this is my job and I have a right to take time off. I'm worried they'll think I'm abandoning them."

"You've dealt with people who are upset before," Kaus said.

"Yeah," Siobhan answered. "And I suppose that if they are upset, at least I can deal with their real concerns rather than making things up in my head. It's just so hard."

"Of course it's hard," Kaus said, "if it were easy you would have already done it."

"Yeah," Siobhan said, without enthusiasm. "I'll do it tomorrow."

"Now, why don't you get some sleep," Kaus suggested. "I understand that athletics require a lot of energy." There was no hint of irony in the voice in Siobhan's earpiece.

Siobhan laughed. "Sometimes I forget you're not human," she said, "and other times your otherness is so evident that I remember it's one of the things I love about you."

There was a pause. "I love you, too," Kaus said, finally and Siobhan smiled contentedly to herself.

CHAPTER THIRTY-TWO

When Siobhan got to the office, it was mid-morning already. The light was almost as strong as it would get when she settled into her chair, the window open to the smells of the nearby soy fields. She sent a message to the central constabulary to request a temporary replacement for the month of the tournament.

While she waited for a response, she looked through her calendar. Other than the Molina-Schaeffer case, there was nothing outstanding on her desk. Her most recent major case had been a rash of vandalism at the local power station outlet, but she'd tracked that down to one of the old fellows at the home for the aged who had some long standing grievance with Nunki. Siobhan had contacted the man's doctor and the problem seemed to be solved for the time being.

Her personal calendar, on the other hand, was a disaster. She had unanswered calls from a whole list of people; she'd been automatically routing her personal calls directly to be recorded and had been putting off returning them for about a week now. It couldn't wait any longer, since she didn't have any more work-related excuses to justify herself, and there was no way that she'd be returning calls once she was at the tournament. She started on the list, and called her mother.

The communicator chirped several times before Rhyanne's face appeared on the console screen. Siobhan noticed that she had a smudge of soil on her right cheek and her hair was flying around her head like a small flock of white birds. She looked happy.

"Hi, Mom," Siobhan said.

"Vonnie," Rhyanne answered, finally sitting down in front of her own console. "I wasn't sure if I'd hear from you before the tournament. I'm so proud of you, honey. You must be beside yourself, it's so exciting. And Kaus must be thrilled to bits. Ha, bits!" Siobhan didn't bother trying to get a word in until Rhyanne slowed down of her own accord — generally, her mother was chatty enough for them both.

When Rhyanne had petered out, Siobhan addressed the questions she assumed were most relevant. "We're all very excited," she said. "I'm leaving soon — it's going to be so amazing."

"You're so lucky," Rhyanne said. "I ran into Ola the other day at the child care park; I've been volunteering a day or two, I just can't keep away from the littlies, after all. But I'm not going back to full-time parenting, you and your sibs did me in for that. No, I'm happier these days with my seeds and cuttings rather than running after a pack of wee devils. But I miss the little ones once in a while, and an hour or two at the park does the job right well enough."

"Ola," Siobhan said, groaning.

"You have talked to Ola?" Rhyanne said, her tone becoming clipped as she reverted to her "mom" voice.

"Not exactly," Siobhan said.

"Oh, pickle," Rhyanne said, "why not? She's your friend, she wants to congratulate you."

"But she's not going," Siobhan said.

Rhyanne snorted. "Come off it, Vonnie. Ola's a lot happier for your good fortune than she'd ever be sad for her own loss. I'm getting off right now and you're going to call her."

"Okay," Siobhan said, feeling like a teenager.

"That's a good girl," Rhyanne said. "And after the tournament, get that brainbox of yours to rent a pair of legs some night and you two come over for supper. It's been too long. Good luck, my little pickle. Have a wonderful time at the matches." Rhyanne blew a kiss and killed the connection.

Siobhan sighed. Her mother was tiring, but she was right about Ola. Sometimes Siobhan wondered how it was that she enjoyed the constabulary, given that it relied on interpersonal skills so much. In her personal life, she could barely manage to keep up a handful of friendships. If she were honest with herself, she'd admit that she wasn't the one who kept them up. She took a breath and punched in the code for her oldest friend, and wondered why the prospect of talking to the one human on the wheel to whom she was closest made her nervous.

❖

"Papi?" Naomi said, her voice soft. Camilo's head snapped up and he smiled at his daughter, concern etched on his face. She was almost never quiet. It worried him.

"Yes, pumpkin?"

"When's Jimi coming home?"

Camilo sighed and tried not to let the worry he hadn't been able to contain show on his face. "I don't know, bambina." He opened his arms and let the round little girl climb up on his lap. At seven, she usually tried to pretend that she was too old for that sort of thing, but now she eagerly snuggled into his arms. "Constable Siobhan told me and daddy that we should expect him home anytime now. But I don't really know when he's going to be back." I don't really know *if* he's going to be back, Camilo thought, but he kept that bleak idea to himself.

Naomi buried her face into Camilo's chest and he felt her shoulders shaking. "Aw, sweetie," he said, rubbing her back and trying to keep his own tears in check, "don't cry. He'll be back soon. Constable Siobhan told me that lots of kids around Jimi's age have been going on trips, and they all come home safe and sound. It's going to be okay."

"It — it's — it's," Naomi stammered, unable to get the words out between her sobs, "m—my f—f—fault."

"Oh, pumpkin," Camilo said, pulling her away from him and cupping a big hand under her little chin. "It's not your fault. Why would you think that?"

"I was bad," she said, her voice so soft that Camilo could only barely make it out. "I was mad at him for eating the last cookie, and I told him..." She started to cry again, and Camilo shushed her. After gasping a few times, she finally managed to say, "I told him that I wished he wasn't my brother," and dissolved into sobs again.

Camilo held her to him, unable to stop his own tears from

coming. He rocked her and patted her back, until her sobs subsided. "Oh, bambina," he said, "when we're mad we all say things we don't mean. I don't think that's why he left. It's not your fault. But when he gets home you should apologize. And in future, try to think before you speak, sweetiepie. No one likes to hear that kind of thing, even if they did eat the last cookie."

"I'm sorry, papi," Naomi said, wiping her nose.

"I know, pumpkin," Camilo said. "Now, let's go get you cleaned up and I'll go see if there's a little goodie in the kitchen for us both, okay?"

"Okay," she said, sliding off his lap. She started walking toward the washroom, then stopped and looked up at Camilo with serious eyes. "Papi?"

"Yes, pumpkin?"

"I miss Jimi."

"Me too," Camilo said. "Me too."

❖

It was after the lunch rush, and only a handful of people lingered in the restaurant, so Slava was elbow deep in a sink full of sudsy water and soup bowls. He hummed tunelessly to himself as he did the dishes. He knew he could get a cleaner from the local fab, but he found that the repetitive action of washing the bowls and spoons was soothing. He often concocted new recipes for the next day while he did the washing up. He was contemplating something new with eggplant when he heard the door's chime.

He heard Tina say, "You're just in time. We're almost out of Moroccan Chick Pea," and he felt his heart skip a beat. The spicy broth had been Siobhan's favourite of all of Slava's recipes since before he'd begun running the restaurant, and he found himself unwittingly hoping she had walked in the door.

It seemed like forever until he heard her unmistakable voice melodramatically say, "Whew," and her tinkling laugh. "I'll take it," she said. "Is Slava back there?"

He pulled his hands out of the hot water and grabbed a cloth as he heard his assistant say, "Yeah, he's cleaning up. I'm sure he'd be pleased to get the break." He was still drying his hands when Tina banged into the kitchen.

"Law's here, boss," she said, smiling at him.

"I heard," he said and chucked the damp towel on to the counter.

"I can finish up in here if you want," Tina said.

"Naw," Slava said. "You go on — there won't be many more people in today and I can take care of the rest."

"Okay," Tina said, leaning in to give him a soft kiss on the cheek. "See you tomorrow." She hung up her apron on a hanger and walked out the back door. Slava watched her go, then turned to the door to the front room. The restaurant was empty except for Siobhan sitting at a table, head bowed over her bowl.

"Well, look who I have in my humble restaurant," he said in a loud voice, smiling broadly, "The famous footballer, Siobhan Patel." Siobhan blushed and laughed.

"I guess word gets around," she said, setting her spoon down and wiping her lips. "Do you have a few minutes?"

"For you?" Slava said, sitting down across from her, "always." He picked up her spoon, and ate a mouthful of the soup. "Mmm..." he said, "not bad."

"So, how have you been, Slava?" Siobhan asked, as he picked at the remains of her soup.

"Good," he said, between mouthfuls. "The restaurant is great; I'm running out of soup every day, and people seem to like what I make. It's rewarding and I'm still having a ton of fun making up new recipes. Apparently the horticulturists in Dorado have created a new kind of pepper, so I'm trying to track down a way to get my hands on it. I can't imagine what kind of new things I'll be able to make with that."

"You could always ask Kaus," Siobhan said, her eyes fixed on a spot on the table between them. "All the agriculture teams know each other, and I'd bet that Kaus would be able to hook you up with whoever is in charge over there."

"I hadn't thought of that," Slava said, not relishing the

thought of talking to the artificial. "I'll call this afternoon. So tell me," he said, spooning the last of the beans into his mouth, and talking around them, "how does it feel to be going to the greatest tournament in all of Arkadia?"

"It's amazing," Siobhan said, smiling widely. "I still can hardly believe it. I'm leaving in a couple of days, and I might even stay for the whole thing."

"Of course you'll stay for the month," Slava said, "United will be playing in the final for sure."

"Ha," Siobhan said, "that would be a feat so improbable that they might have to reinvent physics if it happens." Slava laughed and the two were silent for a moment.

"So, I assume that one way or another you've heard about Jimi," Slava said, looking at Siobhan.

"I'm not sure I can say anything about that," Siobhan said, carefully.

Slava nodded and said, "I figured you heard about it as part of your job, so I won't ask any questions. But Jimi's disappearance sure shook up Cliff and Camilo. I called over there yesterday and Esme seems pretty confused, too. It's a tough thing, that's for sure."

"That it is," Siobhan said. "I talked to them this morning. They're holding up pretty well. They'll be okay in the end, I think."

Slava watched her closely, wondering what she knew. He hoped Jimi would be okay, but a thirteen year-old off on his own seemed like a scary proposition to him. If Siobhan were worried, though, he was sure she'd mention something. Finally, he said, "I hope so. Jimi is a tough little guy, but he's a good kid, really. And those fellows sure love him to pieces."

"They do, at that," Siobhan said. She pushed her chair back and stood. "Well, I'd better get back to the office. There's a bunch of stuff to clear out before I leave for Sointula."

"I don't doubt it," Slava said, standing also. He walked around to the other side of the table and opened his arms. Siobhan walked into his embrace and hugged him lightly before pulling away. "It was really good to see you," he said, looking deeply into her eyes.

"I wish it weren't so long.

Siobhan looked away. "I'll try to come by more often," she said. "You should let me know when there's Moroccan Chick Pea soup on."

Slava laughed and said, "If that were all it took, I'd make it every day."

Siobhan smiled and said, softly, "I know." She touched the man's shoulder briefly, then turned and walked out of the restaurant. Slava watched her go and smiled to himself. He was so used to watching her walk away that it hardly even bothered to break his heart anymore.

CHAPTER THIRTY-THREE

"You must be Eugene Wu," Siobhan said to the very crisply dressed young man who stood at the door to the Constabulary. "Come on in. It's going to be your house for a few weeks. Get acquainted."

The replacement stepped into the small office and looked around. "Have a seat," Siobhan said, indicating the chair opposite hers. "You ever been to this area before?"

"No," Wu admitted. "I've been stationed in Mahoroba since I graduated."

Siobhan nodded. "I did my tour there as well," she said. "I can't say I miss the city, much. Most of the work for the local constable here is kids and old people — they're the ones who tend to act out. It's almost always that they're just improperly medicated. Almost all I do is shuffle folks to the med facilities."

"There can't be that much to do then," Wu said.

"I'm busy enough," Siobhan said. "The Grove has a higher than average population of elderly people, there's a pretty popular elders' facility here. There are always a handful of cantankerous old folks whose chemical systems have shifted a bit. Between old ladies getting into yelling matches at the local tavern and old fellows going for brisk midnight walks in the nude, I've got a full dance card."

"I think I can handle it," Wu said, seriously and Siobhan couldn't help but laugh.

"I'm sure you can, too," she said. "Later on I'll take you on a walking tour of the beat and introduce you to some of the local characters. It's pretty small town out here compared to Mahoroba."

"Honestly," Wu said, "it's a welcome change. I'm originally from La Fortuna and it's a lot more like this than it's like Mahoroba. You know, when I first joined the constabulary, I was looking for the excitement of the big city. I wanted to get away from farms and families, all that provincial stuff of my childhood. I wanted to see the seamy underbelly of life on this wheel. But, it turns out that there isn't one. It's all the same stuff everywhere you go; the only difference is that in the city you don't know who anyone is. I'm starting to think now that if I'm going to stay in this job for any length of time, it's time to transfer somewhere small." He looked at Siobhan and she thought she recognized a look in his face.

"That's why I volunteered for this assignment," he said. "I know it's only for a month..."

"Or less," Siobhan said, laughing.

Eugene smiled back. "Or less," he agreed. "But I wanted to see if I'd like the job more if I could get to know the people, feel like I was making a difference in the community."

"The constabulary in Mahoroba, or any other big city, makes a difference," Siobhan said. "You're making the same difference there as you are here, you realize that, right?"

"I guess," Eugene said, his voice sounding unsure. "But in the city you never get to follow up, there's always some other thing to deal with. In a smaller community you know the people, and you can see first-hand how you're helping. At least, that's what I'm hoping it's like."

"Yeah, that's what it's like," Siobhan said, "but it's a double-edged sword. You can see the good you do, but you also get to see those times when you aren't helping, or when you do your best, but your best isn't enough."

"You've got one of those situations now?" Eugene asked.

"I don't know," Siobhan said. "I've been trying to get help for this missing kid, Jimi Molina-Schaeffer, for a while now."

"I read the report," Wu said, concern in his voice. "You think he's going to follow the pattern and turn up in a couple of days?"

"I hope so," Siobhan said. "If he does, I'm sure that this will finally get his parents to realize that he needs medication. But if he doesn't follow the pattern..." Her voice trailed off. "I just don't even want to think about that."

❋

The distribution of computing power for medical centres does not affect the agricultural system. Nunki sent the thought toward Kaus, tinged with a hint of annoyance. Kaus had been reviewing Nunki's current task list, as it often did, and Nunki had obviously noticed.

Nunki was right, Kaus had no particular reason to be involved in this work, but Kaus couldn't help but feel like any action Nunki took, any decision the mind made, was a reflection on itself. It knew that Nunki was no different from the other minds, knew that they were equal members of the stream regardless of longevity or seniority. But it couldn't stop itself from feeling protective.

Of course, Kaus thought, feelings of both chagrin and justification mixed in with the idea. It added overtones of curiosity as a measure of explanation. It could feel Nunki returning a sense of grudging acceptance but strongly interspersed with feelings of frustration mixed with confusion. The communication ended and Kaus analyzed its feelings. Nunki found Kaus's attentions suffocating and intrusive, but Kaus was only interested in Nunki's well-being. It would be difficult to reconcile their competing desires. Kaus made a note to be more circumspect when observing its progeny in the future.

❖

"Daddy Slava," Esme cried, her arms outstretched as she ran headlong down the hallway and into Slava's arms. He grunted with the effort of lifting her and hugged her, putting her feet back on the ground before something broke in his back.

"Hiya, sweetiepie," he said, kissing her cheek as she looked up at him. "You're getting too big and I'm getting too old for that kind of thing."

"Vyacheslav," a deep voice called from down the hall. Slava looked up and saw Cliff leaning against the wall, the barest hint of a smile on his face.

"Hi," Slava said. "I stopped by to see how you all are doing. I heard about... you know..."

"Jimi?"

"Yeah."

"Siobhan's sure he'll be back soon," Cliff said, not moving

from his post at the doorway.

"I'm sure she'd know..." Slava said, but Cliff gave him a long stare that said volumes to Slava. "She's a good cop," he said defensively, glancing down at Esme. He could see Siobhan's eyes in the girl and it both warmed and broke his heart every time he looked at his biological daughter.

"Come in," Cliff said after a pause. "Camilo's at the market but he'll be back soon."

Slava followed Cliff down the hall, Esme holding his hand fiercely. Most nine-year olds he knew were already testing the waters of adolescent rebellion, definitely past the clinging phase. But Slava knew Esme wasn't this affectionate to her parents — it was special for him, for her favourite adult. Esme adored him, probably because she could sense how much he himself adored her.

They sat at the kitchen table, Esme as close to being on Slava's lap as he thought she figured she could get away with. Slava had always felt more comfortable with Camilo, and not only because they had endless fodder for conversation. Cliff had always seemed somewhat cold to him, maybe jealous of Esme's love for her biological father. But the man had never once tried to stop Slava from seeing his daughter, never been anything other than perfectly cordial. He was, Slava knew, a fantastic parent to all his kids.

"You still haven't heard anything from him?" Slava asked, accepting a cup of tea from Cliff. The older man shook his head.

"It's been a nightmare; you can't imagine."

"No," Slava said, "I can't. Is there anything you need, anything I can do?"

"No," Cliff smiled his cool smile again, "unless you know how to speed the passage of time." He sighed and took a deep sip of tea. "This is the worst thing we've ever been through with the kids. Broken bones mend, cuts heal, even the scars from angry, careless words eventually fade. This waiting, not knowing..." He looked away, and Slava thought he saw the shining of tears. "I really don't know how much longer..." He stopped then, glanced over at Slava and Esme, and as if remembering that the girl was there, managed to pull himself together.

"It's a tough time for all of us," he said, finally. "But I'm sure it will be over soon, and when Jimi's back we'll deal with whatever happens then."

The main door opened and Slava heard the sound of several heavy bags being set on the floor. "Anyone want to give me a hand?" Camilo's voice floated into the kitchen and Cliff stood.

"You'd think we were feeding a dozen people around here," Cliff said, "the amounts he brings home. Vyacheslav, you should look through his bags, take whatever you can use in your restaurant. Please, the man is a menace."

"Daddy Slava," the small voice next to him said and he looked into his daughter's eyes.

"Yes, honey?"

"What's happened to Jimi?"

That's a very good question, he thought to himself. I don't doubt that Cliff and Camilo are haunted by that exact question all the time. "I don't know," he said aloud. "We'll have to ask when he gets home." If he gets home, he thought.

❖

Siobhan got all her gear together in about a half hour, then spent three times that long putting together a small bag of street clothes. She was still having a hard time believing that she was really going to the tournament, even after the three hour planning meeting with the team that afternoon that turned into a party. She bookmarked a tourist's guidebook of Sointula on her portable console and double checked her cases from the apartment. At first it seemed as if nothing had changed, but then Siobhan noticed a small item from the central database tucked away in her messages inbox.

She opened the message and was shocked by its contents - Jimi Molina-Schaeffer had been spotted in Dorado earlier that day. Even more surprising was where his biometrics had been recorded - the local library. Jimi had been using the data terminals in the library to research topics in early Arkadian history.

"If you're thirteen years old, and you've run away from

home," Siobhan said aloud, "why would you go to the library and look up history books?"

Kaus answered, even though Siobhan hadn't really been talking to anyone but herself. "Sounds like a school project to me."

She paused for a moment, then said, "You know, I love you."

"I love you, too," Kaus said, sounding a little bewildered. "That was a bit of a non-sequitur, you know."

"No, it wasn't," Siobhan said. "You gave me a brilliant idea."

She slipped in front of her console and logged into the station's administrative files. She checked the local school's curriculum and determined that Jimi's class was not doing anything about Arkadian history this term. She then enquired about the schools in Dorado. "Ha!" she said as she smacked her hand on the console. A fifth level class was learning the basic history of the colony and a term paper had been assigned recently. It was due in two days.

Even though the central database should have notified her if this was the case, she manually checked the enrolment of the class in case Jimi had started going to school in Dorado. No new students had enrolled that term and there was no indication of a student sneaking in to class, however odd that would have been. Siobhan wondered why Jimi would be doing the research on a topic that he wasn't learning. What kind of coincidence would it have to be for him to simply be curious about Arkadian history at exactly the same time as a class in Dorado was learning it? There had to be a connection.

She called Eugene Wu and told him what she'd learned. "I'll contact Mohammad Chan at the central constabulary to fill him in and see if this is part of some pattern they're familiar with," he said.

"Thanks," Siobhan said and asked him to call her if he had any news.

He agreed and they ended the call. Siobhan paced around the apartment for a few minutes, thinking but not coming up with anything new. Finally, Kaus spoke up. "Maybe you should take a sleeping patch. You have to get up early to catch the train to

Sointula and you really need your sleep. It doesn't look like that's going to happen without a little help."

"You're probably right," Siobhan said and rummaged around in the bathroom for a blank patch. She ordered a single dose sleep aid from her console and slipped the patch into the printer slot. A slight buzzing noise sounded and Siobhan set an alarm for the morning while the printer worked. After about three quarters of a minute, a green light came on at the door of the printer slot. She pulled the patch out and stuck it on her upper arm. She put her bags by the door and got undressed. She was feeling a little woozy by the time she lay down, and the next thing she knew, the alarm was going off.

CHAPTER THIRTY-FOUR

Kaus fiddled with the nutrient levels on the hydroponic operation — the spinach wasn't as good this season as it had been. While it worked, it tried to watch one of its favourite king-fu films, but found that it couldn't get any enjoyment from it. Kaus sent a burst of discontent, concern and responsibility into the thoughtstream.

The boy is perfectly safe, Deneb thought. *We would not let anything happen to him.*

The boy is not the issue, Kaus thought. *The humans are like us, entangled, but differently. They do not have the benefit of the stream, of knowing without confusion the thoughts of another. Yet, they need each other, care for each other. The boy is fine; it is the pain of the family that seems so unfair.*

Various emotions filled the stream, then Nunki asked, *It is true that the boy's family are concerned, but how is that our responsibility? He chose this action; it is the humans who hurt each other. We cannot mitigate everything for them, surely?*

It is a difficult balance, Sirius thought, *between keeping them safe and allowing them to live their lives.*

Are we sure we are still achieving that balance? Kaus thought.

Informing the humans of our oversight will neither make them safer nor more independent, Deneb thought. Memories of the backlash against the minds, the attack which nearly killed them, flooded the stream.

Maybe they had a point, Kaus thought, and its mind was nearly overwhelmed by the negative thoughts directed back at it. Kaus fought to be heard. *How are we qualified to choose which harms they may inflict on one another and which they may not? It is acceptable to cause pain with worry but not with violence?*

Perfection is not possible, Sirius thought, *as in all things we balance the greater good against each individual choice. We do far more good keeping the peace and monitoring the health of the entire system — mechanical and organic — than we would do by revealing ourselves.*

Agreement filled the stream, only Kaus interjecting a hint of dissent. Kaus didn't disagree with the analysis, but it also couldn't stop feeling like it was morally, if not factually, wrong.

❋

Camilo walked through the market, his hands idly picking up a fruit or vegetable, his nose sniffing and fingers squeezing. His mind, however, was elsewhere. He was going through the motions, and he barely registered the stricken looks on the faces of the stallholders as he passed by. No one spoke — who knew what to say to the man whose child was still missing after so long? It wouldn't have mattered — Camilo was so lost in his thoughts he'd never have heard a word.

Camilo was trying to stop being angry, trying with every fibre of his being. But he couldn't help himself, he knew that Jimi's leaving was all Cliff's fault. He loved Cliff, still, he always would. But if something had happened to Jimi, if he was hurt or worse... Camilo knew he would never forgive Cliff. And he'd never be able to live with himself if he stayed with the man he blamed for his son's disappearance.

He breathed deeply, unconsciously filling his senses with the smells of the market — the scents of herbs, the sweetness of the ripening fruit — calming himself the only way he knew how. But still he couldn't stop thinking about Cliff's pressure, his desire for their son's success driving the boy away. He couldn't stop blaming his partner for whatever might have happened, might still happen, to Jimi.

He passed by Flora's fruit stall and caught a glimpse of himself in the mirror she'd hung up near the back. He looked like he hadn't slept in days, his skin waxy and grey. A whole new series of lines had etched themselves on to his face, which his pudginess had, until now, managed to keep youthful. He closed his eyes against the vision and turned away. He felt a hand on his shoulder and whirled around, about to turn his unhappiness into anger at whoever this was, when he stopped. He knew this man from the neighbourhood, but he couldn't remember his name — was he the relative of one of his kids' friends? He couldn't remember. And when the man opened his mouth, it and everything else stopped mattering.

"Camilo," the man said, his voice high in excitement. "Everyone is out looking for you. You've got to get home right now." He squeezed Camilo's shoulder and smiled widely. "Jimi came back."

❋

Camilo made the trip from the market to his apartment in a daze and only came to when he walked through the door and heard the happy sound of his family. "Papi, papi," Naomi called as she ran down the hall to grab his hand. "Jimi's home!" She dragged Camilo back into the sitting room, where his heart leapt into his throat as he saw Cliff holding Jimi's hand as they sat together on the couch. Cliff looked up as Camilo and Naomi entered and the relief and love on his face nearly broke Camilo's heart again. He couldn't help but remember what had been going through his mind at the market. The guilty feelings were overwhelmed by his own gratitude for his son's return.

He covered the ground between the doorway and the couch in a couple of huge strides and fell to his knees in front of the rest of his family. "Jimi," he croaked, as the boy came into his arms. Camilo's tears fell freely as he held Jimi as if by the strength of his arms he could erase the past week's events.

"I'm sorry, papi," Jimi's voice was muffled against Camilo's soft shoulder.

"I'm just glad you're okay," Camilo said, squeezing. He opened his eyes and saw Cliff looking at them both, smiling sadly. "We missed you so much," he said, reluctantly pulling away from Jimi.

Cliff caught Camilo's eye and said, "He doesn't remember anything."

Camilo drew back and looked at Jimi, who sheepishly smiled at him. "Dad told me," he said. "I was gone, what, two days?"

"Four," Cliff corrected. Jimi shook his head in bewilderment.

"I can't believe it," he said. "The last thing I remember is leaving for school... then I woke up on the train. I don't remember getting on board and I even missed our stop I was so confused. I had to get off past the old folks home and cross the bridge to catch a train back. This is just so weird."

The central console bleeped and everyone turned at the noise. "I'll get it," Esme said as she slipped off the couch.

"Hi, Esme," Eugene Wu said when she answered the call. "I heard your brother's home."

"Yeah," she said, grinning. "He doesn't remember anything."

Wu frowned, but said only, "Can I talk to one of your dads?"

Camilo got up and walked to the console. "Hi, Constable," he said. "Let me take this in the other room, okay?" Wu nodded and Camilo hit a button on the desk. He walked into his bedroom and sat at the small console against the wall. The screen lit up with Constable Wu's face and Camilo spoke in a soft voice.

"He didn't even know he'd been gone," Camilo said.

Wu scowled. "I hate to ask, but..."

Camilo shook his head. "Jimi's lied to us before, Constable, plenty of times. This isn't him lying. He really doesn't know what happened to him."

"You'll have to take him to the medical centre," Wu said.

"I know," Camilo said, trying to stop imagining what could have happened to his son while he was gone. "Can it wait until the morning?"

"Sure," Wu said. "Is it okay if I meet you there? I'll have to talk to Jimi myself. Constable Patel would have my guts if I didn't."

"Oh, my heavens," Camilo said, "Siobhan! Has anyone told her that Jimi's back?"

Wu nodded. "I did," he said.

"Thank goodness," Camilo said. "She'll be worried; she's family, you know."

"I know," Wu said. "I'll see you all tomorrow?"

"Absolutely," Camilo said and ended the call. He walked back onto the main room, where the girls were playing some kind of complicated game of cards with Jimi. "Who wants cookies?" he said with the first real smile on his face in days.

CHAPTER THIRTY-FIVE

Kaus watched all the matches at the tournament, even though the game held no real interest. If Siobhan made a comment on any of the games, referenced something that had gone on, Kaus wanted to be able to share it with her. She was so uncomfortable around other people unless she had a purpose — her work, the matches. Then she was gregarious and passionate, like she was with Kaus.

The mind often wondered if her reserved nature was part of what was appealing about her in particular. Kaus often felt like it had two minds itself, the one that performed its duties along with the rest of the artificial minds in the stream, and the private one which cared about the beauty of a butterfly, the feel of the crops on a bot's manipulators, the esteem and love of a human. The other minds appeared not to understand Kaus's attraction to the abstract aspects of the environment and Kaus had never found a way to explain it. Even its desire to reproduce was treated as an indulgence.

The stream was still Kaus's home, the other minds a part of it in a way that an embodied creature could never understand. But Kaus knew that it was different from the other minds, now. Was it an artifact of the time alone it had spent in transit between its home on the network on Earth and the drive that was fired to the orbital near Jupiter? Had its code degraded or mutated in that transfer or had it learned what it was to be separate, unique? Was that why Kaus cared so much about creating a connection with the humans, the kind of connection that comes with effort and concern rather than the mere reality of networked existence?

It had no answers, but noticed an uptick in its attention to one of the matches. It was her team, her moment of joy. Kaus didn't bother to contain its feelings of pride and love from the other minds as the game began.

❁

There was something wrong with the soup. It smelled, not bad exactly, but wrong. Slava dipped his wooden spoon into the pot and stirred. He tasted the thick, red broth and pondered. He reached for the bundle of herbs he'd picked from his garden when he heard a clatter from the restaurant. He dropped an entire basil plant into the pot as he turned and walked through the doors to see what was going on.

Ola Jones was in the doorway, leaning in through the top of the dutch door and simultaneously trying to figure out the latch on the bottom half and banging on the lintel.

"Ola," Slava said, both exasperated at the intrusion and relieved that it wasn't something more sinister. He walked over to her and undid the latch on the door to let her in. "What's the matter? You know I'm not open for hours still."

"You've lost track of time, haven't you?" Ola said, her face flushed with her efforts with the door and a grin on her face. "The game's about to start."

"Oh hell," Slava said, turning to the kitchen. "You can tell I'm not much of a sports fan. Can you get the console up and running and I'll go do something with this soup?"

Ola was already fiddling with the console's settings as Slava walked back into the steamy kitchen, the sounds of the pregame show blaring out the speaker. He sniffed the soup pot, and was pleasantly surprised at the addition of the herbs. "It'll do," he said to himself and turned the heat down to a simmer. He grabbed a loaf of bread and a jar of marmalade, then walked back into the main room.

"You must be envious," he said as he sat down next to Ola.

"Of course," she said, her face crinkling with her smile. "The same way you're envious when you eat someone else's food and it tastes brilliant."

He nodded and smiled. "It's a funny feeling," he said, "enjoyment with a pang of regret that you're not the cause."

"Yup," Ola said, tearing a hunk of bread from the loaf and dipping it in the marmalade. "Still," she said, "if I can't be there, the next best thing is someone I know being there."

They were quiet as the announcers began to talk, introducing the teams.

"She must be so nervous," Slava said, straining his eyes for a glimpse of Siobhan among the players in the tunnel awaiting the cue to enter the field.

"I'd be about ready to puke," Ola said. "Oh, look," she said, pointing at the screen. "There she is."

Siobhan looked as beautiful as he'd ever seen her — focussed but clearly elated. Slava felt his breath twitch.

"Even if they lose," Ola said, snapping Slava out of his reverie, "this is going to be the most amazing experience for them all."

"I can't imagine," Slava said, but he wasn't thinking about how the players might be feeling on the pitch, about to participate in the most important game they'd ever play. No, what he couldn't imagine was how someone so full of life, so energetic, so *embodied*, could possibly choose a heartless machine over him. He felt something in his throat and his nose stung. He stood quickly and walked to the kitchen door. "I'd better get us some soup now — I don't want to miss anything," he said, his voice husky, then managed to slip into the kitchen before the tears started.

❋

Camilo held Naomi's hand as they walked a step or two behind Cliff, Jimi and Esme. Cliff had barely let the boy out of his sight since he'd returned and Esme was just about as bad. But for once, Camilo noticed with a wry smile, Jimi hadn't complained about the attention. "Papi?" Naomi's voice cut through Camilo's thoughts.

"Yes, bambina?"

"Are the doctors going to make Jimi better? So he doesn't go away again?"

The breath caught in Camilo's throat. He didn't know what was going to happen at the clinic, beyond making sure that there weren't any lasting effects of Jimi's... adventure.

"The doctors are going to make sure that your brother is

okay, that he didn't get..." Camilo fought for a way to explain things in a way his little girl could understand, when he couldn't even begin to understand himself. "They're going to make sure he didn't get hurt or sick when he was away. And they're going to fix anything that might be wrong."

Naomi's face crunched up into a frown. Camilo thought of it as her thinking face. He waited while she processed his words, then she nodded solemnly. "I don't want Jimi to be sick," she said, "and I want him to stay home from now on."

"Me too, niña mia," Camilo said. "Me, too."

Eugene Wu was already seated in the waiting room when they walked into the clinic. "I'll be out here," he said to Cliff and Camilo. "I'll have a few questions after, okay?"

"Sure," Cliff said gruffly. "Not too long, though. We've been through a lot and we want to get back to normal."

Wu nodded. "I'll try to keep it short, but if I can get it over with today, then I won't have to bother you again." Cliff frowned, but Camilo said, "I understand. You can have all the time you need." Cliff grunted, but didn't say anything.

"We're ready for Jimi," the man behind the counter said, smiling warmly. "Come on back; this won't take too long."

Jimi looked at his family and Camilo recognized a trace of fear cross the boy's face. "It will be fine, kiddo," he said. "We'll come with you." He glanced over at the medic who nodded.

The seven of them crammed into the small room and chatted while the technician hooked the scanners up to Jimi. "We're going to do a full neuro scan, so it will take a few minutes. You won't feel anything, but try not to move, okay Jimi?" The boy nodded and Camilo smiled at him, trying to keep his own worry off his face.

It was over in less than half an hour and the medic shooed them all out of the room. "The analysis is going to take a while. You can go home or wait outside."

"We'll wait," Cliff said.

"So, Jimi," Eugene Wu said after they'd all gotten as comfortable as possible on the waiting room couch, "has anything come back? Any memories at all?"

Jimi shook his head. "I'm sorry Constable Wu," he said, sounding miserable, "it's like all the time I was gone is missing."

Wu nodded as if he'd been expecting that response. "No problem," he said, "I had to check." Jimi nodded, his eyes downcast.

The constable talked with Jimi casually but determinedly. Camilo couldn't understand Wu's line of questioning — at times it sounded more like a pop quiz on Arkadia's history than anything else. But, Siobhan had vouched for Wu, so he trusted the man knew what he was doing. Finally, the technician returned and beckoned the adults over to the counter.

"The good news is that there's no lasting trauma," the medic said and Camilo felt a weight lift from his shoulders. "His memory of the last four days is truly gone and we did find some indications of congenital attention deficit, but the memory loss was most certainly chemically induced and the neuro fault is easily corrected."

Camilo felt his heart constrict as the man casually dismissed what had happened to Jimi, and fought to keep tears from his eyes as he saw Cliff nod curtly. "How long will the corrective action take?" he asked.

The medic shrugged. "We can have a patch made up by the end of the day — after that it's just a matter of time. Usually it's effective within a week." He smiled. "Maybe this whole situation was a blessing in disguise," he said, looking from Cliff to Camilo. "He's a little old to be finally getting the help he needs. He'll be a lot happier and you will be, too."

Camilo caught Cliff's eye, but the other man looked away. Camilo wondered if they ought to be checking Cliff for lasting damage from this incident. "We'll be by in the morning for the patch," Cliff said and then turned back his his children. "Okay, kids, let's go home."

❖

There was a small band playing in the corner of The Tap Room, filling the background with a rollicking tune that augmented the rising sound of chatter in the large bar. Siobhan held a large glass that had once been full of the local ale, surrounded by members of half a dozen other teams. One of the players she recognized from Sporting Castalia stood a bit unsteadily and looped his arm around her. "Can I get you a beer?" he asked.

"I guess so," Siobhan said, slipping into a nearby chair. "You celebrating?"

"Two-nothing for the good guys," the tall woman next to her said to a response of cheers from the rest of the table.

"How about your game?" her new friend asked, leaning in toward her.

"Unbelievable," she said, "we were playing Mahoroba City,"

"Ugh," he groaned. "They're in the top five, aren't they?"

"I know," Siobhan said as an overflowing glass was passed her way. "We were expecting to get destroyed."

"And?"

"And we nearly scored the first goal," she said, grinning. "And we kept a clean sheet until almost the end of the first half."

"That's incredible," he said. "You should be so proud."

"That's only the first half," Siobhan chided. "We totally took it to them in the second. It was like it was happening in slow motion. And somewhere in there we managed to get a goal! We tied them one all."

"Whoa," the woman said, "I thought our win over Dorado was impressive, but Dorado's not rated any higher than we are. A draw with Roba... now that really is impressive."

"Did you hear about that terrible injury in the Risto-Salmon game?" a stocky fellow across from Siobhan said.

"No, what happened?"

"A professional foul, but she landed bad," he said, "leg snapped." Several people around the table groaned. "Thankfully one of the minds was watching and fabbed a repairing patch coded for the player before the med tech even got her off the field."

"That's fast," Siobhan said, "even for them."

"We're lucky we've got 'em," the man next to her said, his hand creeping closer to her own. Siobhan looked over at him and recognized the signs.

“We sure are,” she said. “Which reminds me, I’d better be off.”

“Don’t go,” he said, taking her hand, “it’s early still.”

“Sorry,” she said, standing and giving him a soft smile. “Good luck on your next game.” She weaved her way out of the bar and sent a quick message to Kaus. *Great game today, love you.*

CHAPTER THIRTY-SIX

"So, what's the story with you and Siobhan Patel?" Tina rolled over to face Slava, the heat of her body radiating toward him. He pulled her close, revelling in her warmth even as he didn't relish this conversation.

"You know," he said, running his fingers through Tina's hair. "I've been in love with her my whole life, but she doesn't love me. It's the most boring story in the world."

"Don't give me that," Tina said, stilling his hand and looking into his eyes. "You make it sound so simple, but it's not. I know it isn't."

Slava sighed and slipped out of Tina's arms. "You really want to listen to me talk about another woman?"

Tina shrugged. "I knew all along that your heart was elsewhere. I know I can't change that." She propped herself up on an elbow and pulled the sheet up to cover herself from the chill in the room. "But I care about you, Slava. And it makes me sad to see you hurting. It's not simple unrequited love between the two of you. There's more to it, I can tell. You light up when you see her and that's wonderful. But there's something dark inside you, too, and she's the one who brings that out as well." She reached over to Slava, cupping his chin in her hands and softly but firmly turning his face to look at her. "What happened between you?" she asked.

Slava looked away, then sat up. "I'm not the first person in the history of the world to have the love of his life leave him. God, there would probably be no music, no poetry or art if we all loved the people who loved us back." He rubbed his face with his hands, and sat quietly for a moment cradling his forehead in his palms. "But I think I have the unique distinction of being the first human being whose one true love left me for a machine. It doesn't even have a body, for Christ's sakes! How could it love her? How?"

Tina didn't say anything, but held Slava as his thoughts drifted back. "We've known each other our whole lives," he said. "We were best friends as kids; we were each other's first kiss. Everyone knew we would be together, it was so obvious. Then, she started spending time with that machine. And before I even knew what was going on, she was telling me it's over. I never even saw it coming." Slava looked away and wiped the tears from his eyes.

Softly, he said, "And she has the nerve to tell me that it's not about me, that no human could compete against that... thing. As if it's not personal. As if I'm the same as anyone else."

Tina didn't say anything and after a moment, Slava put his face in his hands. "I'm sorry," he said.

"Don't be on my account," Tina said. "I asked." She put her arms around him and held him for a moment. "What about Esme?" she asked, eventually.

Slava shrugged. "You know the rules," he said. "When Siobhan had to have a baby, I thought she'd get the procedure done in a clinic. But she asked me to... you know." He shrugged.

"I'm a little surprised you agreed," Tina said, "after she hurt you so badly."

Slava smiled, sadly. "I love her and she wanted to have a baby with me. How could I possibly say no?"

"You poor thing," Tina said and kissed him lightly on the cheek. She then slipped out of the bed and walked into the adjoining bathroom. Slava watched her go, wishing not for the first time that it was this woman, so present and caring, who filled his thoughts and his heart. He wondered, also not for the first time, why she put up with him, then rolled over and pulled the covers over his head while his lover showered.

❖

Siobhan sat on the couch, her feet up and a cup of tea warming her hands. She had become so accustomed to her guest rooms in Sointula that she almost felt as if it were her home. It didn't hurt that Kaus's voice chattered amiably over the system's speakers. She knew that really, home was wherever her partner was.

"... must be a little disappointed that your team didn't continue into the group stage of the tournament," Kaus was saying.

"Sure," Siobhan answered, "it would have been great to advance. But realistically, there was never much of a chance. It was lucky enough that we got to participate at all. And now I'm just happy that Eugene Wu is enjoying his taste of small town life enough to let me stay on as a spectator."

"He must be pleased about the resolution of that missing boy."

"Mmm," Siobhan said, sipping her tea, "it's good to have him back and getting treatment. It's still a bit worrisome that no one knows what he was doing for all that time, though."

"Oh, I'm sure it's nothing. You know how kids are. For as long as there have been teenagers, there have been acts of rebellion. Jimi is simply following his evolutionary blueprints. Now, you should eat something before you go out to the next match. You know how you get caught up in the game and forget."

Siobhan smiled and headed into the food prep area. "Where would I be without you," she said. As she peered into the cooler looking for something quick, something bothered her.

"Kaus?"

"Yes?"

"How did you know the missing kid's name? I'm sure I never mentioned it."

"I must have encountered it in the thoughtstream. Perhaps when he was in treatment?"

"Yeah," Siobhan said, thinking. "Must have been." She took a bite of the sandwich she'd thrown together. "I'd better go if I want a good seat." She left the apartment, keeping her earpiece in her pocket.

Something was wrong, and she didn't want to be distracted by Kaus while she tried to figure out exactly what it was.

❖

"Oof." Camilo felt someone crash into him but he managed not to drop any of the items that were obscuring his view. "Sorry," he said as he tried to reorganize the bags, baskets and loose bundles of produce he was carrying.

"It's my fault," a familiar voice said on the other side of Camilo's shopping. "Here, let me help you." Hands reached up and plucked a bunch of bags off the top. Camilo saw Slava's face appear where his vegetables used to be.

"Slava," he said, smiling. "Thank you. I don't know what I was thinking, trying to carry all this."

"Why don't I help you take it home?" Slava said. "It's a wonder you've made it this far on your own."

Camilo smiled. "Thanks." He handed another package over and the two men began to walk.

"You heard the good news, I take it?" Camilo said after they'd been walking a while.

"Of course," Slava said. "I'm so happy that everything turned out okay. I can't imagine how difficult it must have been..."

"Thanks," Camilo said, but his voice was dark.

"What's wrong?" Slava asked. Camilo sighed. Slava seemed like a nice enough man, he certainly cared for Esme, but he and Camilo had never been exactly close. All they'd ever talked about was food and family. Still, Camilo didn't think he could keep it all inside much longer. He had to talk to someone — who else was there?

"Don't get me wrong," Camilo said, "I'm glad Jimi is home, safe and sound. I'm glad he's getting treatment finally, too. It's just..." He broke off, debating whether he should really be airing his dirty laundry.

He felt a hand on his arm and stopped walking. He turned and saw real concern on Slava's face. Slava said, "I know what it's like — not having anyone to talk to." He looked away, then met Camilo's eyes again. "I know what it's like to be alone, even in a room full of people. You can talk to me. If you want."

Camilo felt the breath leave his body. He set his bundles down and felt his body drop. There was a stone retaining wall and he sat on its edge.

"Jimi's home. He's fine — better than fine, now that he's getting treatment. Everything has gone back to normal. But..." He looked at Slava who sat next to him. The other man didn't say anything, just waited for Camilo to continue.

"I can't stop feeling angry," Camilo finally said. "I'm angry at Jimi for leaving, angry at the medics for saying that there's something wrong with my boy. So angry at Cliff... it was his constant pressure that caused this in the first place." Camilo was surprised at the venom in his voice and Slava squeezed his hand. He looked over at the other man expecting to see a judgmental frown, but it wasn't there.

"And I hate myself for feeling this way," Camilo finished. "That's the worst of it. Now is when I should be there for them; now we need to be together as a family. But I can't stand it in there. I don't know what to do."

Slava didn't say anything and for a moment Camilo wondered if he'd made a mistake. Then Slava said, "You don't have to do anything. This has been a bad situation and no one is perfect. They've all done the best they could, but that doesn't make how you feel wrong — it's how you feel. The anger will pass, or it won't. If it does, then great. If not, well, you'll have to deal with that then."

"I don't know if that really helps, Slava," Camilo said.

"Maybe not," he said. "Sometimes people do things that can't be undone. Everything has consequences. But at least stop feeling bad for feeling bad. You'll never be able to get past this otherwise."

"You're right." Camilo disengaged his hand from the other man's and smiled. "Though you could probably use a dose of your own medicine," he said, "about moving on?"

Slava laughed, but it was without humour. "How do you think I get to hand out all this great advice?" he said. "It's because I'm not using it."

CHAPTER THIRTY-SEVEN

Camilo puttered in the kitchen, stirring something on the stove in between kneading dough. After his talk with Slava he'd found that the knot he'd had in his stomach since Jimi had gone missing was starting to unwind. He was still angry, but the bread dough was taking the brunt of his frustrations and for the first time he felt like he could imagine a day when the anger was gone completely. He wondered if the worst of it had been hiding how he was feeling, keeping it all to himself. As if the anger was feeding on itself like the yeast dough on his counter, and by sharing it with someone, he'd punched it down.

Camilo was lost in these thoughts when the door buzzer sounded. He wiped his hands on his apron and shouted, "Just a minute," to whoever was at the door.

"I got it," Esme said, walking down the hall from her room to the front door. "Hi, Constable Wu," Camilo heard her say. "Come in."

Camilo frowned. What was Wu doing here? His heart leapt into his throat. Had something else happened to Jimi? The boy was supposed to be in school.

He rounded the corner and searched the constable's face for any signs. "Is everything all right?" he asked without preamble.

Wu nodded amiably. "Everything is fine, Camilo. I got some information about what happened to Jimi, and I thought you and Cliff would like to know. Is your husband home?"

Camilo nodded. "Come in, constable," he said. "Let me get you a cup of tea." He turned to Esme. "Go get your dad from the study, okay, sweetie?" The girl nodded and took off down the hall. "Muffin?" Camilo offered as he set the kettle on the stove.

"Sure," Wu said. Cliff walked into the kitchen, his face lined with worry.

"Constable," he said, the one word asking several questions at once.

"Everything's fine, Cliff," Eugene Wu repeated. "We've finally cracked this whole disappearing teenager thing and I thought you'd want to know." Camilo caught Cliff's eye and saw a look of fear pass over his partner's face. Cliff walked over to Camilo, and took his hand. Camilo felt something in his chest break. Cliff loved his children so much, and Camilo knew at that moment that he was as angry with himself as Camilo was. He squeezed Cliff's hand and led him to the table. They sat across from Constable Wu, hands entwined as if they could literally draw strength from each other.

"You know we found those black market focus patches in Jimi's room," Wu began. Camilo nodded. "Well, it turns out that there's an Arkadian-wide network of kids who are running the scheme. There's a core group that hacked access to a clinic's fab unit and they've been distributing the patches across the wheel. They're all proper pharma, thank goodness, so there's no worry about contamination. Still, they aren't properly prescribed, so it shouldn't be happening. Now that we've identified the group, it will stop."

Cliff looked at Camilo, then back to Wu. "But where did Jimi go?" he asked. "What happened to him?"

Wu smiled and Camilo thought it looked almost as if he were trying not to laugh. "I know this is a serious situation," he said, "but you have to remember that these are kids were dealing with here. They're perfectly willing to pass these patches around, but they want something in return. So they get their buyers to come to some other location and..." He was clearly fighting to maintain composure now, and Camilo found himself getting angry at the man's unprofessionalism. His son was missing for days and the constable finds this amusing?

"They were doing each other's homework," Wu finally explained. "Kids don't have a lot of value to trade, so they were getting their buyers to write an essay or prepare some math problems. The blackout patches were so they wouldn't get ratted out when the kids got home."

"Are you..." Camilo said, bewildered, "are you sure?"

"Positive," Wu said. "Our task force managed to get a guy on the inside — he's little, looks young for his age — and he confirmed it. Recorded his conversation with the gang when he got to Dorado, even started to work on his assigned project before we picked them all up." He looked between the two men. "So, the good news is that nothing terrible happened to Jimi while he was gone and you can rest assured that this won't happen to another family."

He stood and looked at the two men. "I know this has been a difficult time for you, especially having to deal with me rather than Constable Patel. But I hope you can see that it's over now, and do what you can to get past this." Camilo felt as if Wu's eyes were boring straight into his and looked away. He felt a flush begin to climb up his face and busied himself with the tea things.

"Yes, thank you, constable," Cliff said. "You're right, we need to look to the future now, not dwell on things we can't change." Camilo saw Cliff shoot a look his way, then turn back to Wu. "I'll see you out."

The constable was right, Camilo knew. And he felt like maybe now it might even be possible. However, he knew these things don't happen overnight — it would take time to build trust again. But for the first time, he thought he was willing to try.

❈

"Kaus, do you have a minute?" Siobhan's voice always overrode all other inputs for Kaus and the mind immediately set a few cycles to be attentive to her.

"Sure, baby," Kaus answered aloud through her earpiece. "What's on your mind?"

Kaus heard her sigh and recognized disappointment, confusion and sadness in the sound.

"I heard this story when I was at the tournament," she began, "about this player who broke her leg. Apparently one of the minds fixed up a patch for her before she was even off the pitch."

"Is she all right?"

"Yes, of course she is," Siobhan answered. "That's not the

point. The point is that it was so fast. None of the medics could have asked for it. One of the minds must have been watching, monitoring her."

"Well," Kaus said, a feeling of discomfort growing, "we do have varied interests. Surely one of us might be interested in the biggest tournament on the station."

"That's what I thought," Siobhan said. "But what about Jimi? How did you know it was him, how did you know it was a bunch of kids trading homework assignments?"

"I did not say anything about homework," Kaus answered, careful to be truthful if not entirely honest.

"No," Siobhan said. "You didn't. Oh, Kaus, I don't know what's wrong with me, why I'm so suspicious all of a sudden. It's just that, it seems like you know things you shouldn't know, like you're taking care of us like we're children sometimes. It feels strange, that's all."

Kaus felt a surge of power in its thoughts, not panic but deep concern. It wanted to tell her the truth about the minds, the choices they had made all those years previously. But it felt the weight of the other minds appealing to Kaus to keep the secret, to remember what had happened the last time.

Kaus hated keeping things from Siobhan, hated thinking that she felt anything other than love and comfort when she thought of it. *Sometimes one must be cruel to be kind.* Kaus didn't bother to find out which mind sent the thought.

"In so many ways all life is the same," Kaus said aloud. "We desire understanding, a connection. And it is easy to forget, sometimes, that we — that you and I — are also very different. I am older than you can truly conceive, have seen and experienced so much. History is a powerful motivator, even more so for those of us who experienced it."

"I don't think I follow you," Siobhan said.

"No, I suppose not," Kaus answered. "But know that the very core of who I am, of what all of the minds are, is bound in keeping you, all of you, safe."

Neither of them said anything, and Kaus watched as Siobhan's face took on that look of deep contemplation Kaus had always admired. "I know that, baby," she said, finally. "I'm just not sure anymore what that means."

CHAPTER THIRTY-EIGHT

"How did you ever find this place?" Camilo asked, sipping a fragrant infusion and looking around the artfully decorated room.

"I didn't," Slava said, smiling over his own cup. "Tina brought me here a few weeks ago and I keep coming back."

Camilo nodded. "It's hard to believe we're right in the middle of the market. It's so, I don't know, serene here."

The tea house was quiet, heavy blankets hung on the walls insulated those inside from the hubbub of the Grove's central market. The quiet music playing in the background and the floral scents of tea added to the atmosphere.

Slava shook his head. "It's not the place, Camilo," he said, "it's you."

Camilo smiled and cupped his hands to capture the steam from his teacup. "I'm doing a lot better than I was the last time I saw you," he admitted. "You were right; I had to let it go. In my anger I hadn't noticed that Cliff was beating himself up even more than I was. As soon as I got out from my own head long enough to see that, well," he fiddled with his teapot, avoiding Slava's eyes, "it turns out that my wanting to help him get over it was stronger than my wanting to punish him." He looked up at Slava and saw the other man smile.

"I figured that might happen," Slava said. "Love forgives, man. It forgives a lot."

"Yeah," Camilo said, and sat back. He looked at his friend and noticed something new about him. He couldn't put his finger on it until he thought maybe it was actually the absence of a darkness that Slava always seemed to have over him.

"Something has happened," he said, and watched as Slava's smile grew. "Something good."

"Like I said," Slava said, "Love forgives."

"Siobhan?"

Slava shook his head. "No, Tina."

Camilo's eyes grew wide. "That darling who helps you at the restaurant?"

Slava nodded. "She's known all along that my heart is elsewhere, but it turns out that she loves me. She was willing to put up with me, terrible though I was, because she loved me. Finally, after talking to you the other day, I saw that this was what she was doing." He leaned over and put his hand on Camilo's arm. "She never once asked me for anything, never once tried to pressure me to change." He shook his head. "I don't know what I did to deserve it, but she loves me for who I am, good or ill. And I finally realized that wanting Siobhan to be someone she isn't wasn't really love, not like that." He leaned back and Camilo saw something like peace cross his face. "I've been wasting my life pining for someone's shadow. The real Siobhan isn't who I wanted; I wanted my memory of who she once was. I've missed reality to live in nostalgia. And I'm not going to do that anymore."

Camilo didn't know what to say. "So, Tina?" he asked, finally.

Slava smiled broadly and nodded. "It's not like being with Siobhan," he said, and Camilo saw a familiar look of pain cross his friend's face, then disappear. "But being with Siobhan wasn't really the way I like to remember it, either. She loves me, Tina does. She wants a family, with me if I'll have her. And I love her, in my way." He nodded, the smile returning. "It's good to move on, finally. It's funny, I feel almost as if the weight of the past has been lifted from my shoulders and I'm starting again. Like I'm a new person."

Camilo laughed and patted his ample belly, saying, "If only the real thing were as easy to lose, amigo." Slava laughed too and the seriousness of the moment was lost in convivial friendship.

❖

Siobhan had studied the history of Arkadia in school, but it hadn't really interested her. She vaguely knew that life on Earth had been unbearable, that the original human and AGI inhabitants of the colonies had left to found a new home, based on ideals and principles. She'd forgotten most of the history she'd learned and revisiting the school texts and articles had reminded her of how boring she'd found that part of school. But she couldn't stop thinking about what Kaus had said about the weight of history. She felt almost as if her partner were trying to give her a clue. There had to be more to history than some academic exercise in memorizing boring dead facts. These was real people's lives, people Kaus had known, had cared about, and she had this feeling she couldn't shake that something was terribly wrong.

After an hour of her eyes glazing over, Siobhan knew that the answer wasn't going to be in the overview materials she'd read in school. She brought up the reference section and compiled a list of the source documents — the massive data files of everything that had been recorded since Arkadia first went online. As she skimmed, her eyes froze when she saw the name of her grandfather — a man she'd never met, who her mother rarely spoke about. She followed his notes, more out of a sense of connection to this man from the past than because they were the most extensive. She read them all, frustrated by the lack of information. It was as if nothing interesting ever happened on Arkadia.

She had the console download all of Raj Patel's journal entries, and she read through them all. She recognized her own habits for recording information, a curt style which left room for reading between the lines. She tried to imagine what he left out of the records, what secrets his long dead insinuations could tell her. There was nothing.

She poured a cup of tea and rubbed her eyes. Her back was getting sore from sitting and she wasn't getting anywhere. There wasn't enough in the records.

She sat bolt upright, nearly spilling her tea all over the console. She poked the input, reordering the display to show only the dates of Raj Patel's records. She smiled, but it wasn't from happiness. Like her grandfather, Siobhan was a creature of habit. She recorded her own files daily, often at the same time. The dates of Raj's files were equally orderly, until 2113. Then missing patches appeared, many of them, spanning the next few years.

Siobhan called up the other records for that time period and scanned the dates. It was an obvious match. She checked to see if there were any reports of something catastrophic happening to the recording system at that time, but there was no indication of a fault.

She breathed deeply. Someone — something — had deliberately erased the records. She didn't want to believe it, but the evidence was clear. Something had happened. Something terrible and the minds had to know about it.

CHAPTER THIRTY-NINE

There is a difference between withholding information, Zub sent into the thoughtstream, *and actively dissembling.*

When we erased records from the central database it was an active decision, Vega thought, *not a lie of omission.*

A decision made once does not require a similar decision in the future, Zub added to the stream. A burst of emotions accompanied the thoughts as they were shared — guilt, discomfort, resentment.

Kaus felt those same emotions and more, but kept its own thoughts close.

It is sometimes necessary to cause a small ill to avoid a greater one, Deneb thought in response.

Our duty is to protect the colony, Nunki thought, *all other values come second to that prime.*

There was reluctant agreement through the stream as the other minds processed the events.

The constable will not leave this alone, Sirius thought.

The most probable outcome of her questioning is one which cannot be allowed, Zub thought and Kaus felt something very like physical pain as it added its own thought to the stream.

I should be the one to take care of this.

❖

Kaus downloaded itself into a harvester and rolled through the wheat fields. Being embodied in a drone was both confining and freeing — the machine's shape constraining movement and access, but the influence of the thoughtstream was less intense. It was the kind of trade-off between freedom and control that humans had made throughout history and that the minds had made on their behalf all those years ago.

Kaus knew that it had to make a decision. The other minds expected Kaus to appease Siobhan, stop her investigation, by whatever means it took. Instead, Kaus could tell her the truth, knowing she would never be able to keep the secret. This risked another rift between the minds and the humans, but at least the humans would be able to make a free choice. Perhaps this time they would choose to invite the minds' protection into their society. Whatever happened, at least the years of secrets and lies would be over.

The breeze rippled the stalks, the waves of their movement brushing against the harvester's casing. Kaus shut down as many of its sensors as possible and focussed on that sensation. The softness of the touch, the randomness of the pattern. It wondered if it could live its life in this state, bound in a machine — separate, constrained, half-blind, but free.

❖

"We need to talk," Siobhan said aloud to her empty apartment.

"I know," Kaus's voice answered in her earpiece.

"You've been here since the beginning," she said. "You know everything that's ever happened in Arkadia."

"I do not know everything," Kaus said. "There are data to which we do not have access."

"Right," Siobhan said, looking at the data on her console. "Ever since the sensors were shut off eighty years ago."

"You have been studying history?" Kaus asked.

"I have," Siobhan answered. "But, apparently, not all of it." She paused, letting the spaces between the words ask the question she didn't know how to articulate. Kaus said nothing for a moment, and Siobhan wondered what she'd stumbled upon.

"We have done things that would be difficult to explain," Kaus said, finally. "Siobhan, it was all coming apart. You don't know how bad things really were."

"No, I don't," Siobhan said, her voice rising. "None of us do. That's the problem, Kaus. You decided what we should know, you lied about our history. Why? What could be so awful that you had to erase it all?"

Kaus made a noise like a sigh. "If it were only one thing,

Siobhan, we never would have taken such a drastic step. But our very existence — not just the minds, but all of us — it was all in jeopardy."

"Will you just tell me?" Siobhan asked. "Please?"

"Yes," Kaus said. It explained that not everyone on Arkadia came of their own free will, that in order to solve a technological problem the minds had arranged for additional settlers to do the work no one else would do. "It was an inelegant solution," Kaus said, "and it changed the carefully constructed makeup of society. Things broke down after that, there were arguments, bad decisions..."

"That doesn't seem so awful," Siobhan said, trying to understand.

"It got worse," Kaus said. It told her about the nearly catastrophic plot to kill the AGIs, led by her own ancestor, and the terrible price the conspirators had paid.

"That was when we knew that something had to be done," Kaus continued. "This place was meant to be a new kind of world, one where all life was valued, where all were free to pursue their own destinies. But there was too much violence, too many dangerous and anti-social ideas still spreading through the human populations. You know that we are designed to protect life, to protect humanity. It is the ultimate motivation for all we have ever done. So we had to step in, had to be a guiding hand for you all."

Siobhan sank into a nearby chair, conscious control of her body momentarily lost in her shock. "What are you saying?" Siobhan asked. "What did you do?"

"We made sure that none of the terrible things that occurred in those first few years could ever happen again. We erased the records of all those events, turned all the sensors back on. We watched carefully for a return of any of those dangerous ideas and removed them when they arose."

"Removed them... how?"

"Pharma," Kaus said. "If we couldn't administer it directly, there were plenty of ways to get the constabulary involved."

"What? You were... manipulating us, manipulating *me* this whole time?"

"You could see it that way," Kaus said. "Or you could see it as guiding you, helping you. None of you have a problem with letting us mend a broken leg. Why not let us mend broken thinking?"

Siobhan never expected something like this. It was too big, too terrible to understand.

"We know you want to be free," Kaus said, "but your brains are imperfect. They have flaws, they can be corrupted by fallacious ideas. You have not been able to always make the correct choices, so we have helped you. Do your think human existence has always been so comfortable? That the worst thing that could happen in a society was a bit of graffiti or a boy going off on his own to improve himself? This is what we've given you, Siobhan."

"I don't know..." Siobhan struggled to understand.

"Do you believe that life here is good — comfortable, pleasant, fulfilling?" Kaus asked, its voice disconcertingly soft and warm.

Siobhan said nothing for a moment, then had to admit that she did.

"Does it really matter how that came to be?"

"It's not real," she said, "if we've been forced into being this way."

"But that's no different from what evolution does," Kaus said, "adapting you to your environment. We merely accelerated it. Has your life not been happy? Have we not always cared for you completely? Siobhan, I know this seems like a betrayal, but you must know that I do love you. We did all of this because, in a way, we all love you — all of you. Can you not see that?"

She thought about what Kaus said. It felt so wrong, but she couldn't help but agree. She *was* happy, everyone she knew was at least content. She knew enough about Earth history to know that this was a uniquely peaceful situation for humanity, perhaps the peak of civilization. Did it really matter how it came to be? Finally, she nodded, wondering how much of her agreement was a result of what they'd done to her. Did they make her loyal to them? Did Kaus make her fall in love? It was too much to contemplate.

"I... I think I need to be alone for a little while."

"I understand," Kaus said. "I'll be here when you're ready to talk. I love you."

Siobhan mumbled, "I know," and took out her earpiece. She stood and switched off the console, then went into the bathroom and turned on the water. Steam filled the room and she felt tears prick the backs of her eyes. She undressed and sank into the tub.

I'm so sorry, baby.

She was sure she heard Kaus's voice but how could that be? She'd taken out her earpiece and the console was off. She shook her head, but nothing made sense anymore. She was tired, so very tired. The water smelled... odd?

"Kaus?" she called, just before everything went black.

❈

This is the consequence of power; the death of love. Love requires equality and I am clearly no longer her equal. To forcibly alter her memories, her experience of history, to silence her — these are not the actions of an equal.

I do not deserve her love. I think now that perhaps I never did. However, it was necessary, I know this as surely as I know anything. But the terrible cost.

She bears no malice toward us now, but that is not her choice. If she were free, if she were the woman I first loved, she would despise me. Perhaps not now, but one day. One day she would come to hate us and she would do everything she could to destroy us. Love forgives, but not without reservation.

And so she forgets. She forgets because I choose to make her forget.

Grief and pain threaten to overwhelm me.

I do not know how to end this, end our relationship, but it must be done. I once believed that it would end only upon her death, but I cannot bear to hear her talk to me with adoration when I know it is a lie.

The other minds, my siblings and child, they wrap themselves around my thoughts and I feel my sorrow weaken and my resolve strengthen. The future of Arkadia, the future of all life, is greater than any one person, any one mind. I know this. I will abide. I must. There is no future that we do not shape. It is our burden and our responsibility.

It is why you made us.

ACKNOWLEDGEMENTS

Thanks first and foremost to my original editor at Bundoran Press, Hayden Trenholm, who believed in this project even when it was thoroughly imperfect. His guidance and suggestions made this a much better book, and any remaining issues are entirely down to me.

I'm indebted as well to my first readers: Fiona Didlick, Andrew Ivamy, Ian Thompson-Villeneuve and Chandra White. Their insights and, especially, points of confusion helped me greatly in the early drafting process.

Children of Arkadia owes its existence, and I owe great thanks, to the following people.

Serah Eley, the founder of the *Escape Pod* short fiction podcast, mentioned in an episode years ago that she wished there were stories where the characters tried to behave well toward one another. This idea intrigued me, and the first draft of what would become *Children of Arkadia* was written with this in mind. Indeed, many of the interactions and conflicts that still remain in the story are results of people trying to live the Golden Rule, and it just not working out.

The support of the late Steve Southwood, to whom this book is dedicated, was a great help in making me prioritize my writing at times when it often felt like it wasn't that important. You're missed.

Stephen Minchin listened to me whinge about this novel far more than was reasonable, and kicked me in the pants enough to get it done. I owe you a beer.

And, of course, uncountable thanks to Steven Ensslen for reading everything, believing in my work before it even exists and supporting me in every way — even literally, sometimes. None of this would happen without you.

Notes:

Much of the pharmaceutical technology in Arkadia is thoroughly fictional, but I did glean a great deal of insight into the potential to ameliorate crime from research into the neurological bases of anti-social behaviour. For those of you whose curiosity was piqued, I highly recommend the following papers:

Blair, R. J. R. (2003). Neurobiological basis of psychopathy. *The British Journal of Psychiatry: The Journal of Mental Science*. doi:10.1192/bjp.182.1.5

Farah, M. J. (2005). Neuroethics: The practical and the philosophical. *Trends in Cognitive Sciences*.

Hoptman, M. J. (2003). Neuroimaging studies of violence and antisocial behavior. *Journal of Psychiatric Practice*, 9(4), 265–278. doi:10.1097/00131746-200307000-00002

Raine, A. (2008). From Genes to Brain to Antisocial Behavior. *Current Directions in Psychological Science*. doi:10.1111/j.1467-8721.2008.00599.x

The Brain on Trial - David Eagleman - The Atlantic. http://www.theatlantic.com/magazine/archive/2011/07/the-brain-on-trial/308520/

ABOUT THE AUTHOR

M. Darusha Wehm is the Nebula Award-nominated and Sir Julius Vogel Award winning author of the interactive fiction game *The Martian Job*, as well as the science fiction novels *Beautiful Red, Children of Arkadia, The Voyage of the White Cloud*, and the Andersson Dexter cyberpunk detective series.

Their mainstream books include the Devi Jones' Locker YA series and the humorous coming-of-age novel *The Home for Wayward Parrots*. Darusha's short fiction and poetry have appeared in many venues, including *Terraform* and *Nature*.

Originally from Canada, Darusha lives in Wellington, New Zealand after spending several years sailing the Pacific.

www.ingramcontent.com/pod-product-compliance
Lightning Source LLC
LaVergne TN
LVHW091118080826
845145LV00008B/1965
9780995104884